FORGOTTEN

ALISON STOKER

ISBN 978-1-0369-1006-8

Cover design by Gill de Warren
Book layout by Andrew Stoker

Typeset in:
Avant Garde Gothic
Sabon

'He's done wrong, he knows it, please can we just leave it alone,' she said.

'I want a happy house as well.'

'Then leave it alone.'

Joseph nodded.

'You promise me you'll leave it alone?' said Eva.

'Fine,' said Joseph.

He looked at his watch.

'Go,' said Eva. She balanced on tiptoe to retrieve the box they kept on the shelf above the stove and pulled out some cash. 'Take a taxi, you'll never make it on foot now.'

'But that money's for us to go out and have a bottle of wine for our anniversary.'

'I don't want to go out, the happiest place I can be is here with my boys,' she put one hand to Joseph's cheek and the other on the tiny bulge of her pregnant stomach and looked down at it, 'and my precious girl, Gabriella.'

'We don't know if it's a—'

'Or Gabriel for a boy. But I know this one's a girl, not that I mind. I just want a big family, as many Goltzes as we can get out,' Eva said. She laughed and Joseph kissed her on the cheek and left. She listened to him skipping the stairs two at a time, down from their third-floor tenement to the hot and noisy sidewalk.

Later at the school gates her boy skipped out. She held up an ice-cream cone and he threw himself into her arms.

'I love you, Mommy,' he said, 'you're the best.'

They walked home along the sunbaked streets. It was the lull between the hot weather coming and the garbage and drains of the city making themselves known. Eva kept stopping to breathe deeply while her son held out his hands to be held for balance as he walked along the top of low walls. It felt like every dog in the neighbourhood was barking, every window

3

was open and family discussions and cooking smells spilled out. Eva had to stop and press her hand over her mouth, the sickness had been gone for weeks but was back again. Aunt Sal said it was good news, the pregnancy hormones were strong which meant the baby was too.

With her head half way out of the window Eva managed to cook some dinner and sit down with her son while he ate. She put him to bed to protests that it was still light outside. She told him he could stay up if he kept to his room and she went to lie down. She must have fallen asleep because it was getting dark when she next opened her eyes.

Eva shifted herself from her back to her side in the bed. She tried to sit but pain streaked through her body and she gasped and fell back down on her elbow. She breathed through the tugging sensation, she waited for the spots in front of her eyes to fade and the pain passed. She rolled over to one side and put her feet on the carpeted floor, carefully pulled her dress between her legs and stood up.

'Joe?' she called out.

She tried to stand but another pain came and she let out a groan. She moved her legs back in the bed again.

There was a gentle knock at the door.

'Honey is that you? Don't come in, is Daddy home?'

She tried to get up again but felt warm blood dribbling down the insides of her legs and if she didn't get to the door before her son opened it he would see.

'Mommy?' said a voice on the other side of the door.

'Don't come in, sweetheart, wait outside. Is Daddy coming?'

Nausea came and she wretched, the pain was back and clawing at her insides. Eva waited it out and pulled the covers up to her chest. Outside on the landing she could hear movement.

'Joe?'

'It's me, Mommy, can I come in now? Daddy's watching TV.'

'No, honey, go and get him.'

'Why?'

The word he said more than any other.

'Because it's grownup stuff.'

It was a terrible answer. Eva knew he wouldn't be satisfied with it. She'd taught him better than that.

'I'm six next week, so you can tell me.'

'If you get Daddy right now, I'll give you a dollar.'

She heard his feet thundering along the corridor. Her body was heavy and she thought she might pass out. Her hands had gone a yellowy white, which she hadn't seen happen in years. They used to be like this all winter when she had nothing to cover them with in freezing temperatures. An older girl in the camp had taught her to blow on them and she tried it now.

Joseph opened the door and put his head around.

'What's the matter?'

'Call 911 will you.'

Eva pushed down the covers. She sat there small and vulnerable, a stain of red on the front of her dress and around her in the bed, like ink spilled on a blank page.

'Again?' said Joseph.

'Again,' said Eva.

Chapter One

Eva Goltz had never visited Rabbi Rovner in his office before. Normally he came to her, or they spoke in the sunny garden at the back of the synagogue. Today summer felt further away than ever. Radiators clicked and gurgled to keep the office just slightly warmer than outside. Eva noticed that nobody else felt the cold as much as she did. Normally she would be preparing to leave Manhattan for some sun. She would visit Lois and Dash, her friends on the West Coast. They'd take Dash's plane down to Aruba and spend a couple of weeks on the beach and she would feel warm again, warm to her bones, a comfort she couldn't imagine now. Eva went over to the radiator and pressed her hand against it. It was hot to the touch but the room was still so cold. She could have visited the rabbi less formally. She'd spent so much time in the living room of his home, fussed over by his wife Jona while Eva took in photographs of his smiling family and marvelled at the bronze casts of his now grown-up sons' tiny feet that stood at either end of the mantelpiece like bookends. When the boys were home they would sit there too, and never disappear to their rooms while a guest was present—they were properly brought up.

She sat down in a plain office swivel chair; her black patent court shoes swung an inch above the carpeted floor. She shuffled forward to put her feet on the floor, to feel something solid beneath her. On the desk there was a picture of Jona and the two boys. They were standing next to a sign that said 'Yosemite National Park'. It was the kind of sign that people waited in line to have their picture taken next to. Eva wondered if the rabbi and his family had had to queue. Or had they been there alone? The picture looked as if it was taken in a highly unconscious moment when Jona was prepared to eschew her usual tight-lipped smile for a huge and goofy grin, when the boys could forget to josh each other and instead reached out behind their mother and linked arms. To have a picture like that, thought Eva, that's something.

She couldn't get comfortable in the chair, it wiggled around too much. She took in a deep breath and stood up. All morning people had been asking her to take a seat. As if the news she'd been given would be any easier to take whilst sat on her behind than it would be doing star jumps, if she still could. Standing, it occurred to her that she'd been sitting on the wrong side of the desk anyhow. The setup of the room was confusing, she thought. The desk sat side on to the door, its end up against the window ledge. Rabbi Rovner's assistant, Adam, had shown her into the room anxiously, concerned that the rabbi wasn't there to greet her.

'I arrived unannounced,' she said, several times.

This hadn't reassured him, she heard him tapping away on the keys of his cell phone before he'd closed the door.

Everyone ran around Eva, in shops, restaurants, exhibitions and fundraisers. It passed through her mind that perhaps they'd sensed something of her limited time with them before she knew it. Then she laughed aloud at herself and at that moment Rabbi Rovner opened the door. She met him eye to eye and with a chuckle, not at all what she'd intended.

'Eva,' he said. His hands reached out and met Eva's and he

received a kiss on the cheek. 'What a nice surprise to see you. I'm glad you're in good spirits.'

He gestured for her to sit. The chair on the other side was better, it was solid and her feet could reach the ground.

Rabbi Rovner's eyes darted quickly around his desk before he looked up at Eva. He sometimes spilled bits of lettuce or meat from his sandwiches and hoped there was none left from lunch. More than once in his career he'd had to create an elaborate story as to why an official document needed to be re-produced when the original had acquired grease spots on it or red sauce and mustard. He was sloppy, Jona said. She regularly ticked him off for being a messy eater even after twenty-six years of marriage. She stuffed wodges of paper napkins in the top of his lunch bag but he was too eager to get to his food and would fish them out and dump them to one side. It was only luck that occasionally they saved paperwork or the walnut desk beneath. Rabbi Rovner had no idea that anyone ate any differently until Jona had pointed it out to him. His mother and father delighted in filling the plates of their children, then filling them again. How they dealt with clearing them was their own concern. As a boy he'd once eaten ten slices of white bread as a snack when he'd been left at home with his two older sisters while his mother and father were at work in their store.

'Let him have as much as he wants,' his mother said to his sisters, Ada and Mag.

'You hear that?' They called in his direction. And so he did. Bread was cheap and nobody waited to feel hungry in the Rovner house.

'You'll be wondering why I'm here, ' said Eva. Her hands rested on the top of her Fendi handbag, perched on her lap.

'Not at all, you're always welcome to drop in. Just the other day Jona said she misses you calling by.'

Eva looked down in her lap.

'I know I've relied on you and Jona heavily in recent times.'

Rabbi Rovner spluttered, so many ways of saying that that's exactly what they wanted vied for expression.

'Eva, no, no, you've blessed us many times over.'

Even that felt inadequate and open to misinterpretation. Despite sharing a language with the people he lived with and served, he often felt he wasn't quite choosing the correct words and, once chosen, he had no power over how they were taken. The story of the tower of Babel came to mind. Before then had people shared understanding as well as the same tongue? he thought. If they had, then mankind had lost more than they realised. What an impossible set up this world could be. He made a mental note to suggest it to Adam as a point of discussion for their weekly study session. What he was trying to avoid alluding to was that Eva had donated generously to the synagogue and projects connected to it. He feared she thought he meant that.

'What I mean is that you're a valued member of the congregation,' said the rabbi. 'We all think so very highly of you. It's an honour to be your rabbi, a true honour. We think of you as the backbone of our community, you're the one so many of us look to. You're the fuel in the fire, the oil that continues to burn.' He searched his mind for more to say, 'When you walk in the room people stand up an inch taller,' no, that's not what he meant, it was true but not what he meant to say, he had to try again. He tutted at himself and shook his head. 'Eva, you're never, ever, ever a burden. Being your rabbi is, it is, it's, it's...' His words had run out so he simply lifted his hands from the desk to the sky.

Eva had come straight from the doctor's office. She'd expected the appointment to take longer and was surprised just how quickly and efficiently she'd been delivered the news and dispatched back to her car, which was waiting outside the hospital entrance. The car windows were down and on the radio a doom-monger declared the year 2000 as the end of the world. Eva wondered— it was an election year and she had a bad feeling about it. The driver saw her and switched off the radio. He climbed out and opened her car door and she got in. She'd forced a smile to the driver and managed to ask him to drive her to the synagogue without displaying emotion. She wondered how long she would keep it up. Would it become more difficult with each person she told, or would it be like a script she'd memorised and read with gestures and inflections rehearsed to show the other person she wasn't kidding. This would be her very first try with the news. She trod carefully.

'It's on my mind that little Maya has only me, not another living soul, only her dull and ageing grandmother,' she said.

'You are anything but dull, Eva.' said Rabbi Rovner. 'And you're sixty-two for goodness's sake, that's not old at all nowadays.'

Eva hadn't considered how she'd manage interruptions so she ignored this one.

'I won't be around forever. Naturally I didn't think much about this when my son was alive, but now...'

Rabbi Rovner interjected again, praising Eva's devotion to Maya, describing what a support she was to the child and how lucky Maya was to have her. Eva waited patiently. Rabbi Rovner ran out of superlatives. The quiet of the room and the street outside surprised her. It was as if everything had taken a collective breath in waiting for her to speak.

'I have about four months to live,' said Eva. And there it was. Like a pigeon thumping into a closed window. Rabbi Rovner recoiled.

'Seems my bad year just got worse,' she said.

'And mine as well,' said Rabbi Rovner.

Then opened out the silence she'd previously hoped for but which she now felt responsible for filling. The rabbi had tears in his eyes and Eva had to look away. Out of the window she could see something flapping around between two branches. It was the last days of October and the branches were getting barer, she squinted but couldn't tell if the movement was a goldfinch or just leaves. It occupied her long enough for her mind to step aside from the piece of information it was trying to absorb. It would be Halloween soon and Maya would wander the streets, with her friends— the smallest child in her class and dressed as a ballerina, blue lipped in the cold. Eva and Maya would go through the annual argument about footwear and Eva would insist on sensible boots over ballet shoes and carry Maya's coat, hoping she could be persuaded to put it on. Eva's only other involvement was to stand a respectable distance away while the girls knocked doors and she would help Maya carry her haul of candy home. Rabbi Rovner had begun talking, offering help and support, trying to comfort her, saying he was glad she'd told him. Eva placed her hand on her chest, trying to decide if disclosure had made her feel any better. She couldn't tell. People said that it felt better to talk things over, to share your troubles. Eva had only just begun and wondered when she'd feel the benefit. Her son's death back in the spring and then her husband's passing months later uncapped the lid tightly screwed on her life's troubles. It turned out they were stored in a heavy vat that all of a sudden she felt the weight of. It was deep, possibly bottomless. Now it was being thrown back and forth like her son had thrown footballs from one end of the pitch to the other. Then her vat was hoisted up on to shoulders and flung about, given the bumps and set down ready to be opened. And all that Eva thought she'd contained and held back, with no more effort than stifling a sneeze had got loose. Rabbi Rovner had been the ear she'd chosen to listen, hoping that with God to lean back on he would be able

11

to manage it in a way that she didn't expect anyone else to. Everyone knew Eva Goltz was a survivor.

Rabbi Rovner was still offering kind words, forcing them upon Eva like a second helping of tapioca pudding, when even the first wasn't asked for.

'It's Maya,' interrupted Eva.

Rabbi Rovner halted mid-sentence. He took a breath and Eva decided she would have to lurch in with what she was going to say before he spoke again.

'I wonder how you'll see this but all I can think is that I'll have to call her mother.'

Rabbi Rovner didn't see himself as gifted spiritually in any way except that he liked to talk and people seemed to like him to listen to them. He felt none of the rush of euphoria that others described when connecting with God. For him God was the steady arm around his shoulder and occasionally a pat on the back. He considered himself ordinary in his devotion and not of great spiritual talent. But whenever Eva mentioned Maya's mother, from the very first day that she talked about the twenty-year-old shiksa who her son was besotted by, he felt the most urgent need to defend her. Under usual circumstances that might be normal. Anyone would argue for a mother to have a relationship with her daughter— but Eva had persistently said that Maya's mother was the worst kind of person imaginable and he could only take her word for it. If anyone knew about terrible people it was Eva Goltz.

Rabbi Rovner thought he might have fallen off his chair in surprise if he couldn't see Eva still sitting opposite him, her handbag now leaning up against the far side of his desk.

'She stopped calling after Maya's second birthday,' said Eva. 'Nothing for more than five years.'

'I recall,' he said, keeping calm while he waited for what she had to say.

He knew Eva's accusations towards Maya's mother chorus and verse. The girl drank and took drugs, lied and money grabbed, targetted her wealthy son and left him broken inside and with a brand-new baby. She'd extorted the family and run home to England hardly looking back.

'The story I told you…' began Eva.

Rabbi Rovner shifted forward in his seat and nodded.

'It isn't exactly what happened,' said Eva.

Eva felt the bottom of her stomach turn over. She'd never managed to convince herself of the story she'd previously told and each time it cost her more energy than it should. Guilt had laid itself down all around the memory so that she had to fight to recall what had truly happened. The first stage of her punishment, as she saw it, would be to re-tell the truth to the only man who still looked at her with an iota of interest; and for her thoughts no less and not her money. And so she re-told it with as much accuracy as she could and by the end she was leant forward, her handbag pressed against the desk and her chin just a foot away from the rabbi's.

'So?' she said.

Chapter Two

The Goltz Residence in Greenwich Village

Eva climbed the stairs and went into what had been her husband's study. It was the first room on the second floor and the smallest in the house. For a man who did so well in business he was never interested in making a show of it. The room still smelled like him; paper, ink and bergamot. Sometimes after supper she would switch the desk lamp on, go downstairs and imagine he'd just left the room. Joseph didn't leave much behind. He didn't hold much stock in owning more than he needed and when he'd gone Eva was astonished to realise that she had little to remember him by apart from the photos he'd been unsuccessful in avoiding. He was no renunciate, he enjoyed his stop sign red Bentley and a good quality steak. He donated as much money as was legal to the Democratic party and he owned more Manhattan real estate than she was able to keep track of. Eva heard a woman refer to her deceased husband as a rock. Joseph wasn't a rock he was a wall that you could throw anything at and it would bounce right off without making a dent.

The desk drawers had been cleared months ago and inside them was a freshly delivered box of her own headed stationery. They'd always had cream paper with black type but now all the sheets that had said Mr J and Mrs E Goltz were gone. She'd chosen dark blue on white paper with a mottled effect. The new sheets read Mrs Eva Goltz. She wasn't sure why all of a sudden, the printer had included her first name as though her solitary initial was insufficient. This was followed by her Manhattan address and email, though she didn't know how to work email yet. If the computers were all going to stop functioning at midnight on 31st December, and people said they might, then she didn't see the need to learn how to use one. Especially not now. She sat down at the desk and pulled out a sheet of paper and wrote the date. 4th November 1999.

'To Deborah,' too cold.

'Dear Deborah,' too formal.

'Hello Deborah,' no.

'Deborah,' is what she wrote.

She crossed it out and tore the sheet in half. She would write the letter tomorrow. She threw it in the waste paper basket, closed the drawer and went downstairs.

Outside in her courtyard garden she looked up at the patch of bright blue sky above her and watched planes pass over the city. She wrapped her coat tightly around herself and sat down in the only patch of sun near the wrought iron patio table. A carved pumpkin grinned at her from the low wall opposite and next to it her pink potted geraniums still bloomed hopefully. A sketchily painted garden gnome that Maya had fallen in love with at her school's table top sale last week was now discarded and lay on one side. Beyond the walls she could hear Lower Manhattan's constant song of traffic, horns, sirens, the bleeping of trucks backing up, raised voices and pigeons flapping from tree to tree.

There was being caught in a lie and then there was having to tell the lie to the person you made it up about. Would she do the telling or let others fill in the gaps when Deborah came back? If she came back. It occurred to Eva that a letter wouldn't do, she would have to call her in person. She would begin by telling her that Maya needed her mother and the reason why. Surely this would calm the girl. After all who bawls at a dying woman, even if she deserves it. Eva had kept a close eye on Deborah when she'd returned to London. She tried to come back a few times in the early years. Once when Maya was twelve weeks old, another just before Maya turned one and finally just before Maya's second birthday. Eva told her nobody wanted her and then paid her off. She always took the money, but she cried a lot too and begged to speak to 'him'- it was embarrassing to listen to.

Keeping such a close eye on her was expensive and difficult to manage because Joseph and her son didn't know anything more than Deborah had left. Deborah wrote him long letters that Eva had disposed of and Connie, the housekeeper, knew to put all calls through to Eva. Eva always knew where Deborah lived and with whom and where she worked and who she associated with. Deborah had been quiet for years and as time passed Eva felt less afraid when the detective called her with an update. The information was banal; where she was going on vacation and how she'd changed her hair style. The telephone calls on Maya's birthday stopped and eventually the cards and letters too. Eva didn't wish the girl any more harm. She just wanted her away. She had hoped she'd get married and have children with the man she'd lived with for a while, that way she would never want to come back for Maya. But Deborah moved out of their home weeks after her son, Maya's father, died.

Eva would be quick to tell Deborah there would be $100,000 in her account to cover her expenses. Eva decided that she would offer half on arrival and the other half if Deborah stayed for a minimum of a month. Surely, she wouldn't be able to leave when her own daughter was going to be as good as orphaned. But Eva suspected she had trained Deborah out of her maternal instincts through years of separation, distraction and shame. She knew what it was like to no longer respond as other people do. Rabbi Rovner said the only way to make it right would be to welcome Deborah back into the family. Eva would need to let her build a bond with Maya and tell her that Maya's father had grieved her leaving, instead of briskly moving on to another woman, as Eva had made sure she believed. Eva gripped the edge of the table, the pain passed through her chest and down, she breathed erratically. It passed, the pains always passed, that was the only thing that made them tolerable, for now. When they were gone she wiped her face dry with the Kleenex that was up her sleeve and looked up again to the bright morning sky.

'You couldn't have just struck me down?' she said to the noise above.

On the Monday before Thanksgiving she finally accepted Rabbi Rovner's invitation for her and Maya to spend the day with his family. This way Connie could take the day off and spend it with her own family instead of kindly pretending she had nowhere else to be. Eva had set herself the deadline of Thanksgiving to call Deborah but it would have to wait. She would string it out and place a bet against God. She had lost almost every other hand; with these odds luck might be on her side. Her symptoms were no worse. She carried on with everyday matters. She took Maya to the theatre where she ate candy hidden in Eva's purse and then asked to go home the moment the bag was empty. She spent afternoons mulling over dinner party menus with Connie and hours in the park with Maya admiring the horses. She sat down with the architect who was designing the new indoor swimming pool complex at her Hamptons home. She could imagine herself and Maya

17

swimming laps in the crystalline waters and looking up through the glass roof at the stars. The project would be completed by next summer. If she was to see it, she'd have to stretch her four months to six or seven. She held court at The Goltz Foundation annual fundraiser, attended drinks parties and private gallery openings and had a different set of friends over every week for Friday night dinner. Like musicians playing on the deck of the Titanic she would sink playing every note in perfect time until she went under.

Thanksgiving came and she got up and put cinnamon rolls in the oven like she always had. They ate them and talked about everything but the people missing. Connie left just after nine and promised to be back to straighten up the house around five. Maya didn't ask to watch the parade and Eva wasn't going to offer to take her, she usually went with her grandpa. They used to come back smelling of the outdoors and hungry for supper. Eva would be putting the finishing touches on the dining table and preparing for their guests while Connie cooked the meal. This time they passed the morning with Maya watching cartoons and Eva flitting from room to room doing all the little tasks that she wouldn't normally make the time for. She overhauled the bar in the den and threw out any spirits that had been pushed to the back and were gathering dust. She looked through the upholstery fabric samples she'd been sent for the new drapes and walked around the house comparing them to the walls and carpets. She telephoned through an order for pure silk bedding and finally took the Halloween candy she'd bought too much of and bagged it up to give to Connie to take home for her boys. She was finished by eleven thirty. Maya got bored of the TV and roamed around looking sullen. They played a game of backgammon and Maya lost and sulked. Eva let her win the next game. This wasn't the day to teach her a lesson. By two o'clock Maya was asking when they could go out and they crossed the road to Washington Square Park where Maya chased down a few pigeons and petted a Labrador while Eva sat down and let her eyes close a moment. So this was to be her last Thanksgiving.

Maya held Eva's hand the entire journey up town to Rabbi Rovner's home.

'What'll I say?' said Maya. 'When I have to say what I'm grateful for?'

'We won't be doing that this year,' said Eva.

They arrived at the Rovners' apartment building and were ushered in by the doorman, past piled up snow topped with the detritus of the Thanksgiving Parade that had happened along the street earlier in the day. Empty hamburger boxes, a child's glove, a crushed traffic cone, a subway ticket and paper coffee cups. Before they got in the elevator they could already smell the multiple Thanksgiving turkeys that were being cooked throughout the building.

'Sometimes you're the pilgrim, sometimes you're the turkey,' said Eva.

'What?'

'It's not 'what' it's 'pardon',' said Eva.

'Pardon?'

'I just said a silly phrase that Grandpa used to use. It means some days are yours, others are not.'

'This is not our day.'

'No,' said Eva. 'But Rabbi and Mrs Rovner have tried very hard so we will too.'

Maya nodded.

They got in the elevator and Maya stood on tiptoe to press the button for the 22th floor. Eva set the bag with a bottle of wine and some chocolates in, down on the elevator floor. It felt much heavier than it should.

'Do you think there'll be dessert?' said Maya.

'If I know Samuel,' she stopped and quickly corrected herself, 'I mean, if I know Rabbi Rovner, there will be dessert. Only if you eat your supper that is.'

The elevator doors opened and Samuel and Jona Rovner were waiting in the doorway of their apartment. Both opened their arms to receive Maya running towards them. And for a moment, just a moment, Eva thought she might be saved from the call she didn't think she could make. Samuel and Jona had no daughters, they were both fond of Maya. Would they?

Samuel broke free from Maya's grip and came over and kissed Eva on both cheeks.

'Quite a day,' he said.

'For you,' said Eva. She held out the bag and watched Samuel take it to see if he found it heavy too.

'Thank you, you didn't need to bring anything,' he said. He took the bag without seeming to notice its weight.

The dining room table had been laid with a deep red cloth and tartan napkins. There were twin squat silver candelabra holding two green candles either end of the turkey. It was already sliced. The Rovner boys, now at college in their freshman and sophomore years, sat at the table. They stood up shook Eva and Maya's hands formally. Eva hadn't seen either of them since Joseph's funeral. Their expressions were unchanged. She didn't know how to tell them that they didn't need to put it on for her. They all sat down and the food was passed around. Samuel poured Eva a glass of Pinot Noir and even though it had been months since her last drink she took a glug. She used to enjoy a glass with supper but the gentle release that she had once felt now had a malevolent quality. The room was silent except for the sound of cutlery clanging.

'Sometimes you're the pilgrim, sometimes you're the turkey,' said Maya.

'What?' said Rabbi Rovner.

'It's not 'what' it's 'pardon',' said Maya.

The adults eyed each other and Eva started laughing.

'It's something Joseph used to say,' said Eva.

Rabbi Rovner put down his knife and fork and lifted his glass.

'To Joseph, our dear departed friend,' he said. Everyone except for Maya lifted their glasses in the air and then drank; Eva to the bottom.

'I'll have another, Rabbi, if I may,' said Eva.

Rabbi Rovner obliged and Eva took another sip.

'Let's all say something that we're grateful for,' she said. 'I'm grateful for Maya.'

'I'm grateful for dessert, will there be dessert?' said Maya.

'I'm grateful for your company,' said Rabbi Rovner. 'And yes, there will be dessert.'

'I'm grateful for turkeys,' said one of the Rovner boys.

'I'm grateful for booze,' said the other and then knocked back his glass of wine.

Jona tutted.

'I'm grateful that Samuel hadn't eaten *all* of the cheesecake after I caught him standing at the refrigerator,' said Jona.

Eva had known the rabbi and his wife since they were newlyweds. They were as pleased with themselves as any happy couple. Then Jona fell pregnant and her manner changed completely— nobody knew why. She couldn't say a kind word to her husband's face but behind his back it was 'my husband the rabbi came top of his class', 'my husband the rabbi advises a senator', 'my husband the rabbi could choose a post any place he wants one.' But she was kind in a way that Eva thought nobody else noticed. She made an appliqued baby blanket for Maya when she was born, and new one every year on her birthday. She handed the blankets over furtively— not wanting to make a show of the gift that it would have taken her hours to create. In some of the Goltz family's rawest times Jona took over school pick-ups and drop offs. And she gave hours of quiet company— saving Eva the harassment of a person who tries to fix the unfixable.

Eva and Maya got home just after nine o'clock. The house looked nothing like it normally did at Thanksgiving. There were no guests and no music, no smell of pecan pie or spiced cranberry sauce. Connie had pulled the drapes and turned the lights on. A festive bouquet sat on the hall table. Eva read the card, 'We are grateful for your friendship, Love Lois and Dash.' Eva felt herself surrounded by the love of wholehearted people and at the same time ashamed that it wasn't enough.

Eva put Maya to bed and went to Joseph's study. She picked up the phone. It would be the middle of the night in London. Who cares, she thought, life never changes when it's convenient.

Chapter Three

Five weeks later in Essex, UK

Deborah stood on the damp front steps of her mother and Patrick's concrete McMansion. It was at the bottom of a cul-de-sac nestled incongruently between a bungalow with a front garden full of gnomes and faded plastic fairies, miniature wishing wells and bird tables and another with a clapped-out motorhome on the driveway. She rang the doorbell. She didn't hear it chime so she pressed her ear against the front door. Through a glass panel on the door she could see the burglar alarm light flashing so they weren't at home. She called the house phone and got the answer machine.

'Mum, it's me, Deborah,' she stopped, 'I thought you'd be home. I thought you said you'd be home today.'

Her mother and Patrick had been on a Mediterranean cruise since the middle of December and now it was the very last day of the month, the year, the century, she'd expected them to be back or to have called her. Patrick liked telling people how much cruising he'd done. Deborah liked to be there and watch his audience hide a smile.

Deborah hung up and went back to her car. She switched on the ignition in the hope that the heater would kick in and clear the misty windows.

Her mobile phone rang, it was a number she didn't recognise.

'Hello?'

'Deb-o-rah,' said the voice at the other end. It was Patrick. He sounded as though he was grinning from ear to ear.

'Hi Patrick, is Mum with you?'

Her mother was never far from Patrick.

'I'll wish you a Happy New Year before the phones go mad,' he said.

'Is Mum with you? Can I speak to Mum? I just called the house phone.'

'We've got all our calls re-directed to our cabin.'

'I thought you were coming home before New Year. Can I speak to Mum?

'We're in Madeira, leaving tomorrow. I won't make you feel any worse and tell you that it's wall to wall sunshine and twenty-one degrees here.'

'Can I speak to Mum?'

'We played miniature golf this morning and there's a gala dinner tonight. Your mother's bought a frock and my dickie bow matches it. What are the chances of that?'

Deborah was silent.

'Is everything alright with the house? Did you check on it like we asked you to?'

'It's fine, I'm here now.'

'Don't try and go in again. I can't face re-setting the alarm system.'

'Can I speak to my Mum?'

'Wait a minute, she's in a bit of a state of undress. No, no, no, don't get the wrong idea. She's changing into her bikini and we're going up to the pool.'

Silence.

'Did you hear me? I said we're going up to the pool, it's warm enough to swim outside.'

She heard muffled voices as Patrick and her mother chatted in the background as though there was nothing else in the world to do. Eventually her mother's voice was loud and clear enough for Deborah to assume she'd picked up the phone.

'All alright?' said her mother.

'I thought you were coming home before the new year?'

'No, the 2nd, the day after tomorrow.'

Her mother laughed at something Patrick said but apart from that the line remained silent.

'Christmas was alright,' said Deborah. 'I went to Kirsty's place for lunch, there were a group of us, stragglers I suppose.'

'You ought to have seen the spread they put on here. There was every meat you can imagine, not just turkey and roast beef. There was duck, pork belly, lamb, partridge, chicken, salmon and veal. There was every type of wine as well. A different one for every course. And the puddings, there was an entire pudding room. Oh, the decadence Deb, the feasting, it was like the last days of Rome. I mean total excess all of the time.'

'That's not what it means, Mum,' said Deborah.

Her mother had a habit of picking a phrase that she didn't understand but liked the sound of and using it liberally. The afternoon tea at the Savoy that Patrick had taken her to had been like the last days of Rome. So had the cocktails at the rooftop bar in London they went to for Deborah's birthday and the dinner dance at Patrick's golf club.

'I'm going to New York for a month tomorrow.'

'Are you really?'

'Yes.'

She heard Patrick's voice in the background saying 'what for?'

'What for?' said her mother.

'Do you think I could speak to you alone?' said Deborah.

'What do you mean?'

'Out of Patrick's earshot?'

'It'll be about my birthday,' he said in the background.

'He's gone to the balcony,' said her mother.

Deborah took a deep breath.

Then her mother squealed excitedly and she could hear her playfully scolding Patrick and telling him not to creep back in.

'For fuck's sake, Mum,' said Deborah, under her breath.

'Oi, I heard that. Don't let me hear you say that again. What is it? I'm listening.'

'It's not about Patrick's birthday.'

'It's in two weeks, you know.'

'I know.'

'Oh Debs, you should see the view from our cabin.'

'I'm sure it's spectacular.'

'You should see it.'

Deborah paused.

'Come on then, spit it out, poor Patrick's waiting around, we're going to the outdoor pool. What is it then? Why are you going back there? You came back bloody miserable last time.'

Her mother had a way of making everything she said sound like both a bore and an accusation.

'Work.'

'That's the big secret?'

'Yes, that's all. See you in February,' she said and hung up.

Deborah pulled down the sun visor and studied herself in the mirror. She looked like herself. It just felt like she was visiting in someone else's body, someone who'd had seventeen cups of coffee.

She drove back to London, through the thick New Year's Eve traffic as revellers flocked to the capital to see if anything was going to happen as Big Ben struck midnight and 1999 turned to the year 2000. She got back to her flat by seven and finished packing for the morning, assuming there would be one. Or perhaps time would spin out into a wild and immeasurable force that nobody knew how to manage anymore. If nothing happened and everything stayed the same, in the morning there would be a taxi outside ready to take her to Heathrow airport.

At nine thirty she left for Kirsty's house party. Kirsty lived with her boyfriend Jonty in a flat over-looking the Thames. The party's selling point was that at midnight they could go up to the roof and watch the river of fire that London had been promised. The flat was already full of people from the modelling agency Deborah worked for. They hung over sofas as if they were on a magazine cover and sipped champagne from any clean vessel. Kirsty kissed Deborah three times, Parisian style, though she had grown up in Inverness.

'You invited the models?' said Deborah.

'Jonty did. He said they'd get wind he'd had a party and not invited them. Don't worry about it, they'll be too pissed or too high to talk work. I saw a glass over there, grab it,' said Kirsty. 'Have some fizz, we took that case from work.'

'I'm not drinking.'

Kirsty laughed.

'I'm not drinking, really I'm not.'

'Then, my friend, you will remember your last night here as a harrowing display of leering, bragging conversations that last three and a half seconds— and puking.'

'I'll have one.'

'Good girl.'

Kirsty swiped the glass she'd spotted on the window ledge and filled it up.

'Cheers,' she said.

'I hate toasting,' said Deborah. 'It's bullshit. We drink for everything.'

'Everything is bullshit,' said Kirsty. She smiled and swigged down her drink and re-filled. 'Do you want to tell me why you're going to New York?'

'I have.'

Jonty came by and beckoned Kirsty and Deborah in close.

'Venetia just excused herself to go and have a bath,' he said and collapsed into giggles.

'Here?' said Kirsty. 'In my bathroom?'

He nodded his head.

'Fucking models,' said Kirsty. She took hold of Jonty's face and studied his eyes. 'You've peaked too soon, my love, don't take anything else.' His pupils were huge.

He kissed her on the cheek and wandered off.

'What's the time?' said Deborah.

'A quarter to eleven.'

'Why is New Year's Eve always like this? Do you think we'll ever be the kind of people who remember what the year before was like and instead stay home and watch TV and order a takeaway?'

'What's the matter with you tonight?'

'Nothing.'

'Are you going to prison or something? The dying relative in New York's a cover story, isn't it?'

Deborah finished her drink and held out her glass. Kirsty poured her another.

'Are they really going to set the Thames alight?' said Deborah.

'That's what they say.'

'I bet it's a flop, a fiver says it goes tits up.'

Kirsty held out her hand and Deborah shook it.

'I've got big plans for that fiver,' said Deborah.

'You can't spend it in New York,' said Kirsty. She took a swig from a miniature bottle of Moet. 'Is your mum going to see this dying relative too?'

'She's with Patrick in Madeira.'

'Is it like the last days of Rome there?'

Deborah smiled at her friend. She was so close to telling her. Instead she threw back her drink and poured another.

At a quarter past midnight Deborah and Kirsty hugged goodbye. Kirsty held Deborah so tight she thought the pressure might squeeze out the tears that were in her eyes.

'Say bye to Jonty,' said Deborah

'He's gone to bed; I'll say it in the morning.'

Deborah bit her bottom lip to stop it from wobbling.

'Where the fuck are you going?' said Kirsty, 'really?'

Deborah shook her head.

'Will you phone me or email, write a letter, just tell me you're alive?'

Deborah nodded, said goodbye and went to the tube station to join queues of the tired, pissed and pissed off as they made their way home to tell everyone what a night they'd had in town.

She got home just after one and put on the television to watch rolling footage of the firework displays from Sydney, Japan, Russia, France and Spain. She took the fiver she'd won out of her purse and unfolded it. She recognised Kirsty's scrawl across the Queen's chest.

'Last days of Rome?'

Chapter Four

It might be her imagination but, Deborah thought, the air stewardesses' smiles were just a little brighter once she'd turned left and walked through business class and into first. The morning had brought with it a collective, bashful sense of relief as the year 2000 arrived and nothing except for littered streets and hangovers needed tending to. Deborah had travelled in first class once before but she didn't remember much of the experience. She entered her cubicle and set her Chloe handbag down. It was several seasons old and looked a little tatty next to the luggage being stowed away by the passengers around her. They were settling down but nobody paid much attention to anyone else. It wasn't like economy class, where everyone eyed each other, wondering if there would be enough room in the overhead lockers for their belongings and whether or not the person in front was the kind of arsehole to jam their seat back the moment the plane took off.

Once they were in the air she stood up for a while and walked the spacious corridor to the bathroom and back. A fellow passenger gave her a polite smile as she returned to her seat. Deborah normally avoided the talkative types who she almost always found herself next to on a long flight. But this time she wished someone would ask her where she was going and why. She wanted to hear herself tell the third cover story she'd created, hopeful that she could tell it well enough that someone would believe it. She couldn't settle enough to watch a film or read the magazines she'd bought at the airport. She wanted to call the bank and see if the money was there. Eva had promised $50,000 would be in her account by the time she landed, and if the money didn't make it on time her credit card bills and rent would go unpaid. She'd overshot her overdraft long ago. Despite the bank sending letters saying they wanted to help the charges kept on coming. If she did have someone to talk to about her trip she would leave out the part about the money. A menu of cocktails was put in front of her and she picked out a vodka martini. It was delivered in a tall open glass with a plate of salted pretzels. She sipped it to begin with and ate the pretzels. They made her thirsty and she threw back the rest of the drink and was almost immediately offered another. The next was gone in a few sips.

'I need to make a phone call,' said Deborah to the stewardess who delivered her next drink.

'I'm sorry madam, that's not possible,' said the stewardess, discreet and apologetic.

'In that case I'll have another of these please.' Deborah lifted the martini glass to her lips, knocked the drink back in one and handed it back to the stewardess.

What if the money wasn't there? she thought. She should have asked for it in advance. The money Eva had given her over the years was gone. The trouble was she'd got used to a certain style of living, dinners out at good restaurants, clothes bought from Bond Street and holidays to Meribel and the Maldives and her salary wasn't enough. The money that was coming could start her up all over again. The conditions it came with were that she visit Maya; that was all, just a visit, a month out of an entire lifetime. She couldn't plan what would happen at the end of the month. All she knew was she needed the money offered her and she wanted to see her daughter— and that those two desires ought to be the other way around.

With a bump of turbulence Deborah's fourth martini was sent down in one gulp and she ordered another. She wasn't hungry but said she'd have some cheese and biscuits because the stewardess asked her what she wanted to eat so many times that she got tired of turning her away. After the next martini she realised that if she stopped now she'd have a hangover by the time she got to JFK, so she kept going. She would outrun it until she was ready to feel it. The onboard beauty therapist came by to offer her a treatment. Deborah looked down at her fingernails and then at the nails of the beauty therapist and agreed to a manicure. She must have fallen asleep because when she woke there was a landing card on her tray table along with another drink. She threw the drink back and lifted the landing card close to her face. It didn't make the print any clearer. She'd filled one out before, she would guess what information went where.

'Just one more,' said Deborah to the air stewardess and passed her the glass. 'And can I have that glass of champagne you offered me earlier?'

The plane began its descent. Deborah was politely refused another drink. She gripped her seatbelt and pressed her forehead against the window to look at the New York skyline. She murmured the names of the landmarks below as if she was pointing them out to a child. Then they were above the tarmac. The plane landed with a gentle shudder and Deborah had the same thought she always did when taking off or landing. This plane could blow up any second and if it did what would people have to say about my life when they found out about what I did?

The captain's voice welcomed them to JFK airport where the local time was five o'clock and it was just above freezing outside. No matter, thought Deborah, this time she wouldn't be waiting for a bus or pulling a suitcase for sixteen blocks. Eva said her driver would be there. The plane came to a standstill and everyone took their seatbelts off, stewardesses were on their feet helping passengers with luggage and thanking them heartily for choosing to fly Virgin Atlantic.

Deborah instinctively picked up the eye mask and pouch of free toiletries she'd been given and put them in her handbag, she noticed unopened packs lying around and wondered if she could scoop them up too. Around her people were turning on their cell phones and talking to relatives, she heard dinner plans and meet ups in the park, the start time of a child's birthday party and the corralling of friends to go for drinks. The door opened and fellow first and business class passengers left behind them balled up napkins, newspapers and empty water bottles. Deborah waited until last, sure she'd left something important behind. She was looking in the overhead compartment and all around her seat but couldn't remember what she'd lost. She sat down in the empty cabin with her elbows pressing heavily against her thighs and her head in her hands. She felt a hand gently touch her shoulder; it was the stewardess who'd refused her the last drink.

'What?' said Deborah. Had the stewardess seen her swipe two of the cosmetics bags other passengers had left behind?

'Can I help you with anything, Miss Foster?'

'No, you can't,' said Deborah.

'Have a safe onward journey.'

Deborah stood and tried to stride away from the stewardess but her bag got caught on an arm rest. She shook it free and stumbled into the galley between first and business class. She was offered a bottle of water which she took. Then tripped out of the plane and fell to the ground. She hadn't known she'd fallen or felt a thing until she was suddenly on all fours on the rubbery floor between the plane and a carpeted tunnel that would lead her into the terminal. Her knees were scuffed black and the contents of her handbag had scattered. Another stewardess stepped out to help her recover her phone, wallet, make up bag and the freebies from the plane.

She didn't realise this was part of travelling first class but she was offered a lift on a buggy that took her through the airport terminal to the customs and border control line. She was ahead of most of the passengers on her flight. But she felt queasy and she knew that she should have eaten something more than the cheese and biscuits. It was only the afternoon and her hangover was already rapping on the door. Her eyes were stinging and tiredness was coming for her. She looked around for somewhere she might make a break to if she was going to throw up. There was nowhere and she waited, nauseous and impatient. She tutted and shifted from foot to foot, trying to distract herself from the vomit that was rising in her throat. Every time she thought she was going to be sick she held her breath and pinched her nose. Then she realised that was what you do when you're holding back a sneeze. Either way, it worked. Eventually she reached the desk. The stern official, shorter than she was by several inches, looked her up and down. Behind him two other men appeared and she couldn't remember what she might have said or done once they'd informed her that they were detaining her for questioning.

The cameras in Jon's section had first caught sight of Deborah when she strutted to the back of the existing queue. She walked like a pre-teen trying on her mother's high heeled shoes and knocked into the people in front of her. Fifth in line, she stood tapping her right heel and looking around the room. In his training he'd been taught to notice nervous behaviour and this young woman caught his eye. It was his second job after leaving the military, he'd just passed his probationary period and was no longer shadowing a more experienced member of staff. The tapping continued and was punctuated by an occasional flick of her hair and a pursing of her lips. To Jon she looked rich, well-dressed at least, though on closer inspection he could see that her clothes were dirty. Normally rich people didn't sweat this much over immigration. They were usually the most gracious about the queues. He supposed, this was because they were normally at the front of them.

'Are you just looking at tits or do I need to be informed, son?' Jon felt a nudge behind him. His immediate boss pressed his wide form against the back of his chair, a smell of Cheetos on his breath.

'I don't know, sir.'

'Then what are you doing in the job?'

'She's acting nervous, sir, maybe drunk, maybe not.'

Jon moved forward, an inch away from the bulk of his superior. He had closed up the gap between his body and the desk. His boss moved in even closer and was looking over Jon's shoulder.

'That she is,' he said.

Suddenly Jon wanted to defend her, give her a little more time, let the people at the desk decide.

'Let's call her in,' the breath announced.

Inside the holding room at JFK the light cast shadows on the faces of its occupants. Jon thought it made them appear sinister. Had he met the young woman across the table from him on a bright winter day, walking through Astoria Park, he'd have accepted her as a fellow resident of the neighbourhood he'd lived in for most of his life. Here he must treat her as a suspicious person.

She staggered around the room, once again searching for the water cooler she'd been back and forth to several times in the last hour. Jon leant his elbows on the table and winced as she tripped but miraculously landed back in her seat with only a little water in her lap. Her eyes met his and narrowed. He pulled his elbows back and sat up taller in his chair.

'You're not even a cop,' she said. 'Weren't you bright enough?'

Jon didn't answer. He was told to say as little as possible to detainees.

'Is your new year's resolution to be a prick?' said Deborah.

She threw back what was left in the tiny white plastic disposable cup and lines of water dribbled down either side of her chin. She slammed the cup down empty and it buckled beneath the force and spun off the table.

'I'll have another,' she said.

She plonked her chin on her hands on the table and closed her eyes for a moment.

'This place is a dump and you people are idiots.'

Jon lifted his palm from the table and held it out before he spoke.

'I would refrain from saying anything more if I were you, Miss; my colleague will be back soon.'

'Has he gone for donuts? No, donuts are for real cops, he's gone for cookies, milk and cookies.' She laughed at her own joke. Jon thought that she was the kind of girl who could be pretty if it weren't for the nonchalance she worked hard to present. Her laughter trailed off and turned into a bored sigh and she searched out Jon's eyes again.

'You should be watching out for drug dealers, not tipsy English girls. You're making arses of yourselves.'

She tilted her chair, balancing on the back two legs and just the tips of her stilettoed heels.

'Ma'am please sit on the chair properly.' Jon almost laughed at his own request. What was he, her babysitter?

But she acquiesced. She slammed the front legs down, and jolted. A surprised hiccup escaped her mouth and she took a deep breath and swallowed hard.

'Do you need another sick bag?' said Jon.

'Fuck off.'

Deborah could remember throwing her handbag down in disgust and being manhandled into the room where she vomited on the floor and immediately felt better, though no less drunk. She got up and went over to the water cooler again. She filled and re-filled her cup and glugged down the water. The numbness of the alcohol was wearing off and her feet ached. She thought about the money again and the bills that might not have been paid. She'd seen enough TV shows to know that they had to give her a phone call. Or did they? What if they thought she was a drug dealer? She scanned her mind for the last time she smoked a joint and wondered if it could still be in her system after more than a year.

'I want my phone call. I have to phone the bank,' she said. 'I know the number by heart, it's…' she reeled off the number.

'Most people call friends or a family member, perhaps an employer if you're travelling for work?' he said. 'Is there someone who can help you out?'

'No,' said Deborah. 'Absolutely nobody,' she added, 'Nobody in the world.'

Jon looked down to the table between them. He hoped his supervisor wasn't listening in. This girl wasn't a drug mule or an illegal. She was as frightened as either would be, but it was something else.

'Where are you staying?'

'Washington Square.'

'A hotel?'

Deborah shook her head.

'I'm trying to help you. Who can you call here? A friend? A relative?'

'I suppose I'll have to call Eva Goltz, though she's none of those.'

Deborah stood in front of a call box phone that had been bolted to a wall and put her ear to a receiver that had taken a few blows in its time. She listened to the tinny sound of the phone ringing.

'If nobody picks up can I call someone else?' she said.

'Give them a little time,' said Jon.

'How about if I change my mind? I think I want to call someone else. Actually, I do,' she said.

'Who is this Eva Goltz?'

Jon looked around to see if any of his colleagues were listening in. He shouldn't ask questions like that.

Deborah took the receiver away from her ear and looked up at Jon.

'I want to go home,' she said.

'We're going to let you go.'

'I want to go home, to England, home.'

But it was too late, Eva had answered the phone.

From the dimly lit, wood panelled landing of her home Eva watched through the crack of Maya's bedroom door as Maya cycled down the covers. Maya flipped on to her side. Lithe and small for her age, like her father had been, she could, Eva thought, almost be mistaken for a preschooler. Eva waited until her granddaughter was still and her breathing soft and regular before she slipped in to cover her against the cold that wasn't present in the well heated room. She sat on the bed and took in the room in darkness. Pictures of Eva and Maya on horseback were printed on to canvases around the room. On the bedside table there were framed pictures of Maya's father and another of her grandfather. The toys cast shadows and Eva remembered her own childhood fears of the dark in a place where there were no toys and the people looked as much like shadows as the shadows themselves.

'I don't want to die in the dark,' she thought again.

She lay her hand on Maya's forehead. It felt warm against the cool of her own body. Downstairs the phone rang. They had expected Deborah long before now. Connie had left an hour ago, the driver had driven to and from the airport twice to see if she was there. Eva made it to the hallway phone just a ring before the caller would have hung up.

Chapter Five

Deborah awoke, drowsy and parched. She gulped down the tumbler of water by her bed and looked at the clock, it was nearly eight, so she'd slept for twelve hours.

She quickly got up and flattened down her hair. She tidied up the make-up that the pillow had mostly rubbed off and went downstairs. She stepped inside the living room, which Eva called the den. She wondered what Maya called it. Either way, any room with a crystal chandelier was too grand to be called a den in Deborah's opinion. She glanced out to the hallway and could see no one so she sat in one of the armchairs and looked about her, taking in the room. She was looking for a change, something different from what she'd seen nearly eight years ago. How could the room have stayed the same, she thought, with everything that had happened. She folded the draping sides of her dressing gown over her cotton pyjamas, feeling exposed and yet afraid of being alone.

Around her was a collection of brown leather chesterfield sofas and chairs and a dark mahogany coffee table with an arrangement of white and lilac flowers in a vase and a mirror beneath to reflect them. In one corner of the room there was an antique sideboard that was used as a bar. A dark marble fireplace with a shining brass grate drew the eye to the far wall. Another wall was given over to leather bound books. Opposite, a pair of large windows framed by cream velvet curtains, looked out on Washington Square. The low winter sun projected prisms of light through the gaps in the vertical blinds and outside the snow was melting on the window ledges. Connie appeared from the entrance to the kitchen and took a step back when she saw Deborah.

'Deborah,' she said. 'Forgive me, I mean Miss.'

Deborah took in Connie's altered appearance and wondered if Connie was doing the same to her.

'Can I get you anything?' Connie said.

'Something for my head,' said Deborah.

'Yes Miss.'

Connie left the room.

Deborah remembered Connie as young and lively, her jittery activity in stark contrast to Eva's stateliness. Eva was the conductor of the family and everyone would rise or fall like notes on a scale depending on her mood. Connie's strawberry blonde hair had turned almost completely white. She'd filled out and done away with the Cuban heeled black leather lace up shoes Deborah used to hear coming as she walked the halls. Now she wore flat, silent moccasins.

Connie returned with a silver tray. Balanced on it were a crystal tumbler of water, a dish with slices of lemon, a tiny sugar cube bowl full of ice and some tongs and on a small silver saucer, an unopened pack of painkillers Deborah didn't recognise.

'Very good,' said Deborah. She'd seen people on television say 'very good' to their servants. She wanted Connie to remember her place and forget the last time they'd been together and Deborah had trusted her and been betrayed. There would be no pally exchanges between them. Not after what Connie did.

She allowed Connie to place the ice cubes in her glass and shook her head to decline a slice of lemon.

'That's all,' she said.

'It's good to have you back,' said Connie.

Deborah sipped her water.

Connie turned and walked back to the kitchen. Deborah swallowed down two pills and emptied her glass. She went over to the mantelpiece above the fire which was newly lit. It was yet to give off any real warmth, though the underfloor heating was on and the room hotter than Deborah would have expected. She picked up a framed picture of a handsome young man and her eyes couldn't leave it no matter how much she knew it would be better if they did. She hadn't seen his face for so long, he looked just the way she remembered him; the picture could have been taken on the day she'd left.

She didn't hear a sound until Maya's ballet-slippered feet hit the squeaky floorboard at the hallway entrance to the room. Maya came to an abrupt halt. Deborah's grip on the picture stiffened and her eyes met Maya's. They glanced around the outside edges of one another as if inspecting a curious unknown creature. Deborah's eyes cast down and Maya's up until they had taken in each other's almost identical features. Deborah took a half step in Maya's direction and Maya stepped back. The floorboard let out a wince.

'Maya,' Deborah whispered, as if her voice might break.

Maya's head tilted, like a dog trying to comprehend its babbling owner. But there was no eagerness in her gaze.

'Hello, Maya,' said Deborah. She extended her hand and with the other clutched the picture to her chest.

She edged a little closer. Maya stepped back, her face deadpan.

'No school today, Maya?'

Maya continued to stare Deborah down. At the same time Connie walked into the room and ruffled Maya's hair as she passed her.

'Maya goes when she feels like it, which isn't very often,' she said, rummaging down the back of one of the armchair cushions.

'Why don't you go to school, Maya?' Deborah asked.

Maya blanked Deborah and turned to Connie who had fished out a pair of Eva's tortoiseshell rimmed reading glasses and was buffing them against her skirt. Maya took hold of Connie's free hand and asked in a whisper if they could go out and have something from Soho Sushi for lunch. Connie smiled and shook her head. Then Maya asked Connie to bake her some of the chocolate chip cookies she liked. Connie pinched Maya's cheek affectionately.

'Alright, but what do you say?' she said.

Maya rolled her eyes and gave a withering 'please'.

Deborah suddenly felt faint, as if she'd taken another drink on an empty stomach. She steadied herself on the back of the leather sofa.

'Will you let me get you something else?' Connie said.

'I'll have a coffee,' said Deborah.

Connie nodded and left the room, adeptly avoiding the groaning floorboard.

In the near distance Deborah heard Eva's voice calling out to Maya. Deborah dashed across the room to the mantelpiece and replaced the photograph just before Eva's head appeared around the door frame. Her body, always slim but now almost hollowed out, followed.

There was no time to take her in, to begin again or remind her that she was lucky to have got her way. Eva had hold of Deborah's hand and was shaking it, the other hand took hold of Deborah's other arm. That was Eva; she could own you, place you and arrange you so that you'd look a fool to question her. She let go as quickly as she'd taken hold and turned to Maya.

'Now didn't I ask you to wait until Deborah was dressed and had had breakfast?' she said to Maya.

'It's not her fault, I was in here already,' said Deborah.

Maya walked over and slipped her hand into Eva's. Eva smiled down at her.

'Have you said hello, then?'

Maya pointed to the mantelpiece and Deborah caught a look from the corner of her eye.

'She was hugging that picture of Daddy to her chest,'

There was a moment where nobody's eyes could meet.

'I'm sorry, I...' said Deborah into the void.

Maya scuffed the toe of her ballet shoe along the grain of the wooden floorboards.

'Can Connie bring you anything?' said Eva.

Before Deborah could answer Connie came back into the room, this time carrying a silver tray with a coffee cup and saucer, a cafetiere, both milk and cream in small silver jugs and sugar cubes and tongs in a matching pot.

'It's a Kenyan blend, Miss. It's Mrs Goltz's favourite. I hope you enjoy it. Will there be anything else?' said Connie, a smile on her face.

'No,' said Deborah.

'Please sit down,' said Eva to Deborah. Deborah did so. She poured herself a cup of black coffee.

'Thank you, Connie,' said Eva and Connie left the room. Eva turned to Maya again, 'Have you said a proper hello to Deborah?'

Eva was still standing so Deborah had to look up to her. Maya slinked behind Eva, contorting Eva's arm behind her back. She lolled against Eva's legs while her gaze travelled around the ceiling as if following a lazy fly. Eva turned her body and shook Maya's arm,

'For goodness's sake, say hello, Maya,' she said.

'It's alright,' said Deborah. She stood up. 'This is pretty

strange for me too, Maya.'

Maya's eyes couldn't be moved from the ceiling.

'Are you looking at the chandelier? Doesn't it sparkle.'

It had been the hottest day of the year the afternoon that Deborah had first looked up at the chandelier. The rest of Manhattan, Deborah's Manhattan at least, was fractious and fraught. The lazy breeze came only in wisps and maddeningly flipped up the hems of sundresses. Deborah had followed Maya's father into the town house. A town house on one of the island's most prestigious streets, flanked by homes owned by New York royalty and celebrities. In the cool hallway there had been a smell of freesias along with a subtle lemony verbena. When he closed the front door and placed his hand in the small of her sweat-speckled lower back there was a quiet that Deborah hadn't enjoyed since she'd arrived in the city. The rest of the family were away at their summer house. They came later. First came Deborah's attachment to what they had. In the room, which he told her was called a den she was transfixed by the chandelier that cast little circles of rainbow coloured light around the room as the sun came in. She ran her hand along the glossy wood, leather and marble surfaces and he fixed them a drink from the bar in the corner. She willed her senses to remember every detail of this place. She wanted to wrap her body around it, encompass it.

'What do you think about living here, Maya?' said Deborah.

She was immediately aware of what a puerile question it was to ask a seven-year-old. It was all she had ever known and a house like any other. Maya didn't give the question the dignity of an answer.

'Maya, where are your manners?' Eva said. 'She's been so excited,' she said to Deborah again.

'No I haven't,' said Maya, her eyes still wandering.

45

'She's tired.'

'No, I'm not.'

Deborah smiled because it was all she could do. What had she expected? Not this. She excused herself to take a shower and get dressed. And she must find her phone, call the bank and hope.

Eva watched her leave and walked over to the mantelpiece. She picked up the framed picture. Using the edge of her Hermes scarf she buffed away any fingerprints and replaced it on the shelf.

'When is she leaving?' asked Maya.

Chapter Six

After a fitful night in her overheated bedroom Deborah woke up too early. The day ahead was a terrifying stretch, nothing to do and nowhere to go. It was the 3rd of January, twenty-eight more days until her flight home would leave. Maya hadn't spoken to her at dinner the night before and she had nothing to say to Eva. She would keep to her room as much as she could. It's early days, she told herself again, things might get better. She reached out to the phone and dialled the bank again. The automated voice she'd come to dread practically sang to her now. She thought of all the people hauling themselves out of a warm bed to go to work so they could just about pay the bills, buy a coffee and get through the day. She felt ashamed about what she was willing to do not to be one of them. Deborah got up and dug through her suitcase for her workout clothes. She'd go for a run, turn down King Street and then Hudson, down to Tribeca to see the streets that had once been her neighbourhood. Then she remembered throwing out her trainers and running clothes at the very last minute when the cab was sounding its horn and she was still trying to close her suitcase.

She couldn't bring herself to unpack properly. Nothing she

owned looked good enough to sit on the mink velvet hangers in the walk-in wardrobe. To while away some time she took a bath in a tub that was big enough to fit everyone in the house inside it. She sniffed the miniature toiletries and poured a splash of a few of them into the running water. The room smelled of peach schnapps, raspberry and coconut; after half an hour the smell overpowered her and she got out and sat on the edge of the bed wrapped in a towel. On the television there was an animated anchor woman with teeth so white they were luminous. She ought to get dressed, she was hungry and hoped she could slip into the kitchen and get something to eat without a fanfare. Sifting through everything she had brought with her she eventually found an outfit that was the best of a bad lot, she put on her make-up and styled her hair. She studied her teeth in the bathroom mirror, opening wide and then pulling up her lips and baring her teeth like a snarling dog. Maybe it was her teeth that were too stained and not that the anchor woman's were too bright, she thought.

Deborah was alone at breakfast. It was too early for Eva and Maya. Connie wouldn't let her so much as pour her own juice and cheerfully took her order. Connie delivered oatmeal and melon along with a cup of the best coffee Deborah had ever tasted. Connie lingered at the front door as Deborah buttoned her coat. Deborah refused to tell Connie where she was going or when she'd be back. Let Eva ask her own questions. She stepped outside to a gust of wind and watched a couple of soda cans and a lottery ticket, some potato chip wrappers and a plastic water bottle skitter along the sidewalk. No matter how much money you had everyone had to dance around litter and clean out the black grit from inside their noses after a day in the city.

She walked a block to Dean & DeLuca. She bought a coffee and sat down on a tall wooden stall at a bar that looked out on the street. She'd sat there many times before. Nothing much had changed in the time she'd been away. The Banana Republic store seemed to have expanded and there was a small tapas place she didn't remember, but she didn't completely trust her memory. There was a lot she hadn't seen back then. Across the street a chauffeur driven car pulled up and a woman about Deborah's age stepped out accompanied by two children. Both were younger than Maya and trussed up in woolen coats and furry mittens. Their mother wore a fur-trimmed poncho, matching hat and gloves and she was carrying the handbag of the season. Her life could have been like that, Deborah thought, if only she could have held on tighter. She twirled the corrugated cardboard looped around her paper coffee cup and thought about going back to the counter for an almond biscotti. But she wanted her seat more and so she stayed put. Just then a delivery lorry pulled up and obscured her view of the street. Denim covered legs slithered out of the cab and landed with a spring on the pavement. The man looked like he delivered diet coke on adverts and Deborah stared. He caught her looking at him and smiled. He went to the back and unloaded several boxes on to a trolley which he wheeled in through the door. A barista called out to him from the counter and a conversation started about his holiday to Bermuda. Deborah turned a little to watch him then quickly looked away when he caught her staring. She wasn't equipped with a newspaper or a friend to talk to, so she studied the inside of her coffee cup and listened in to the conversation. She sneaked a look over her shoulder at him and once again he was turned in her direction.

'Hey,' he said.

'Hi,' said Deborah.

He went back outside for another stack of boxes. There was nowhere to look apart from out to his truck. On his way back Deborah watched him as he stopped in the doorway letting in a gust of cold air. He broke the seal of the top box and reached inside. He pulled out a cellophane wrapped biscotti and leant over the boxes to hand it to Deborah.

'Thanks,' she said.

He was flirting with her. But what now? She was used to the attention of men and would play along. With an absence of feeling it was always just a game. Sometimes she played it easy and other times she delighted in making it difficult. Nobody won because if they wanted her she didn't want them back. The one person she'd wanted had let her leave and never come after her.

She didn't want the biscotti anymore and stowed it in her coat pocket.

With the spell broken, she went back to stirring around the bubbles on the top of her coffee. She looked up for a moment and he was lingering in the doorway. She looked away— it was better than him asking for her number and going out for an excruciating date where she would confirm her suspicions that he had nothing for her and she had nothing for him either. He climbed back in his cab and drove off.

Across the street the woman and her children were getting back in their car. Deborah studied her outfit then looked down at her own. She drank up and left. She hailed a taxi outside and felt the thrill of a yellow cab sliding to a halt at the curb next to her.

Inside the taxi she told the driver to take her to Saks Fifth Avenue.

'Oh, it's pricey in there,' he said. 'Fine for a visit but not for shopping.'

'I'm going shopping,' said Deborah.

'If you're looking for souvenirs you won't find any,' he said.

'I'm not,' said Deborah.

'You live here?'

'Yes,' said Deborah. What else could she say? If she'd said no he'd have asked her where she was staying because he was, she could tell, the chatty kind. It would be as much of a deviation from the truth to say she was staying with a friend.

'Whereabouts?'

'Washington Square.'

'Very nice. You and your husband, or your parents?'

She saw him sizing up her age in the rear-view mirror. And there it was, the double punch, the assumption that she could only live in such a salubrious area with someone else to pay for it. And the reality that it was true.

'Has it been a cold winter?' she said. She had to change the subject. Because if he asked if she had kids she might tell him the whole sorry tale just to shut him up.

'You weren't in town?'

Shit, Deborah thought, she wasn't keeping up with her own story.

'No, I was away for a couple of months,'

'Yeah, it's been a cold one. But people still turned out in Times Square for the millennium. I was there with my wife and some buddies, where were you when the clock struck?'

'London,' Deborah said.

'Very nice.'

'It was crap actually. They said there was going to be a river of fire along the Thames but it didn't work out. I won a fiver out of it though,' said Deborah.

The taxi pulled up outside of Saks. She paid and said goodbye, relieved this exchange was over. The moment she touched the handle to push the door open into the shop she felt the way she used to when she'd got home from school and shut the front door behind her. It closed out the pasty-faced girl and her mother who walked her home every day and found as many ways as corners turned to make comments about Deborah's mother. Once in the sanctuary of her home all she had to do was wait until her mother got home from work and when she did it would all be ok.

It was getting dark when Deborah got back to Eva's house. She was able to get through the door and to the bottom of the stairs undetected. Her arms were full of bags which banged against the bannisters and she heard Connie call out. She ignored her and made it to the top and into her room without anyone seeing her. She closed the door and wished there was a key she could turn. Without stopping to take her coat off she set about unpacking the bags. From black and white boxes she pulled out two cashmere sweaters, wrapped in tissue paper. Her heart was racing in her chest and she began unpacking her shopping with greater speed. Three dresses, two skirts, a blazer, four pairs of jeans, a bag full of blouses and fitted t-shirts. A winter coat, scarf, hat, gloves, underwear, tights, a handbag, two pairs of boots, three pairs of heels. The store had sent out two shop assistants to help her load all her purchases into the taxi they'd hailed for her. She hadn't realised how much her arms ached until now. But she carried on. She pulled out the hangers from inside the empty wardrobe and quickly the room concealed her extravagance. There was still plenty of space to fill. But this was a start. She got down on her knees and slid her finger down the heels of the shoes, then she smelled the soft grey leather of the gloves and ran her hand over the dresses. Each item was full of enchantment, a promise that she could be made new.

She stood and took out a mulberry skirt and cream cashmere sweater, selected a pair of tights, underwear and pulled out the inner packaging from the pair of knee-high boots. She quickly undressed and scrambled down on all fours to find her suitcase which she'd stashed under the bed. She opened it up and jammed the dirty clothes inside. She felt nothing but disdain for the clothes she'd brought with her— they looked used. They had no place in this life. Not until she was dressed in her new attire could she stop. She looked herself up and down in the mirror. She would need new make up too and a different hairstyle. Nothing too drastic, she liked her long dark hair, she just needed to look different from the person who'd left London. Better.

She smelled like a teenage boy's bedroom just before a girl was due to come over. Her hair had gone lank in the humidity and she'd laddered her tights with the urgency of getting them down.

'Have you got another man in there?' he said, smiling.

'I've got to go,' she said, without looking up.

'Hang on, Deborah, you're sick.'

'Will you call me a cab? I can't face going to look for one at this time of night.'

'Sure,' he said and went to the phone in the hallway. 'Would you let me get you something first?'

'I just need to sleep.'

'I've got a spare room, stay, I'd feel better if you did.'

Unable to hold herself up any longer Deborah sat down on the chair in the hallway and put her head in her hands.

'I feel like shit.'

'You smell like shit,' he said, laughing.

'This is the worst date of my life.'

'It's not going too badly,' he said. 'I was kidding by the way, you smell like me but stronger.'

'I won't stay but I need to lie down for a while.'

He showed her to the spare bedroom and pulled back the covers. Deborah kicked off her shoes and lay down. He covered her over. She closed her eyes and when she awoke it was getting light. There was a pint of water next to the bed along with a note.

'Warning— I have declared a state of emergency in the hallway bathroom, use the en suite.'

She drank down the pint of water and then shrunk back into bed. She heard footsteps outside the bedroom door and then it opened. She peeked out from under the covers.

'I liked your note,' she said, 'very gallant.'

'You haven't seen what I've done in there.'

'You too?'

He nodded.

'We should have that restaurant closed down,' she said.

'I'm going to tell my mom,' he said.

Deborah laughed.

'No seriously, she'll rip them a new one.'

'What? Does she work there?'

He laughed.

'She owns the building,' he said.

'Big shot,' said Deborah.

How funny, thought Deborah in that moment. That this is how she fell in love with him.

Chapter Eight

Jon had finished his night shift at the airport. He was in the locker room where he changed from frozen faced Immigration Officer to himself again. The job wasn't what he'd expected. He was surrounded by the most embittered men he'd met since the army. They spoke to travellers moving through JFK Airport as if they were inmates; a menace, a nuisance and not to be trusted. He'd known people like this at Rikers Island Correctional Centre. That job wasn't what he'd expected either. He worked eight months, five hangings, three overdoses and countless times where he'd witnessed a fellow guard taunt or abuse a prisoner. Eight years in the military and nobody else wanted him. He was turning thirty in a week and all around him friends were winning promotions, getting married and having kids. He was still in his probationary period at the airport and he wasn't even dating anyone. He felt like the kid held back in high school while everyone else graduated. At least he'd moved out of his mom's house.

He noticed a plastic storage box in the corner of the room. Lost property was jammed in like a load of laundry. It would go to Goodwill at the end of the month if nobody claimed it. A grey and silver knit scarf hung down one side, the bottom of it curled up in a pile on the tiled floor. It belonged to a Deborah Foster, the first person he'd called in. He didn't know if she was still on his mind because she was the first or because of the way she went from obnoxious drunk to jittery wreck when it was time to leave. He looked around the corner of the locker room to be sure nobody else was there and then went over to the box and took out the scarf. She had practically begged him to send her back to London on the next plane. Wherever she was going, it might as well have been hell. But a lawyer had collected her, Jon had seen his card and made a note of his name and address and they left in a chauffeur driven car. He could find out where she was staying, take the scarf back to her, it might put his mind at ease. But what would he say when he was asked why he did it? He put the scarf back in the box and went to his locker.

It was 7.15am. He would drive home then walk to the new juice bar that had opened on 38th street, Astoria. He would order the green smoothie and sit looking out of the window watching people go about their ordinary lives and take comfort in the regularity of school runs and daily commutes. His pals bemoaned their ordinary lives but he didn't think they had anything much to complain about.

'Fuck it,' he said aloud to the empty room.

He went over to the box and pulled out the scarf. He balled it up and zipped it into his coat. He turned the key in his locker and went to the empty back office where he logged out. He quickly flicked through his keys to find the one for the filing cabinets. F for Foster. There it was. Washington Square Gardens. There would be a juice bar down there some place, other people to watch and a new rhythm to drum his fingers to.

Deborah finished her first Pilates class at the exclusive Mind Body Blend Studio and struck up a conversation with a clique of women who were getting ready to go out for coffee together. They were polite and half-hearted in their responses to her. Deborah retreated. She'd forgotten how hard these clubs were to get in to even once you've paid your membership fees. She took a cab back to Washington Square. The moment the door clicked closed she heard Connie's voice and took the stairs two at a time up to her room. Just outside the door there was a brown paper bag with a formal looking note written in Connie's handwriting stuck on top. It read,

Caller— Jon Venuto. Date— January 4th 2000. Time— 9.30am. Message— he would like to return your scarf. Caller's number— 646 669 6642.

She held the note in her hand and read the name again, she didn't recall who he was. The night she arrived in New York City came back to her in pieces that had been scrambled. She couldn't put them together in any coherent order and she didn't care to. It took some doing but she came back into the city as ignominiously as she'd left it. Deborah held the scarf between two fingers and lifted it up to sniff it. There was a faint whiff of vomit. She took it over to the bin and mashed it down with her shoe, then she balled up the paper bag and threw it in. She whipped a handful of tissues from the dressing table and laid them over the top and finished the job with a spritz of her new perfume. Still, it was a kind gesture. It was only mid-morning and she had nothing to do except shop or sit in a café. Because of the jet-lag and a persistent feeling of being displaced she wasn't sleeping much. She woke at five every morning and by lunchtime she felt as though she'd been in the house for a week. She went out to the landing and called for Connie. Connie appeared at the bottom of the stairs.

'Miss, a man came to the door with your scarf, he said it was left behind at the airport. He works there.'

'Oh,' said Deborah. 'A pilot?'

'I don't know, he didn't say, Miss,' said Connie. 'A nice

young man though.'

'What does he look like? What was he driving?'

'He was on foot... maybe five ten or eleven, dark hair, dark eyes, he had a friendly face when he smiled. He was kind of Italian looking.'

Connie looked absurdly happy with herself as though the caller's pleasing demeanour was a credit to her.

'Is there anything else Miss?' said Connie. Still grinning.

'No, thanks.'

Deborah was beginning to feel that Connie was trying harder than anyone else to make her feel welcome. She was the closest person she had to an ally in a house where nobody else spoke to her. Connie walked away purposefully and Deborah went to her room. She sniffed the air, afraid that the soiled scarf was going to make itself known all day. She could have asked Connie to empty the bin or she could have done it herself but she feared the unwanted attention that could bring and she knew that Eva was watching her. She read the note again and picked up the telephone and dialled the number. It rang and rang before an answerphone picked up the message.

'This is Jon, leave a message,' the bleep came and Deborah hung up.

She waited a moment then dialled again. He sounded straight-forward, honest and decent enough. The bleep came once more.

'This is Deborah, Deborah Foster. Thanks for returning my scarf.' She paused. 'I wonder if you'd let me buy you a cup of coffee to say a proper thank you? I'm very busy and I'm sure you are too so maybe not, but maybe. This is my number...,' she read the number out and hung up quickly.

It wasn't until Jon got to the place below Houston Street that he realised he'd suggested they meet at a restaurant and not a coffee shop. He'd never been there before but his buddy said it served coffee and was the kind of place you take a girl on a first date, not that this was a date. He was under-dressed in converse and jeans but the woman on the door beamed at him and offered a table at the window. He slid behind the table and flipped the menu over. Five bucks for a cup of coffee. No wonder the woman was smiling. Deborah got out of a taxi just outside the door and Jon stood up. She hadn't remembered him when they spoke on the phone and he didn't expect to be recognised. She was on the sidewalk adjusting her shopping bags in her hand and he realised he'd got up too soon and drawn the attention of the waitress, who was walking in his direction.

'Just waiting to greet my friend,' he said. 'We're not ready to order anything just yet.'

The waitress nodded and he stayed standing, feeling conspicuous. He shifted from foot to foot. Deborah paused in the doorway and was beckoned in by the smiling woman who gestured in Jon's direction. Deborah walked over, her bags brushing the shoulders of other diners as she jutted her elbows out to unwrap a new scarf. It trailed the heads of the other diners and she narrowly missed knocking several glasses over as she finally unravelled it from around her neck. Jon was enjoying the scene. His mother said you could always spot a Catholic in a public place. A Catholic would have picked their way through the diners apologising as they went, 'sorry to disturb you,' 'sorry, did my bag brush you ever so slightly?' 'sorry, sorry, sorry.' He found it kind of irritating when people made a fuss about the most minor infractions. Deborah did not. She sat down, leaving her shopping bags in the thoroughfare and shrugged off her coat.

'Have they got soy milk here? Because I went somewhere the other day and they didn't have it and I was like, honestly, is this the 80s? Am I in the sticks? No, this is New York City, walk to the nearest store and buy some. Where do you live?'

she said. No greeting.

'Close to Astoria Park,' said Jon.

'That's not Manhattan, right? I don't know it.'

'It's in Queens.'

'What's it like?'

'It's like here I guess, but east of the river.'

The waitress came over and Deborah ordered a latte made with soy milk. As she walked away Deborah smirked.

'I find waiting staff funny,' she said.

'How so?'

'They're too chatty here, you've got to wonder if they just...' Deborah pressed her finger against her right nostril and did a little sniff through the left.

'Maybe they're just happy.'

'They make what? Six dollars an hour.'

A pause, Jon wondered if he was supposed to laugh. Deborah turned her head to look out of the window.

'What brings you to the city?' he said.

'My daughter lives here,' said Deborah.

He paused, searching his mind for another question.

'She's seven by the way, just in case you think I have a grown-up daughter and have just had a lot of work done.' Deborah lifted the skin under her chin with both hands. 'She lived with her father after we split up, he passed away last year and her grandmother has been taking care of her.'

Jon nodded.

Silence. Deborah started looking over Jon's head at the blackboard with the day's specials written on it in a loopy scrawl.

'I'm starving, I'm going to have lunch. Will you let me buy you lunch, as a thank you for returning my scarf?' said Deborah.

'There's really no need.'

'You went to some effort.'

'It was nothing.'

'I wouldn't have done it, you're a nice guy, I appreciate it. Oh god, I'm not what you were expecting am I? You're just being polite. You want to leave?' said Deborah.

Jon saw the same anxious look on her face that she'd left the airport with on New Year's Day.

'No, sure, you are. I mean, I didn't expect to be bought lunch.'

Deborah's coffee arrived and Jon tensed when the waitress started a perky little pitch about the specials. She sashayed off and Deborah rolled her eyes.

They ate three courses and sat through a few renditions of perky waitress patter. Deborah ordered wine and she stopped criticising the waitress after her second glass. Jon sipped one glass carefully, afraid of appearing unsophisticated if he refused and asked for a beer instead. She probed him about the night she'd arrived and been detained in JFK. He told her a sanitised version of what had happened and she was willing to accept it. She was talking incessantly which was a relief because he ran out of things to say. His mother said he was the strong silent type. She also said he'd been the last kid in his kindergarten to speak a full sentence.

'There's this party later. Would you like to come? It's in Queens but the journey's not too bad on the train,' he said.

'I prefer cabs,' said Deborah.

'It's a buddy of mine's birthday, his wife will be there.'

And now he'd made it weird. Why did he have to mention a wife? He'd been too concerned with not sounding like it would be a bunch of guys drinking beer in a basement to realise what a strange comment he was making.

'Right,' said Deborah. 'Will there be a sewing circle for me to sit in?'

Jon smiled and shook his head. She was ragging on him as if they were buddies.

'What do these people do?' said Deborah.

'Shaun works at his dad's scrap yard and Jess is a receptionist at the hospital. Me and Shaun went to school together.'

Deborah was folding her napkin in her lap, she placed it down on the table.

'It'll be fun, some drinks, games, we'll order in,' he said.

Deborah gestured to the waitress that they wanted the bill.

'Honestly,' said Deborah. 'It sounds a little homey to me. You're kind to take pity on a foreigner but there must be someone else you can take?'

'Oh sure,' said Jon.

Deborah excused herself and went to the bathroom. Jon fiddled with the sugar packets in the white enamel container on the table and asked the waitress for the cheque again. He still didn't feel like he knew much about Deborah except that she said she liked jazz but couldn't name any of the artists she listened to. She had a lot of money, that much was clear, but said nothing about a job. And she slipped up, just once, and said serviette instead of napkin and it made her blush. Not that Jon cared, he used kitchen towel or the top of his jeans to wipe his hands on. But he liked her. Not because she was thoughtful or kind or for any of the reasons you're supposed to like a girl. She didn't waste anyone's time; she was who she was. She could be rude but real.

Deborah came back from the bathroom and Jon saw the other men in the room notice her as she walked through the central aisle with tables either side. The waitress arrived with the bill at the same time as Deborah got back to the table and Deborah opened her wallet and put down the cash. As they left they walked past new diners with Deborah's elbows sticking out and her scarf trailing the tops of their heads. Jon liked the way she talked. Not because of the accent or even what she said but she talked as though it was important that somebody listen, like you were doing her a solid by letting her vent.

Outside the sky weighed heavy and at just past three o'clock it was already getting dark.

'Where's a cab? It's going to snow,' said Deborah.

Jon raised his arm at a passing taxi. It flew straight past them but the next one stopped.

'Enjoy your party,' said Deborah. She opened the car door and climbed in.

'You're sure I can't give you the address?' he said. 'Just come if you want to, it's fine if you don't.'

'You're not selling it,' said Deborah.

He searched his mind for something else to say but settled with a gesture, his right hand raised like he was asking for a high five. Deborah closed the door of the cab and it pulled away.

As soon as it turned the corner she wished she could go back and say something nicer. Pain makes you funny shaped, she thought, all teeth and elbows. Like Connie said, he was Italian looking, sweet, earnest and much humbler than she'd expected. If she'd have met Jon nine years ago she wouldn't have noticed him. He'd have been too ordinary, predictable and wholesome. Deborah had learned there are young women who notice men like him and know what they're looking at. They don't have any high fences to jump, cartwheels to perform and balancing acts to perfect. She wondered what that life would be like. Though, if she could have gone back and chosen again, back to a time before Maya's father, before the Goltz family, would she?

Chapter Nine

Connie arrived early. It was Saturday morning, the busiest of the week what with Maya's dance class, Eva getting ready for synagogue and a lunch to prepare for any guests she might bring back. She got to work getting Maya's dance bag packed with ballet shoes and leg warmers, a bottle of water, an apple and a packet of raisins. She spent ten minutes running a lint roller over Eva's winter coat and buffed a pair of shoes that had been left in the hallway. She heard the creaking of floorboards above and started preparing the coffee. She ground the beans noisily and crashed around with the new-fangled coffee machine that she was still getting used to. By the time she went to the dining room she'd been in the house for a half an hour and was surprised to see Eva sitting at the table, a mess of papers around her.

'Mrs Goltz,' said Connie. 'I'm sorry to disturb you.'

'I've got something to talk to you about Connie. Will you sit down a minute?'

Connie sat and searched her mind for all the things she might have done wrong. The lid she lost from the 2% milk, the day she lay down on the kitchen floor because her back was aching, the points she sometimes forgot to fold on the end of the toilet paper or the cookies she burned a little but served to Maya all the same.

'All this is my will,' said Eva.

'That's a lot of paper.'

'The lawyers say I'm a very precise woman— apparently not everyone has as many requests.'

Connie didn't know how to respond so she nodded.

'You are incredibly important to this family, I want to tell you that.'

Connie felt her face flush. She mumbled,

'Thank you, Mrs Goltz.'

'And I plan to leave you some money.'

And then she was on her feet.

'No, no, Mrs Goltz,' she said. 'You pay me, that's enough, people will say—'

'I don't care what anyone says, I'll leave my money to whomever I like.'

Connie was at the door.

'I'm sorry, Mrs Goltz, I can't, I can't.'

Connie backed out of the room and hurried away. She found sanctuary in the cool and quiet kitchen. She opened the window above the sink and turned her face towards the incoming stream of cold air. She earned more working for the Goltzes than she ever expected to. She wouldn't take advantage. She wouldn't have anyone say she took advantage.

Connie left breakfast in the kitchen and took Maya to ballet class. While she watched the troupe of pastel clad little girls twirl and sashay around the room she imagined what Eva might say to her when she got back. Connie could barely hear anything Maya talked about on the way home, she was too nervous of what would happen once they got through the front door. Eva was in the hallway on her way out. Connie felt a heat in her throat that travelled upwards to her sinuses, along with a sensation like a coughing fit waiting to happen and hot tears tried to come out. She jammed her tongue to the roof of her mouth and forced them back.

'I'll be home around twelve thirty or one o'clock. The Cohens are coming back for lunch, possibly Mrs Hellick and her daughter and if Rabbi Rovner and Jona don't have plans they'll come as well.'

'Yes, Mrs Goltz.'

Eva gave her a re-assuring smile. Connie's shoulders dropped an inch.

Connie went upstairs. The door of the bedroom sat ajar just enough for Connie to see that Deborah was inside. The guest room, which was still referred to as such even though Deborah had inhabited it for a week, was painted white and had vintage art deco furniture and a specially commissioned shell grey chaise longue and matching chairs. The décor wasn't to Connie's taste but she'd heard guests rave over it and say how much it reminded them of one of the tower suites at the Waldorf Astoria. This pleased Eva and that was enough for Connie. Connie had been waiting all morning for Deborah to leave her room. Though it was not the largest, the room was the most labour intensive. Deborah dropped her clothes where she took them off and left soggy towels balled up on the bed. Daily the dressing table was strewn with make-up smeared cotton wool pads, spilled loose powder and smears of lipstick and nail polish which took a plastic putty knife, wire wool and all of Connie's patience to remove without damaging the furniture.

She lingered outside the room dusting a picture on the landing wall and humming in the hope that Deborah would notice her. Deborah was perched at the end of the chaise longue. A crystal tumbler of water was balanced on the upholstery and she was flipping through a little book with a gold 'D' embossed on the front. She dialled a number from the book on her cell phone.

'Hi Carla, it's Deborah Foster again. I wonder if you got my last message…'

Connie had heard her making calls for the last few mornings, all in the same desperate, slightly agitated tone. Deborah repeated her phone number twice over, said the address of the house and then, all too late, adopted a breezy tone and said goodbye. Deborah's gaze lifted from the display of her phone and landed on Connie.

'Have there been any messages left for me, Connie?'

'No, Miss,' said Connie. She took the opportunity to stand with one foot over the threshold of the bedroom.

'Are you sure?'

'I'm sure Miss. Not while I've been here. Are you expecting someone in particular?'

Deborah shook her head and Connie saw her shoulders slump a little.

'If those people you're calling aren't calling you back perhaps you don't really want them to. If you don't mind me saying. '

'I mind.'

Connie lifted her hands in surrender, a slightly dusty white cloth hung from the right one.

'I'm sorry. I'll be sure to tell you if anyone calls here.'

Connie backed out of the room. Deborah called her back.

'Connie, you don't think Eva has anything to do with this, do you?'

'No.'

'You wouldn't tell me if she did.'

Connie froze. Deborah searched her face.

Connie felt bad for the girl. She thought she knew what to say to cheer her up.

'I baked English scones at home yesterday evening, but it's

the first time I've made them so you'll have to tell me how I did. They're in the kitchen if you want to try one,' said Connie.

Deborah paused.

'Great, I'll be fat as well as friendless,' she said.

Deborah got up and left the room. On the chaise longue lay her phone, the book and a sketchy list with lots of crossings out, arrows and question marks between the names. Beside each name were scrawls detailing how she knew the person and how they knew her. Most referred to him. His name was no longer used and if anyone spoke it Eva flinched as if physically hurt. She held it sacred and so everyone did. As if it were her property and nobody else's.

Connie mopped up the spilled tea on the dressing table and rescued a precariously balanced tray with the remnants of Deborah's scrambled egg breakfast on it. The bedsheet was dusted with crumbs and there was a splash of tea which had gone through the padded mattress cover below. It would be another complete overhaul, thought Connie. She went to work stripping the bed completely. Bunched at the bottom were Deborah's pyjamas. Connie rescued them from the bed linen pile and added to it a couple of make-up smeared towels that were at either end of the en suite bathroom. She went to the large chest of drawers to find another set of pyjamas and laid them out on the corner chair in the bedroom, just as she did for Eva and Maya. It was almost midday by the time she finished and she was going to be pressed to have lunch on the table for one o'clock.

Before Deborah had arrived, Connie could usually get home for a couple of hours in the afternoon before she returned to prepare supper and clean the kitchen for the night, before the same process began again at 7.30 the following morning. She was off on Tuesdays and Fridays from twelve and all day on Sunday. Connie mostly ate her meals by herself in the kitchen, leafing through a newspaper she'd carried off the metro earlier that day. Eva once invited Connie to sit with her and Maya in the dining room but she couldn't bring herself to do it. She made up an excuse and after that Eva didn't ask again.

Eva's guests came and went and in the den Eva sat back on a cream and gold upright armchair that she had rested upon moments ago. Her legs felt tired and her chest heavy and she was wondering how she would get up without making a fuss. Maya stood in front of her dressed in a powder blue leotard with a red cross over cardigan, white tights and her favourite pink satin ballet shoes. On cue, Eva clapped a rhythm as Maya moved her feet from first position to second and third, fourth and fifth. A movement which began in her torso spread up through her chest and head and out to her arms which glided around striking a pose in time with the clapping and positioning of her feet. Deborah stood in the doorway a moment where she could observe Maya unaware. The clapping stopped and Deborah walked into the room with half a buttered scone on a small china plate. Both Eva and Maya looked up at her.

'Aren't you good, Maya.'

Both were unmoved by the compliment. 'Deborah,' said Eva in place of a greeting.

'Am I interrupting?'

Neither answered.

'Have you tried the scones Connie made? They're amazing.'

'They're not as good as her cookies,' said Maya shooting a conspiratorial smile in Eva's direction.

'I'm afraid we didn't care for them,' said Eva.

Eva turned her body no more than an inch in Maya's direction. Maya's eyes were upon her and she began to clap again in time with Maya's footwork. Deborah ate the rest of her scone in two bites and watched Maya's fluid body float from one position to the next. This time she added plies and ronds de jambes and other movements that Deborah didn't know the names of, Maya's feet, body and arms flowed as one. Suddenly Eva stopped clapping. Maya rested her arms and shook out her feet.

'I'm sorry Deborah, is there something you need? ' said Eva.

'No,'

'Are you sure?'

'Sure,' said Deborah and she backed out of the room hitting the squeaky floorboard and jumping a little in fright at the sound of it whining. Eva and Maya listened to the sound of Deborah's heels fading along the marble hallway. Maya's eyes rolled and a grin filled her face.

'You told her, Nana.'

Eva took as deep a breath as her lungs would allow and cast her eyes down.

'I did, didn't I.'

Maya began her practice again and Eva clapped along but more quietly. The fatigue was becoming harder to shake and alongside it she felt shame cutting at her insides. She had prayed for the willingness to let Deborah in to their lives again. Summoning her wasn't so hard, neither was the first couple of days. At that point anything could have happened, she could have retreated, sent her home again and the girl would have taken the money and run.

But now she saw curiosity take the place of indifference in Maya's eyes. One afternoon she discovered Maya sitting at the opposite end of the sofa to Deborah watching her watch mindless television. Then there was the evening when Deborah had grilled her about her day at school and Maya had regaled her with a story of her least favourite teacher falling in the fishpond. Eva doubted it was true but Maya had wanted to impress Deborah. She knew children will say anything to keep an audience with them. Maya had started asking questions about Deborah, out of her ear shot. Did she have any other children? Why not? Would she be staying? Would she get a

73

brother or sister now? Would Deborah let her have a puppy? She wanted to learn about the woman who was called her mother. There was nothing Eva wouldn't have done to know more about her own. How could she keep away nature's most addictive bond? In this moment Eva wanted to cast her out again. But now she couldn't be sure Deborah would leave without a fight and Eva would lose. Whatever happened she was going to lose. Rabbi Rovner often reminded Eva that it was entirely up to her whether she lit up a life for Maya that went beyond her own presence in it or let Maya believe that when she was gone that light was extinguished.

The next time I want to smack Deborah down I'll think of Maya, she thought, and she hoped it would be enough to stop herself.

Chapter Ten

Connie could hear the phone ringing down the hall in the den. Layered on top was the noise of excited infant voices and party whistles being blown. Grownups cooed over two-year-old Maya and the children's entertainer was straining his voice to perform his one-man show. She strode down the hall, her heels making a purposeful crisp sound against the muffled noise she was leaving behind. She stepped over the creaky floorboard and wiped her glitter covered hands on her apron before picking up the receiver.

'Good afternoon, Goltz residence.'

Her chest contracted. She glanced around the room as if she was looking for someone who could rescue her.

'No Deborah, this isn't Eva, it's Connie... the housekeeper.'

Of course, she knew that Deborah knew who she was. She said it to try and remind her that she was talking to staff. It did nothing to restrain Deborah and she wept down the phone. Just then Eva walked in carrying a tall stack of prettily wrapped birthday presents. A party hat sat askew on her head and she stopped and balanced the gifts between one hand and knee as she freed up the other to catch the hat just before it fell off completely. Connie heard her let out a laugh and she set down the presents next to the pile that started on the coffee table and spilled down to the floor beneath and spread all the way to the bar.

Deborah's voice continued in Connie's ear and she put her hand over the mouthpiece while she searched for the mute button she couldn't fathom. Instead she had to rest the phone down and go over to Eva.

'Mrs Goltz, it's Deborah, she's asking for him,' she said in hushed tones.

Eva nodded and snatched off her party hat. She walked over to the telephone table, set the hat down and picked up the receiver.

'Deborah, this is Eva,' she said.

A voice from down the hall called out, 'Come on Mom, we want to light the cake.'

Connie looked to Eva. Eva glanced at the door that led back to the hallway and Connie went over and stood in it just in case anyone came to find them. Eva flashed her a smile and she felt the tightness in her chest slacken. It would all be alright.

'Deborah, honey, slow down,' said Eva. 'Listen, nobody expects you to send cards and gifts. What does a two-year-old care anyhow? He's just fine Deborah, Joseph too... No, he isn't here right now...Deborah just listen, I've been thinking that I want you to feel more settled in a place of your own...of course you weren't calling about more money but let me make things easier for you...sweetheart, you can't speak to him, he isn't here.'

Connie saw that Eva had moved the receiver a little way from her ear.

'Calm down...well yes I'm afraid he's still very angry with you and he's moved on Deborah, people move on. You ought to do the same.'

Connie heard the sound of a distant yelp coming from the phone that Eva was now holding even further away.

'Take a deep breath... that's it... I'll get my lawyer to call you, how's that? It'll all feel better when you're more settled in somewhere of your own...you will Deborah, I'm certain of it. I'll wish Maya a happy birthday from you...Bye Deborah, goodbye.'

Eva hung up and shook the tension from her neck and shoulders.

'We should go,' said Eva. 'About that call...'

'Who was it?' said Connie.

Eva looked at her, puzzled.

'Who was it on the phone, I didn't catch the name?'

'Oh, it was Nancy from the homeless charity I'm doing some fundraising for.'

'So it was,' said Connie.

Connie couldn't imagine how it would have felt to be separated from her sons. They were grown up now. Though they lived at home she really only saw them when they wanted something. Was the bond always so transactional between mothers and sons? She thought. They needed and she wanted to be needed. With Eva it was different. Eva was always grateful. There was only one time when Eva had asked too much of her. She wondered if things would have turned out differently if she'd followed her conscience and refused to escort Deborah back to London and away from baby Maya. It had all happened too fast, an early morning phone call with the news of Maya's birth. A moment of elation followed by the horror of what Eva was asking her to do.

From the hallway Connie could hear footsteps coming and in the distance a voice calling out for Eva. Eva fastened the party hat back on.

'I think I hear the rabbi's voice,' said Eva. 'Do you know, when everyone I love is in one room I feel like I want to seal up the doors and stop time.'

Eva walked into the dining room smiling. Her husband and son were standing behind Maya who was sitting in a high chair at the head of a long table covered in a powder pink cloth and plates of half-eaten party food. Just out of Maya's reach was a cake in the shape of a Disneyesque castle. In one of the turrets the baker had iced little people at a window; a man, a woman and a little girl.

'Look, Maya,' said Eva, pointing up at the iced people. 'Who is this?' she said pointing to the little girl.

'Maya,' she said. Her own name still a novelty.

'And this?' said Eva, pointing to the man.

'Daddy.'

'And this?' said Eva, pointing to the woman.

'Nana,' said Maya.

'Grandad's probably hiding somewhere else in the castle reading his newspaper in peace,' said Eva. Everyone laughed, except for her son.

Her son was a loving father when he was around. He never changed a diaper or nursed Maya when she was sick but he made her laugh and bought her gifts and her eyes lit up and arms flew skyward whenever he walked in the room. Somehow Eva loved him even more because of it, because someone else delighted in him as much as she did. He still lived for his cars and travelled a lot. Whether or not it made him any money Eva didn't know and it didn't matter. He would never need it. He must have had women since Deborah, she thought, but nobody he'd introduced to the family. She could have fixed him up with the daughters of friends a hundred times over if he'd let her. He refused, though she didn't push too hard. All the time he was single and carefree she could be sure Maya would remain in her care.

Maya was reaching out for the cake and swiped a little edible glitter off the side, she immediately put it in her mouth. The youngest in her own family, Eva didn't have any little girls to compare Maya to. When she was born, she reminded Eva of her older sister Judith. They had the same chin that came to a point and eyes that were always asking a question. Maya would have been named Judith if Eva had had her way, but now she was glad her son had ignored her pleas. Her memory of Judith's face was the clearest of all her family members. Perhaps because it was the last she saw when Judith let go of her hand to be swept away in a flock of unfamiliar children. She replayed the memory often because if she forgot that moment she might lose Judith's image in her mind forever. The picture of her parents had altered over time. Their faces had been invaded by traces of her Uncle Ira and Aunt Sal who had taken her in when she arrived in America. They had no children of their own even though they were in their forties. It can't have been through choice she'd decided, because they loved her as fully as she would let them. They'd never quite managed to make her want to seal up the doors and stop time but that wasn't their fault.

Two tall candles were lit and a round of Happy Birthday sung. Maya made a spitty attempt to blow them out and Eva stood over her shoulder and blew hard so Maya thought she'd done it. Maya let out a squeal of joy and clapped her hands and swung her legs vigorously, Eva held the back of the highchair tightly. Eva posed for pictures behind Maya and then her son and Joseph. Finally, they set the timer of the camera and everyone scooched in shoulder to shoulder, ducking low and clinging on to each other to keep their balance as they waited for the flash. At the last moment Eva broke away and pulled Connie into the picture and the camera caught them all looking in Connie's direction while Maya triumphantly stuck both hands into the birthday cake while nobody was watching.

Later that evening, when Eva had got Maya to sleep and she was in the kitchen surreptitiously cutting another slice of birthday cake for herself her son came in. She put the knife down quickly and turned to him. He lingered in the doorway.

'Nothing came from her did it? A card? A gift?' he said.

'No card or gift, honey,' said Eva. She went over to him.

'How could she forget?' he said.

'Some women just aren't built to be mothers.'

'But if she could see, if she could see what we saw in there,' he said pointing towards the dining room. He choked.

'Maya's better off without her. She couldn't be more loved by us and your father. I won't see my dear girl messed around, you either.'

She hugged her son around his middle and he let his arms rest across her back. She would eat cake today and fast tomorrow.

Chapter Eleven

The rain had pounded down since daybreak and the grey clouds were so dense that it felt like dusk all day long. Deborah had to leave the house. She borrowed a clear plastic umbrella from the hallway stand and walked through the quiet streets to an internet café on Sullivan Street. It smelled of cheap office carpet, hot machinery and oily coffee. She gave a dollar fifty to the guy at the front computer who didn't look up. She sat down and started writing a fictitious report to send to her mother. She was having a wonderful time in the city and very busy with work. They were pleased with her and might ask her to stay for longer. She purposely omitted any mention of Patrick's birthday and instead bragged about the bars and restaurants, the museums and galleries, all things she hadn't had anything to do with this time around. She clicked send and imagined her mother sitting down to it with Patrick hovering over her shoulder, reading it aloud to her as if she was an infant. She had a message from Kirsty. It was just one line.

'Can you send emails from jail?'

Deborah smiled and pressed 'reply'.

'Jail's fine, the guards are mean and the fellow inmates boring but the food's good and you ought to see my room.'

She pressed send.

To her surprise an email came right back.

'Now you *have* to tell me more,'

'I feel like I've been invited to a party in order to be closed in a cupboard,' she wrote. 'Except for 'good morning' nobody has spoken to me all day. I want to come home, I need someone to look at me kindly, just a look would do. I know I could call you but you'll ask me to tell you why I'm here again and I'm not strong enough to lie to you at the moment. Please don't ask again. One day I'll tell you, I know I'll have to. I might have to tell everyone but I'll tell you first. I promise.

'I hope everything's alright at work and the temp isn't as annoying as me. She's bound to make better tea but I bet she doesn't take you out for drinks at lunchtime and spend the afternoon making you paranoid that you're outrageously drunk and everyone knows it. Why do we enjoy torturing the people we love? What's that about? I hope Jonty has managed to put himself back together after New Year's Eve. Is it me or is the year 2000 under-whelming?'

Then she highlighted what she wrote and deleted it. In its place she typed,

'One day,' and pressed send.

The clock counting down the minutes and seconds she had left to use the internet kept catching her eye, the time moved faster here than it had all day. She could buy more time if she knew what to do with it. She looked up the class timetable at her gym and there was nothing on until five. She had two and a half hours to fill. If she went home she would feel in the way and sit in her room wondering if Eva and Maya were talking about her. She could go and watch a film or sit in a coffee shop if isolation didn't make her feel conspicuous. She let her time run out and sloped on to the unusually quiet and water-logged street. Walking around the streets was easier, they were

82

different on a Sunday. The rain hadn't let up and the people outside dashed from door to door, not looking up.

She walked purposefully as if she had somewhere to go. She ignored her new boots rubbing her right heel and the rivulets of water that poured down the back of her coat. She turned down Prince Street and past The Mercer Kitchen where she had gone for her first date with him. He wasn't as flash as she had expected but he paid the bill on a card that she knew only sat in certain wallets. She reached in her wallet to get out some cash to leave a tip and he stopped her.

'No way,' he said.

'Why not?'

He shook his head and she never tried to pay for anything again. That's how it ought to be, her mother said. He's a good one, she said, don't let go of him.

She passed the subway station she used to walk to every day when she was still working and just along from there the grocery store that stocked their pantry for the occasions when they would cook together. He could cook spaghetti and poach eggs. She had a wider repertoire so he would sous chef for her. She liked to dine in, he watched her with greater appreciation when nobody else was around and he couldn't be distracted or have his sleeve tugged by acquaintances who hoped to become something more. Perhaps she was no better than them. Or her mother, she thought. Her mother barely looked alive unless she was hanging off a man. Deborah had grown up listening to her mantra, 'if you can just find the right man everything falls into place.' The rain got heavier and the street quieter. She could stop and look around. The other shops in the neighbourhood had changed but the feeling of the place stayed the same; energised, affluent, confident. She kept on walking until she got to his building, their building for a while. It never felt like home unless he was in it. The last time she was there she'd been doubled over waiting for a lift to the hospital, about to deliver Maya. Like a child making a wish she closed her eyes tight for a just a moment and willed her younger self back. She wanted to tell her how it all ended, well what had happened so far. Even if she had been told, would she ever have been able to see Eva off? Or was she supposed to commit her sin against motherhood and marinate in shame until it could do nothing more to her. Then she could look into Eva's eyes and not be afraid of what she would see there.

Chapter Twelve

Monday came as a relief. Eva stood at the black and white flecked marble kitchen counter with a half pint glass of water. In front of her was her open pill box. The box was dotted with stickers Maya had attached; rainbows, ponies, puppy dogs and a large holographic sticker that read 'Get Well Soon' in the centre. One of the Os had a smiley face and a thermometer in its mouth and in biro Maya had written 'Nana' on its forehead. Eva began with the biggest pills first. They scratched her throat as she tried to gulp them down with the water. Her mind knew she needed them but her body was not convinced. It took a few tries to swallow them all. She took a break; she was out of breath. She'd have to tell her doctor about the breathlessness when she saw him later. He would stiffen up and look downcast while he explained the next stage of Eva's disease and what she could expect.

Deborah swung the door on the opposite side of the kitchen open.

'Sorry Eva, I'll come back,' she said.

'Don't worry about it, these are just my appetizer,' Eva said.

Eva put another pill in her mouth, as much to prevent conversation as to get this tedious and increasingly painful ritual out of the way. Although it was one of the smaller ones it hit her gag reflex and she coughed it back up. She continued to cough until she could barely breathe. Deborah was calling out for Connie but she'd swapped her day off and they were alone.

'I'm alright,' said Eva, between gasps.

Deborah poured herself a glass of water and perched on a stool on the opposite side of the kitchen island. Eva's breathing settled down.

'Don't tell Maya you saw this,' said Eva. 'It's bad enough she's got to come to the hospital with me.'

'I'll have her while you go,' said Deborah.

'I thought you were going to a Pilates class.'

Eva suspected this was an excuse.

'I didn't think she wanted to stay with me. She's still so distant.'

'She doesn't know you, Deborah. Give her time.'

'Do we have time?'

Eva left a long enough gap before she answered to give Deborah a chance to feel awkward for asking.

'That's a reasonable enough question,' she said. 'A couple of months, perhaps.'

A couple of months, a space of time that could be frittered by most. If the end was drawn out she might see in March. Still she hadn't cancelled the trip to France she and Maya were due to take in April or halted the renovation work to the house in the Hamptons.

'I should have called you sooner,' said Eva.

'You don't say.'

Eva laughed a little and Deborah did too. For a moment they were united. She knew Deborah had once been fond of her. She hoped that the fondness of the past pushed hard against the bitterness of the present. Though she was doing little to deserve it.

'The therapist she saw after her father's death says she's a reflective child, there's nothing wrong with that.'

'She was always this way?'

'I think it's because she spends a lot of time with adults.'

'Which is why she ought to go to school more.'

'She doesn't like it.'

'There are some things we all have to do that we don't like.'

'Yes, there are,' said Eva.

'You're not helping her by letting her stay home,' said Deborah.

And there was the bitterness. Eva was caught out by the smiling tiger— she and Deborah were similar in that way. Eva put another pill in her mouth and forced it down along with many of the words she'd like to say.

'She's been worse since her grandfather died,' said Eva. 'We all have.'

Joseph Goltz had had a cardiac arrest in the elevator on the way up to his office on the twenty seventh floor of the Chrysler building three months after his son's death. People thought they were being poetic when they said Joseph had died of a broken heart. Eva resented it, nobody loved her boy like she did. If it weren't for Maya she might have found a perverse satisfaction in her diagnosis and rapidly declining health. She would have to forgo the element of surprise her son and husband had brought to their passing. She didn't want Maya to see her right at the end so like them she would be alone. The first few years and what she knew to be the last few of her life drew parallels that made her suspect she'd learned nothing at all in this life.

'It's no excuse,' said Deborah.

There was a spiteful glint in her eye that reminded Eva of Maya when she was preparing to pitch a fit. Her son had been a straight-forward tantrum thrower but Maya was different. She thought hers through before she began so as to maximise the affect.

'I've done my best,' she said. But now she wasn't sure she had. Was all this really her best?

'You have?' said Deborah.

Eva swallowed down another pill. The argument she'd been having over in her head for the last seven years was looking set to manifest. She realised she probably wouldn't win it as she did the one in her mind.

'I didn't say anything to anybody back home,' said Deborah. 'Do you remember when we first told you I was pregnant? You left the room and wouldn't speak to us for the rest of the evening.'

'I was in shock.'

'The next day you took me to ABC Carpet & Home and bought everything in the baby department.'

'I was in shock.'

'I didn't say anything to anybody back home because I was ashamed. If only I'd known that I had nothing to be ashamed about then but you were going to make sure I did eventually.'

Eva knew she should just apologise. She'd talked it over with Rabbi Rovner several times. But it was the gooey Princess Diana look in Deborah's eyes, the righteousness and selective memory that baited her. She stood up from the stool she was sitting on to look down on Deborah.

'I have less than three months left of my life. I will not spend it going over old ground. If it's therapy you need I'm sure the generous allowance I've given you can cover it.'

The blow was delivered with precision and Deborah got up, turned her back on Eva and walked over to the window. Over her shoulder she could see there had been new snowfall and two robins flitted around on the windowsill.

'Maya's not Jewish you know,' said Deborah. She turned back to face Eva.

Eva's hands clenched. 'To all intents and purposes, she is,' she said, trying hard to keep her voice steady.

'No Eva, she isn't. I'm not Jewish, she's not Jewish.'

Eva stood with her hands in fists, her finger nails digging into her palms. The years of wealth, comfort and preferential treatment had insulated Eva from people who argued with just as much gusto as she did.

'It's not as absolute as that,' said Eva.

'It is. Even I know that.'

'She's been raised Jewish, she's part of a Jewish family.'

'That's not the way though, is it?'

Eva knew she should say nothing more. Deborah stood looking at her with one eyebrow raised. They held the silence a while, long enough for Deborah to smile a little because she had won.

'Maya can come to Pilates with me. I'd rather she didn't inherit the Goltz family paunch,' said Deborah.

Eva tried to stand a little taller and pull in the tiny pot belly her immaculately tailored clothes did a good job of hiding. She felt her body disconnect from her will. It was preparing for her departure, she thought, when it wouldn't have to hold any of this anymore. She began to panic, what if she had even less time than anyone thought. Three months ago she thought she was healthy, what else was going on inside of her that nobody could see?

'Deborah, I've been rude to you. It's the pills they...'

'It's nothing to do with the pills.'

Of course it wasn't, Eva thought. This girl wasn't going to take anything less than a grovelling apology.

'You lured me over here with a promise to make amends,' said Deborah.

'And a hundred thousand dollars,' said Eva.

The words were slipping out before she could censor them. Deborah had turned away and Eva saw she was wiping the edges of her eyes.

'It's hard for me,' said Eva. 'Last time you were here I had a son.'

'He might still be here if you hadn't chased me away.'

'I've thought of that,' said Eva.

She went over to her handbag and pulled out a ring box.

'When he died, I found this,' said Eva.

Deborah turned around. Eva handed her the box.

'I'll be back in a few hours. Maya will tell you she's hungry constantly, make her wait for lunch,' she said.

Eva snapped the lid of the pill box closed and locked it away in a drawer. She dropped the key in her handbag and left calling out to Maya as she closed the front door.

Deborah flipped the Cartier ring box open. The light that bounced from the spotlights in the kitchen off the three-carat diamond ring caused her to look away for a moment. It was Eva who had won. Deborah was shaking, hollowed out, stifling sobs. There were spots in her eyes from the brightness.

Just then Maya walked in. Deborah wiped her face on her sleeve.

'I'll tell you now, I am not going to Pilates with you,' she said.

'What's that?' she pointed at the ring box.

'An engagement ring, my engagement ring,' said Deborah. She showed Maya.

'It's pretty,' said Maya. 'So sparkly.'

'Daddy was going to give it to me,' said Deborah.

'Why?'

'Because he wanted to marry me.'

'Why didn't he?'

'Because I went away.'

Maya climbed up on to one of the stools around the kitchen island and came close to Deborah, their arms almost touching. She lowered her voice to a whisper,

'Was it because Nana said you're not good enough to be a mother?'

Deborah nodded.

In an even quieter voice Maya whispered, 'what's the matter with you?'

Deborah whispered back, 'I don't know.'

Deborah cancelled Pilates class; they'd never have let Maya in anyhow. Instead they walked to the store and bought Pepperidge Farm white chocolate and macadamia nut cookies and ate them while they took a walk in the snow. In the park they scooped up enough to make a snow dog with a stick for the tail and two stones for eyes. With their noses pink and fingers tingling with the cold they walked home. And for the first time since she had arrived Deborah felt something for this cold fish of a child who was meant to belong to her. Deborah saw how naïve she had been. She was an only child and none of her friends had kids yet so she hadn't anticipated just how much of a fully-fledged person Maya would be. She felt foolish for imagining that she could arrive and ruffle her hair and let Connie do the rest. When they got to the main road Deborah reached out her hand to be held. Maya looked up at her and half smiled, but left her hanging.

Chapter Thirteen

14th October 1992

Deborah writhed against the firm hospital mattress. Between contractions she looked out across the Manhattan skyline which was beginning to become visible as day dawned. Eva stroked the back of her hand, a contraction came and she wanted to smack her away but resisted. She assumed it was tiredness, hormones or the pain, not her instincts. In spite of the initial shock Eva had been attentive throughout the pregnancy. The family had insisted on taking care of her medical bills, she was sent to the best hospital in the city for all her appointments and Eva and Joseph paid money into her personal account so she didn't need to work anymore. Their son talked about teaching baby G to sail and ski. But after the first trimester she felt his attention drift.

'When I had my son, I had a C-section,' said Eva to the midwife, who she'd treated like an old friend from the moment they arrived. 'It was much more dignified.'

'Sometimes it's all you can do,' said the midwife.

'When you're chicken,' said Eva and they laughed together with Deborah panting between them. Deborah let out a guttural moan and her bent legs collapsed down. Eva and the midwife quickly propped them up again. The midwife moved

92

down the table to examine Deborah.

'You made it here just in time because that baby's nearly here. Two or three more big pushes and it'll be out,' she said.

'Where is he?' said Deborah to Eva. 'He didn't come home last night.'

Then she moaned and tears fell down her cheeks. The midwife gently wiped Deborah's face. It froze and she gripped the edges of the bed and let out a roar. She couldn't hear what the midwife was saying but her body knew what it was to do. Eva grimaced and walked over to the window. Deborah was certain the pain would never stop and she was too petrified to pray for its end. The sensation took her over and she kept pushing and let out another roar.

'Would you take a look at that sunrise,' said Eva.

The pain was lessening and suddenly she could breathe normally again. She looked down her body and out of it the midwife was lifting a writhing, tiny baby. The baby let out a wail and Eva ran back to the bed, her hands thrust out in front of her, and headed for Deborah's child.

Deborah hitched her feet up into the stirrups and the midwife ducked down.

'You're lucky you didn't tear,' said the midwife.

'When can I go home?' said Deborah.

'You can both go home in a few hours. Baby's doing well and you'll be up and about in no time.'

Eva carried the pink bundle around the room, talking and smiling at it.

'It's like looking at your Daddy,' she said, 'same eyes, same nose, same forehead. And Judith, you look like Judith, are you Judith? Are you my Judith?'

'We ought to latch her on soon,' said the midwife, without looking up.

Deborah lifted the sheet that was covering her legs and hid

her face beneath it.

'Formula,' she whispered from beneath the sheet.

Eva turned sharply to look at Deborah.

'Do you have any with you?' said the midwife.

'No.'

'My husband will bring some,' said Eva.

'We have it,' said the midwife. 'I'll get a nurse to make some up.'

The midwife moved back and guided Deborah's legs down to the bed.

'Well, my shift ended at six. I'm going to hand you over to another member of the team now but it was a pleasure to meet you Deborah, and you too Mrs Goltz and congratulations.'

Deborah peeked from behind the sheet.

'Thank you, Barbara, we appreciate you staying on,' said Eva. She turned to Deborah. 'Say thank you.'

'Thank you,' said Deborah from beneath the sheet.

'She's tired,' said Eva.

The midwife paused a moment and gently squeezed Deborah's hand.

'You'll be fine honey, I promise. You've got a beautiful daughter there and a besotted grandmother.'

Deborah nodded.

The door was gently closed, leaving Deborah, Eva and the bundle.

Deborah fell asleep and awoke to Eva bottle feeding the baby.

'Did you reach him yet?' said Deborah.

'Not yet honey, it's early, he's probably sleeping.'

Deborah pictured him sprawled out on a hotel bed. She imagined someone else there with him. A clique of young women permanently circled him and his kind. The image of him with another woman solidified in her mind until she decided it was a vision of the truth. Joseph pushed open the hospital room door just enough for his voice to be heard, but not enough to see Deborah. She wished he'd come in but didn't say so; Eva was taking care of things, Eva always took care of things.

'Eva, have you gotten hold of him yet?' he said. His voice was sharp with irritation. Deborah had never heard him speak that way before.

Eva went to the door.

'I'm trying,' she said

'Where in hell is he?' he said.

'This isn't the time Joe, get out of here will you.' She shooed him out and closed the door.

'What's going on?' said Deborah.

'Nothing, stop worrying,' said Eva.

Deborah felt a pull in her stomach and an empty feeling was filling her chest. She gasped. Eva's hand went to hers.

'Don't worry sweetheart, the baby's fine, she's sleeping now,' said Eva.

'He isn't coming, is he? He meant what he said about leaving this time didn't he?' said Deborah, her voice laboured in panic.

Deborah searched Eva for some hope.

Eva revisited that moment often because it was, she was sure, the juncture between heaven and hell. A week before, her son and Deborah had had another fight and he'd taken off, leaving her in their apartment alone. They were either fiercely in love or sworn enemies, entwined in one another or bereft. They broke up with such regularity that it became hard to care. It would usually happen after one of the regular parties they attended. Eva knew her son had weaknesses; women, alcohol, recreational drugs. He wasn't ready to be a father and Eva couldn't stand to think of her tiny, sweet grand-daughter in a home full of high drama and selfishness. They didn't deserve her.

'I thought it was just another of our fights,' said Deborah.

'We always say unforgivable things to each other when we're angry. He can't have meant it when he said he didn't want anything to do with me or the baby.'

'He said that?' said Eva.

Deborah erupted into deep uncontrollable sobs.

'Poor Joseph, he's dying of shame out there,' said Eva. She passed Deborah a fistful of tissues.

'What am I going to do? I can't cope with this,' Deborah cried. 'I don't feel the way I'm supposed to about the baby, what's the matter with me?'

A nurse popped her head around the door and Eva sent her away before Deborah lifted her head from her tear-soaked hands. It alarmed Eva how quickly she was concocting a plan. Perhaps, she thought, it had been quietly forming in her mind from the day her son told her he'd got this girl pregnant. She'd liked Deborah well enough; she was a change from the waspy, label-clad pouters that her son usually went for, but she wasn't the sort of girl she wanted him to marry. Deborah tried but she wasn't tough enough to take on her son or malleable enough to do it just the way Eva instructed. There were things Eva liked about Deborah, she was sparky and she acted like she belonged even when she was leagues out of her depth. But there was one thing Deborah was not and it was almost the only thing that really mattered.

'What am I going to do?' Deborah said, her voice barely audible between sobs. 'I didn't want this.'

Eva stroked Deborah's undulating back.

'I want to go home,' said Deborah.

Eva found her gentlest voice.

'Listen, honey, I think that might be what you need.'

Eva waited, Deborah was crying more quietly now.

'The midwife said you're in great shape, so you could go back to London, rest up for a while.'

'It's impossible now,' said Deborah.

'It's not if I help you. I insist.'

Deborah stopped crying and looked up at Eva, wide eyed and trusting.

'You're exhausted, you need a good rest.'

'What about Maya?'

'You're calling her what?' said Eva.

'Maya,' said Deborah. 'It's the only name we both agree on.'

Eva wiped a tear away from Deborah's cheek. She was only twenty, so young to have a child. The tears would pass, young girls gave up babies all the time. Her friend Lois had given up a son before she was married and she went on to have a wonderful life. It was merciful to set someone free from a prison of their own making. Deborah had years ahead of her to have a family of her own and this, Eva knew, was her own very last chance.

'If you want me to I can make it happen, tonight,'

'But...'

'All I'm saying is, go home, rest and think about what you want to do. I can sort everything out but you're in charge here honey, you tell me what to do.'

'He's not coming, is he?'

Eva held her breath and looked down at her shoes. Deborah's tears began again.

'What sort of mother would I be abandoning my child,' she said.

'Hang on, you're not abandoning her, I'll take care of her. In some cultures grandparents are as important as parents. You'll be convalescing, that's all. You need to rest and when you're better you'll be a wonderful mother to our gorgeous girl.'

'And he's definitely not coming?'

Eva put her left hand to her heart and shook her head.

Deborah's crying got louder but had changed. It was a cry of defeat, like a child who had found herself in the dentist's chair despite spirited protests.

'I'm a god-awful person,' said Deborah.

'You're not, lots of women have wet nurses and nannies for their new babies. New mothers need rest,' said Eva.

'Did you?'

'Yes,' said Eva. But this was a lie. When her son was born they were living in a fixer upper high up in the Bronx. They couldn't have afforded help even if she'd wanted it.

'What about my things?' said Deborah.

'I'll have Connie pack them for you.'

Deborah wiped her face with the tissues.

'But I'll be back,' said Deborah.

'Of course you will.'

Eva took a plastic cup and filled it with water from a jug on the nightstand and she fed it to Deborah in sips. Then the door opened again. Eva could have thrown the plastic water jug at whomever it was interrupting this moment, threatening to break her spell. Joseph popped his head around the door. Eva got up and went over to him.

'What did I say Joe? Get out,' she hissed.

'I'm going out there to find him myself,' he said and closed the door.

Eva went back to Deborah's bedside.

'What did he say?' she said.

'Nobody can find him, he's taken off,' said Eva.

Deborah began to weep, this time a tired and resigned cry.

'Eva, I don't have anywhere to live,' she said.

'Leave that to me, I'll rent you somewhere. I'll put some money in your account for you and make sure you have a doctor to see when you get back. Just think, you'll be surrounded by all your friends,' said Eva.

'I'm not sure I feel strong enough to travel.'

'Connie will go with you, she's had two babies. She knows what she's doing. You'll fly in first class of course, tonight.'

Deborah stopped crying and looked straight into Eva's eyes.

'You would do all of this for me?' said Deborah.

Eva beamed with relief and then stopped herself.

'Maya is my grand-daughter and she needs you rested and recovered. I would be delighted to help.'

Deborah maneuvered herself off the bed and walked past Maya in the hospital's see-through crib to the window.

'Just for a while.'

'Just for a while.'

Deborah looked worn out and Eva had to help her back to bed. She lay back on the white, oversized pillows behind her and closed her eyes.

To Eva it felt like the first night of Hanukkah; there would be many good days to come.

Chapter Fourteen

Rabbi Rovner went out of his way to find Deborah after the Saturday morning service. She was out the back looking up at the grey sky and jogging on the spot to keep warm. The thermometer next to the mezuzah said it was barely thirty degrees, not even freezing.

'Will you join us for some refreshments?' he said.

'I'm only here until Eva and Maya want to leave,' she said.

He opened the door to the hall adjoined to the synagogue and ushered her in. He could smell the nutty cinnamon fruit cake that had been delivered warm earlier that morning.

'What did you think of our service?' he said.

'Like I say, I'm here until Eva and Maya want to leave.'

Eva said Deborah didn't put on airs or graces with anyone whom she didn't think she could get anything from. But I'm your loudest supporter, thought Rabbi Rovner. Inside everyone had gathered around a table of food donated by the catering company of one of the congregation. Rabbi Rovner hoped there would be some of his favourite salmon mousse rolls left by the time he'd done the rounds and then admonished himself for putting his appetite ahead of service.

'How are you finding being back here?' he said.

'Fine,' said Deborah.

'I'm glad you came today.'

'You're the only one.'

She was right, he thought, nobody else had spoken to her. Everyone knew the story of the girl who seduced Eva's son and broke his heart, delivered a child and then ran away with the expensive gifts they'd given her. Their scorn had been compounded by his tragic death and Joseph's too. We are sloppy, he thought, when it comes to attributing the right amount of blame to the right people and places. He didn't suppose Eva was going to set them straight now.

'If I can be of any assistance to you please call, always,' he said.

'Assistance with what?'

'If you need to talk. Though naturally, you might have a priest or vicar you'd prefer to seek the counsel of.'

'Why is it that religious people assume that everyone else is as well.'

'Alright, call me as a friend.'

Deborah stared at him for a moment, as if waiting for the punchline.

'I know this isn't easy,' he said. 'Eva told me what happened. She's a good woman you know, she's been through more than any of us can comprehend.'

Deborah looked in Eva's direction then back at the rabbi.

'She took my child and separated me from the man who was going to ask me to marry him. Is that a good woman?'

Rabbi Rovner scratched his head. He wasn't used to hearing anything but praise and adoration for Eva; she was untouchable. If he'd heard Deborah's story from anyone else he'd characterise the perpetrator as a highly-flawed individual with great amends to make.

'She's been through more than any of us can comprehend,' he said again.

But that doesn't give her a free pass, he thought.

'That might work with some people but not me,' said Deborah.

And maybe she was right, he thought. Maybe we're not granted clemency for our wrongs no matter why we might have committed them in the first place. But that was not the God he knew. His God yearned for every soul to make the best of life and understood that there were worldly reasons why sometimes we didn't.

'I believe that Eva is sorry,' he said.

But did he believe it? Would she ever have confessed if she hadn't been diagnosed with an illness she couldn't fight. Was she sorry for what she did or sorry that she'd been pushed into a spot where she had nothing else to do but face it? Jona came up to him and tapped him on the shoulder. On a paper napkin were three salmon mousses which she handed to him. He thanked her and introduced her to Deborah. Jona stretched out her hand and shook Deborah's but he could tell from the attempt at a smile on her face that she had no intention of liking this girl.

'I'm told Maya has a ballet exam coming up, Eva says she's got quite an aptitude,' she said. Jona looked Deborah up and down. 'Did you dance?'

'I did, as a child. I do a lot of Pilates now.'

'And that's all is it?' said Jona.

Rabbi Rovner could do nothing to stop her. She too had heard every detail of Eva's previous story about Deborah and not an utterance of the updated version.

Deborah excused herself to use the bathroom.

'You couldn't think of anything else to say?' Rabbi Rovner said to his wife.

'You know me, I speak as I find.'

You do, he thought, but sometimes you don't look far. He thought about going over to stand near the bathrooms so he could catch Deborah when she came out but he knew it would look strange.

'It's not up to you to try and smooth things over with that girl,' said Jona. She said the word 'girl' like she'd searched her mind for vile and derogatory terms and come up with nothing better.

'It costs me nothing,' he said.

'I disagree.'

He could see out of the corner of his eye that the plate of salmon mousse rolls was being replenished.

'Eva has been through so much, if I can make this last test less onerous I will.'

That kept her quiet while she thought of another angle.

'You're a terrible pig Samuel, I can see you making love to that buffet with your eyes.'

'I have my faults,' he said.

'Yes, you do,' said Jona. It was her final word and she turned and walked over to the food table for a second helping.

Rabbi Rovner and Jona had met in the early seventies. Samuel was still in rabbinical school and she had a job in a bank after her parents refused to let her go to college and she had obediently gone to work while she waited for a husband. Jona had been sharp and funny and once she told him, though denied it afterwards, that she had wanted to be a rabbi. She was still sharp enough and he supposed that some people must still find her funny but since he was the butt of many of her jokes he didn't enjoy them much these days. They got married six months after they met and though Samuel vowed to send Jona to college their sons came along and she bawled at him every time he mentioned it after that. Instead she came to Saturday services and criticised him. Perhaps she thought she could have done a better job.

He reminded himself to have mercy, Jona's father had been a terrible bully and her mother did nothing but put her down.

He went over to the buffet table and placed his hand in the small of her back.

'What's good, sweetheart?'

'Take your eyes off my plate, you beg with as much discretion as a dog.'

Deborah sat on the closed lid of the toilet in the ladies' bathroom looking up at a skylight that was cracked. She took her passport out of her handbag and leafed through it looking at the various stamps. She'd brought it because Eva said she'd need identification to get into the synagogue. It was, unlike any place of worship she'd ever been to before, nervous about who it let through its doors. There had been bricks through windows and spray painting on the walls. Eva said there were regular threats telephoned in, though none carried through as yet. Deborah wished she'd feigned illness and refused to come. She would have got out of it if Eva hadn't put her on the spot in front of Maya.

'You'll want to see where Maya goes to temple,' she said. 'Because one day she'll need you to take her.'

Eva was wrong. The Goltz family were surrounded by people who looked at them beatifically, any one of them could do it. Deborah pushed away any thoughts of what would happen when 31st January came. She had fifteen days left before her return ticket was supposed to take her back. Maya didn't want her and turned her away at every opportunity. She was either repaying rejection or she was copying Eva. A better mother would be able to take it, but Deborah knew what she was.

Right now she was sitting in a cold lavatory while she waited to go back to the house. She was almost as uncomfortable there but it had become familiar. Maya had run off to play as soon as the service was over and Eva sat surrounded by a coterie of women who eyed Deborah suspiciously. The only person who'd showed her any kindness was the rabbi and she suspected he was just doing his job. The door into the ladies' room was flung open with such force that the partition around her cubicle shook. Deborah was on her feet, afraid of the stories Eva had told her about the threats. It was Maya and her friends chasing each other.

'Deborah?' called Maya.

Deborah unlocked the door and opened it to Maya and a couple of younger girls. One was dressed in a cream corduroy smock that she'd dribbled chocolate down the front of and the other in a red velvet rah-rah skirt with matching waistcoat and a white blouse with black collar and cuffs. They stood staring at her. Maya pointed at Deborah.

'That's her,' she said.

The two girls looked her up and down and then turned their attention back to Maya, their leader. Maya turned on her heel and sprinted out, followed by the two girls. The door thudded against the wall again.

'What did you want?' said Deborah to their backs. She closed the toilet door and sat back down.

Rabbi Rovner's sermon hadn't been as boring as Deborah thought it would be. He kept saying, 'What do you want? What do you really want? What if what you want is what God wants for you?' Too late, thought Deborah, it came and went. Most people prayed during the service but Deborah closed her eyes and folded her hands in the toilet cubicle. 'God, what do you want? Because I don't know what I want.' She felt her bottom lip quiver and her throat was hot. She didn't know if she believed in God but she kept on going. 'God what do you want?' Hot, heavy tears fell down her face. 'What do you want?'

Just then the door of the toilets thudded open again and someone rapped hard on the cubicle door.

'Deborah, come out!' said Maya's voice.

Deborah hastily pulled toilet paper from the dispenser on

105

the wall and wiped her face, then she opened the door.

Maya was there with the two little girls from before. Behind them was a gangly teenage girl with glasses, another girl Maya's age who clung to Maya's wrist and identically dressed twins.

Maya pointed and they inspected Deborah then followed her out of the toilets.

'What do you want?' said Deborah.

But now she thought she might know. As a girl she used to gather new friends and take them to see her mother who was invariably chatting to another adult and would ignore her visitors. Look what I have, she'd think— you couldn't start to imagine how wonderful it is.

The line she refused to cross had been stepped over by the other side. She hadn't experienced the hundreds of moments of surrender most mothers do as they get shaped by their offspring. She'd had nine months, a little sickness and fatigue and towards the end a bump so low that it made her sit with her legs splayed like an overconfident man on the subway. This was nothing to prepare her for the subtler ways a child would stretch her from the inside out.

When everybody was gone and Jona was making sure the caterers had cleaned the kitchen to her satisfaction Rabbi Rovner closed his eyes and said a silent prayer. Let me right the wrongs, he thought, Eva doesn't have enough time, give the burden to me. Let us keep Maya, though she was stolen and bring Deborah back to her daughter. That is what I want.

Chapter Fifteen

5th November 1991

Deborah was being led blindfolded through their apartment and every time he stopped to open a door or move a piece of furniture out of the way she almost fell over.

'I hate surprises,' said Deborah.

'You won't hate this one.'

'I hate it already, if it's a party I'm not going to act surprised.'

'It's not your birthday, why would I throw a surprise party?'

'What is it then? Come on, babe, I've just got home from work and I'm dying for the loo.'

They changed course and she was delivered to the hallway bathroom. He turned her to the door and took off the blindfold. He guided her in and she tutted. He waited outside. She emerged backwards as he requested and he re-tied the blindfold. It was a black or navy-blue silk like material, though not real silk. Cheap, like the kind of neck scarves you can buy from the sellers in the park who lay out their wares on a gaudy blanket and gather them up fast when the police are coming. Once the blindfold was secured they walked further along the corridor towards the living room. Deborah could tell because the light changed. She wasn't going to let on but she could see a little through the bottom of the makeshift blindfold.

When they were in the living room he stood her still.

'What now?' she said.

'Wait.'

'Can I at least have a drink while I'm waiting?'

'Any second.'

She heard him shuffling around and then he came back to her side and took the blindfold off. In front of her eyes and beyond the wall of windows that surrounded this side of the apartment fireworks exploded. Behind them the Manhattan skyline was solid and staid. He stood behind her and wrapped his arms around her.

'Happy 5th of November,' he said.

'It's Bonfire Night,' she muttered.

'Look,' he said and produced a pair of toffee apples.

'Get you,' she said, and they stood together crunching through the hard and brittle toffee to the sweet apple beneath and watched the show of colour, silent in the sky.

Chapter Sixteen

It was the first day of the school term and much to everyone's surprise Maya was ready and waiting to leave at eight o'clock. The car was idling out front and Maya skipped down the steps. The driver got out and opened the door for her. Deborah called out the promise of a treat when she got home. Connie stood behind Deborah; it was usually her job to see Maya off.

'Let's hope this lasts,' said Connie.

Deborah pulled her dressing gown tight around her. She stepped back and closed the door against the cold of the late January morning. The city had thawed and everybody hoped it was the end of the snowfall.

'The winter's harsher here than I remember,' Deborah said. 'Everything is.'

'You're weathering it,' said Connie. She put her hand on Deborah's back and was surprised that it wasn't shrugged off.

Deborah went upstairs to get showered and dressed so she could have breakfast in the dining room with Eva. She came down to Eva eating a hard-boiled egg and reading the New York Times.

'I shouldn't do it but I read the obituaries,' said Eva. 'Misery loves company as they say. I've dictated mine to Connie.'

Deborah searched Eva's face for a sign that she was joking.

'I thought I'd let you know just in case you were thinking of writing something,' said Eva and then smiled. 'You'll go away and think what an egotistical witch I am but who else would write it for me?'

Deborah took a piece of toast from the wire rack.

'Rabbi Rovner?' she said.

Eva shrugged.

'He'd gush.'

'He would, and it would go on and on.'

Deborah buttered the toast but couldn't eat a thing until she said what she'd come to.

'I'll stay a bit longer,' said Deborah.

'How long is a bit?' said Eva.

'I can't say— a few months.'

'How re-assuring. I'll tell that to Maya, shall I?'

Deborah pinched the corner of her piece of toast between her thumb and forefinger until it was flat.

'Your allowance will continue all the time you're here. Though I hope that's not why you'll stay.'

Deborah put the toast down and got up from the table.

'I'm going out for breakfast,' she said. 'Have a good day, Eva.'

Deborah felt guilty every single step of the way to Dean & DeLuca, for there were so few days left for Eva and Deborah was still wishing them away.

After school Deborah and Maya wedged themselves in a corner of an ice cream shop— or gelateria as Maya called it. The café area felt unhealthily hot after the bitter chill of outside and they both peeled off their layers of coats and sweaters. Deborah didn't remember being taken out for ice cream as a child. Having an ice cream might happen if it was a hot day and the ice cream van came by. Ice cream had become like coffee, something you went out for, it was a strange concept to Deborah but she was glad of something to do with Maya when everything else she'd suggested had been rejected. Maya bit hungrily into a double cone of mint choc chip and rocky road. Deborah had a scoop of cherry and amaretto in a cup.

'Doesn't the cold hurt your teeth?' she said.

Maya shook her head and wiped her chin with a paper napkin.

Deborah was learning to live with Maya's silences. At first she thought they were a snub, but unlike Deborah, Maya was growing up in a household where she didn't need to shout when she wanted something. Maya need only look up and Connie or Eva would rush to her. What appeared to be poise was really only Maya's expectation that her every need would be met before she had to ask.

'You know, I was much chattier than you when I was a kid,' said Deborah.

'You still are,' said Maya.

Deborah laughed and she thought that if anyone looked over they'd see a mother and daughter having a good time together.

'We've got an hour before we need to be back to change for dinner, I mean supper, shall we do some shopping?'

Maya shrugged.

'What would you like to do?'

Maya was quiet for a while, engrossed in chewing on a marshmallow.

'You won't want to do it,' she said.

'I might, what is it?'

Maya shook her head.

'Tell me, Maya, go on,'

Deborah found Maya easier to talk to when neither Eva or Connie were around. She could feel them assessing her.

'You won't tell Nana?'

Deborah held her breath a moment. 'No, I won't tell Nana.'

'I want to go to Daddy and Grandpa's graves.'

Deborah could no longer eat her ice cream. It was melting into a red gloop and even the sight of it made her feel nauseated. She balled up a napkin and pushed it into the cup.

'That's wasteful,' said Maya. 'I might have eaten that.'

'You wouldn't have liked it.'

Deborah hadn't liked it all that much either. She chose cherry and amaretto because it sounded like a flavour that a grown woman would enjoy. In the same way, she drank gin and tonic and ate olives. It wasn't the pleasure of the taste that she was looking for but the enjoyment of knowing that she was joining the other grownups, sophisticated people, who looked forward to these things. She liked chocolate chip ice cream and Malibu and orange juice.

'It'll be dark soon, maybe we should go another time.'

'Doesn't matter.'

'How far away is it?'

Maya looked at Deborah with derision.

'I don't know.'

Deborah thought for a moment.

The café was getting busy with children slotting themselves behind empty tables while their mothers waited in the line to be served. Deborah took out her phone and dialled the number Rabbi Rovner had forced upon her before she left the synagogue. It rang and rang until it reached voicemail and Deborah chanted out loud the office number she was told to call to speak to his assistant. She quickly hung up and redialled, it rang for a while before she heard a young man's voice.

'It's Maya Goltz's mother here, Deborah Foster. Is Rabbi Rovner there?' There was a brief pause and she guessed the young man was working out who she was. She was told the rabbi was out and to Deborah's irritation the young man asked after Eva's health. 'She's fine. Listen, this is a sensitive matter and I know I can trust your confidence here but I'm with Maya and she would like to visit her father and grandfather's graves and I don't know where I can find them.' There was another pause, surely he couldn't deny her. He didn't and sounded pleased as he read out the address, though past the first couple of lines Deborah didn't need it. It was one of the city's most well-known cemeteries and the place she imagined he had been laid to rest in.

The cab dropped them off at the entrance to the cemetery. It was dusk and the lights along the edges of the paths were illuminating one by one. The air turned colder the moment the sun dipped below the buildings and Deborah and Maya's breath came out in clouds.

'I don't suppose you know where to head to?'

'I haven't been here before,' said Maya.

'You've never been?'

'No.'

For a moment Deborah wondered if this was a trick, Maya's collusion with Eva to prove her a bad mother; selfish, stupid, unfit.

'Don't tell Nana,' said Maya.

'Why not?'

'She'll be mad.'

Maya walked closer to Deborah. Deborah reached out her arm to rest it around Maya. Maya ducked in and they walked pressed together looking like two mourners holding each other up. Deborah wondered what Maya knew and what had been kept from her. Perhaps, she thought, there would have been trouble between her and Eva even if she'd stayed. She found Eva permissive to excess in some ways yet secretive and controlling where it really mattered.

'Do you think the headstones are in alphabetical order?' said Maya.

Deborah laughed.

'That's good logic but no, I don't.'

'Then how do we find them?'

'We'll walk around and keep looking until we do.'

'Do you think it's cold underground?' said Maya.

'Yes, it's very cold underground,' said Deborah. 'But you don't feel the cold anymore when you've left your body.'

'What happens to you?'

'I don't know.'

'What do you think?'

Nobody had ever asked Deborah that.

'I think you meet up with everyone you love who has died and have a party.'

'You think dying is good?'

'No, just different.'

'You should tell Nana.'

'I don't think she'd like to hear it from me.'

Maya stopped a moment and Deborah looked back at her. She was twisting the edges of her scarf around nervously.

'She said you're a liar.'

'She must have been very upset with me at the time. I'm sure she didn't mean it.'

'Here,' said Maya and ran down one of the rows. There they were, seven rows back from the front— a row of Jews, some names that Deborah knew and then Joseph Goltz and him.

'We should have brought something to put down,' said Deborah.

'We need to find two rocks and put one on each of the stones,' said Maya.

'Alright.'

They searched the ground. All Deborah could see were a couple of small green stones that must have found their way on to the grass from another grave. Maya went further afield and came back with a rock in each hand. She placed one on each of the headstones, stepped away and looked at Deborah. Deborah offered her the green stones and Maya shook her head.

'You want me to do it?' Deborah said. She rolled the little green stones around in her hand. 'What's it for?'

Maya shrugged.

'Strange custom,' said Deborah.

'You're being rude,' said Maya.

'Maya, I'm sorry, I didn't mean it,'

Maya smiled, 'Got you,' she said.

In the distance a man called out that he'd be locking the gates soon. Deborah promised him they wouldn't be long.

'What now?' she said to Maya.

Maya didn't answer.

Deborah offered her hand but Maya dug hers deep in her pockets and they stepped back from the grave. They stood in silence and Deborah watched Maya as she tracked the birds flying overhead and smiled.

'What do you think happens?' said Deborah.

'The same as you,' said Maya. 'And you catch a ride on the wings of those birds and they carry you up to the party.'

'Or on the back of a flying horse,' said Deborah.

'That's silly,' said Maya.

Deborah laughed.

'You're not meant to laugh in graveyards.'

Deborah pointed down to the ground.

'They're all too busy partying to mind what's going on down here. Do me a favour and when I go don't bury me under those ugly green stones,' said Deborah.

Maya looked up at her and gave a grin.

'I might,' she said.

It was then that Deborah realised that the patch of land they were standing on between the two grave stones was wider than between the others in that line. Another space, maybe two.

Chapter Seventeen

11th June 1976

Eva was standing with her hands on her hips and her chin jutted out, like a washerwoman bellowing at her errant children playing in the street.

'Will you listen to me Joe, put that drink down and get your head out of those newspapers and look at me while I'm talking to you,' said Eva.

Joseph looked up and took off his reading glasses.

'I'm right here, Eva, you don't need to shout,' he said.

'Your son is crying himself to sleep down the hall.'

'My son? Oh shit.'

'Don't you care?'

'Not this again.'

'Oh 'this' just 'this' to you, the boy's been thrown off the football team, Joe. That's a pretty big deal to a nine-year-old. Can you imagine just for a second in your otherwise perfect life how it would be to have the one thing, actually the only thing, you really want taken away.'

Joseph looked down at his newspaper.

'It's disgraceful,' said Eva. 'You should be on his side.'

Joseph looked back up at Eva.

'He goofs off in lessons and he gives the teachers sass, what does he expect?'

'You're his father, you should be supporting him.'

'I'm not talking about this with you now. You know my views.'

Eva turned away from him and walked to the window in their new apartment on the Upper East side. It didn't feel like home yet. The view of the park was what she'd wanted, but when she got it she realised that it didn't bring her any more peace than anywhere else she'd lived. Nothing felt like it should. They'd stopped drinking champagne every time Joseph made a deal or sold a development; it was too often and too normal. For the first time in her life she had help, a young woman from Brooklyn called Connie who did everything so efficiently that sometimes Eva felt surplus to requirements. She picked up a picture of Uncle Ira and Aunt Sal and angrily buffed the frame until it shone. Joseph put his reading glasses on and opened up his paper.

'I'm going to tell them we'll take him out of that school,' said Eva. 'We pay enough for it, they ought to take my wishes into consideration.'

Joseph took his reading glasses off again and stood up.

'It's a good school,' he said. 'No school worth going to will do what you ask them just because we're paying. I might add that I'm not too happy about paying for him to spend his afternoons in detention and his days sitting with his tongue hanging out.'

Eva strode over and stopped within spitting distance of Joseph's face.

'Well I'm sorry I can't have more children who can live up to your standards.'

'Eva,' he warned.

'No Joe, this is about me not being able to have another isn't it?'

'Eva, it's not, you know it's not.'

117

'I'm a disappointment and so is your son, how awful it must be to be you.'

Joseph rubbed his forehead and sat down again.

'Eva, I don't like this,' he said.

Eva had folded her arms and was staring him down.

'I spoke to Rabbi Weil, his wife knows the principal, she's going to talk to him, just a word in his ear. Let's hope this doesn't have to go any further. I've promised him he'll be back on the team by the beginning of the season.'

Joseph nodded and picked up his newspaper.

Eva went down the hall to check on her son. His nightlight had gone out and he'd fallen asleep. The covers were off and she tucked him in again, kissed his forehead and switched on the nightlight. It shone beams of golden light around the room. She went to the chest of drawers where his sweaters were kept and took them all out and re-folded them. She re-arranged the shirts in his closet and brushed down his school uniform. She checked his shoes and sneakers were clean and double checked his school bag was packed with what he needed for the next day. She went to the linen closet on the landing and took out fresh towels to lay over the towel rail in his bathroom and found that Connie had already taken care of that.

Perhaps she should get a job. Everyone said getting pregnant happened when you stopped thinking about it. But what a betrayal of her son, she thought, to pray so hard for him and then leave him with a babysitter. She sat down on the chair in the corner of his room and watched him sleep. She drifted off herself and awoke with a start. For a moment she didn't know where she was except for in a dark room. She clawed through the darkness to the light switch and turned it on and then stood for a moment with her fists clenched.

Then she realised she was in her son's room, perfectly safe but for the finger nails that dug into her palms.

Chapter Eighteen

Eva got back from the doctor's office minutes before Deborah and Maya came home. She was still in the hallway when she heard them coming up the steps and Maya's words,

'Promise you won't tell Nana.'

'I promise I won't,' said Deborah.

They were bonding and it was what she told Rabbi Rovner she wanted; it was what they prayed for together. The front door opened and Maya looked surprised to see her.

'Come here then,' said Eva, her arms outstretched.

Maya leant into Eva's arms and received a hug reluctantly. Eva held her close and planted kisses on her cheek.

'How was school?' she said.

'We went for ice-cream after,' said Maya. 'It was really cold.'

Maya was an awful liar. Eva had to save her.

'Go upstairs and change for supper,' said Eva.

'Alright.'

Maya bounded up the stairs and Deborah hurried after. She stopped mid-way up.

'She said school was fine, that's as much as I could get out of her on the subject.'

Eva nodded and then walked away mouthing 'nobody asked you,'.

It had been three weeks since Deborah had arrived and Eva knew she should be happy to see her more comfortable. She was ashamed to miss the fragile Deborah whom she could reduce to tears so effortlessly. There had been comfort in Deborah's grief for him, as if she shared a burden that Eva had carried alone until then. Deborah still flinched a little when she had to get anything from the shelf where his pictures were. Eva had found one of him and Deborah together and put it in a frame but Deborah said nothing about it. Take baby steps, the rabbi said, make small amends. Eva knew she must try. Every moment she indulged one of the thousand little irritations that were getting larger and larger in her life was a moment she was missing and who knew how many more she had left. She'd just been to her weekly check-up. The doctor had been pitying but blunt with her. He said he expected her to have weeks rather than months of visiting him at the hospital. After that he would be coming to her. She acted as matter of fact about it all as she could but she still burned with shame that in the last minutes of her appointment she asked him if there was anything at all that might save her.

'Anything,' she said. 'At any cost, any place in the world. At *any* cost.'

He shook his head and looked down at his desk.

'I'm sorry, Mrs Goltz.'

There had been almost no symptoms until it was too late. How could she have known nothing about the execution until the cool blade was resting on the back of her neck? She wouldn't call the disease by name because it made her feel ordinary. Everyone she knew had lost somebody to it. Perhaps, she thought, she was being ungrateful, she'd had many more years than her parents and siblings. She'd hoped for ten more, at least if she'd made it into her seventies and Maya was in college, she could have taken it. But could she? Did anyone, ever?

She went upstairs to change for supper. She didn't insist on formal dress but Maya had to change out of her school uniform and everyone was expected to wear something neat and presentable. Deborah seemed to delight in the opportunity and paraded a new outfit nightly. So that, Eva thought, was how she was going to spend the money. She was like a child in a gift shop buying every trinket her money could afford. It was distasteful.

They sat down at the laid table. Two candlesticks topped with long cream candles burned and there was an appetiser of mixed salad in each of their places. Each place was set with a glass for wine and one for water, two forks on one side and a table and fish knife on the other. Connie delivered a main course of salmon in a lemon and dill sauce, new potatoes, green beans and asparagus. She put them on a hot plate on the table and wished everyone a good evening. Eva listened out to hear Connie close the front door.

'That woman is an absolute wonder,' she said. 'Connie is like a member the of the family to us isn't she, Maya?'

Maya didn't answer. She put a cherry tomato in her mouth and chased another around the plate with her fork. When the salads were finished, Eva got up to gather the plates.

'I'll do it,' said Deborah.

'Sit down,' said Eva.

Deborah sat back down. Eva took the plates and cutlery into the kitchen and Deborah served each of them a fillet of salmon and herself and Maya vegetables.

'I want potatoes,' said Maya.

'Try again,' said Deborah.

121

'May I have some potatoes?' said Maya.

'You can have two,' said Deborah.

Eva walked back into the room.

'She can have as many as she pleases,' she said.

Maya looked between Eva and Deborah.

'Two is fine...for now,' said Maya.

Maya ate one of her potatoes and only a few mouthfuls of the salmon before she put her knife and fork together.

'Have you had enough?' said Deborah.

Maya shrugged.

'You should eat some more, it's really good.'

'Are you full, honey?' said Eva. 'The ice-cream probably ruined your appetite.'

Deborah didn't speak for the rest of the meal and Eva got tired of asking Maya questions about her day and getting one-word answers so they ate pretty much in silence. Eva wouldn't be dissuaded and got out a box of chocolates after dessert. This lifted the mood a little and they picked through, choosing the best ones. She wished Connie was here, there was something about her presence that diffused the tension.

'Do you have any homework?' Eva asked Maya.

'No,' she said.

'Do you want to read to me?'

'No.'

'Alright then, you're excused.'

Maya got down from the table and went upstairs.

'You had a good time together this afternoon?'

'I think so,' said Deborah.

'And where did you go, apart from the ice-cream parlour?'

'That's was all.'

'I see.'

Deborah lied more casually than Maya.

'How was it at the doctor's office?' said Deborah.

'It was immense fun.'

122

Eva stood up and gathered their plates. She carried them to the kitchen. Deborah followed behind with a water jug and glasses on a tray and began loading them into the dishwasher.

'You can leave that,' said Eva.

'I don't mind.'

'Just leave it,' said Eva.

'Let me help, it won't take a minute if we do it together.'

'Do you think, perhaps, I could have a few moments in my kitchen by myself?'

'Sorry,' said Deborah and put the glass she was holding down. She walked out of the kitchen.

Eva knew she was being impossible but right now she hoped Deborah had gone away soaked in shame, an unwanted presence in the house. Like a nuisance dog clattering around her feet that she has to nudge away because it lacks the sense to move on its own.

Deborah had gone upstairs and it wasn't until Eva noticed it was Maya's bath time that she realised Deborah must have drawn the bath for her. Eva climbed the stairs and had to stop twice to catch her breath. She got to the landing in front of Maya's bathroom and gently knocked on the door.

'Can I come in, honey?

'Yeah.'

Maya was laid back in the bath and up to her ears in bubbles.

'How was school?'

'Ok.'

'Who did you play with at recess?'

'I can't remember.'

'But you did play with somebody?'

'Yeah, there was a group of us.'

'Good, it's important to have friends.'

The term before her father's death Maya had been part of the dance all groups of little girls have to do from time to time and was left out of their games for a few weeks. She confided in Eva and the school principal received a phone call at ten o'clock at night on an emergency number. By 8am the next morning all the girls and their parents were in the principal's office apologising. Maya had risen to the top of the social chain but that had proved almost as trying because now it was Eva's turn to be summoned when another girl accused her of bullying.

'And you had a good time with Deborah after school?'

'Yes.'

'Where did you go, really?'

Maya was silent, she gathered up a handful of bubbles and entertained herself by patting it into a ball. She stuffed it in her mouth.

'Yuk, Maya. That's soap,' said Eva.

'Tastes good, like marshmallows,' said Maya with bubbles spitting out.

There was a gentle tap on the bathroom door.

'Can I come in?' said Deborah from behind the door.

'Nana's here,' said Maya. She finally spat out the rest of the bubbles.

'Ok, I'll come back in a while,' said Deborah.

They heard her footsteps fade away down the hall.

'Where did you go?' said Eva.

'I don't want to say,' said Maya.

'That makes me very sad,' said Eva. 'Very sad indeed.'

Maya submerged her head under water and then bobbed back up again.

'Remember that I don't like lying.'

'I don't want to say.'

'Why not? Listen, I won't be angry, no matter what.'

Maya spread the bubbles up to her fingertips then flung them off.

'To Daddy and Grandpa's graves.'

Eva stood up, much more quickly than she should and had to catch herself on the towel rail which was hot and burned her hand. She strode out of the bathroom, flinging the door closed. She set off down the landing towards Deborah's door.

Maya climbed out of the bath, a stream of bubbles ran down her legs and on to the floor that Deborah had forgotten to put a bath mat on. She wrapped a warm towel around herself and made a trail of bubbles over to the bathroom door. She opened it and poked her head out. She couldn't see anyone but she heard Eva screaming at Deborah. She heard her Nana say words she'd never heard before. Deborah's voice was quiet and she couldn't hear what she was saying back. Maya tip-toed down the corridor closer to Deborah's room and then took a few steps back when Eva's shouting became too loud.

'Go home,' she heard Eva say, 'get out of my house, get your filthy hands away from my grand-daughter, you're the worst thing that ever happened to my family.'

Maya went closer again but didn't dare look in.

Eva went quiet.

'Eva?' said Deborah.

No sound.

'Eva?'

Still no sound.

'Eva?'

Deborah sounded panicky.

'Nana? I'm frightened,' said Maya, still standing on the landing.

'Hold on Maya, don't come in,' said Deborah.

Maya started to cry. Then she heard a sound that started like a moan and moved up in scale to a scream. This was followed by sobs, loud and gasping. Deborah came out of the room.

'Maya, Nana is feeling unwell. Will you go and dry yourself

125

and put your pyjamas on and I'll come and see you in a minute.'

Maya was still crying but she knew what to do.

'You have to call Rabbi Rovner,' she said.

She wiped her eyes on the corner of the towel and searched her mind for his number.

'This has happened before?'

'One time'.

Maya waited for Deborah. She counted thirty-three minutes before she came. Rabbi Rovner had arrived.

'Is Nana feeling better?'

'Yes, she's very tired, she's in bed now.'

'She has a broken heart,' said Maya.

'Yes, I think she does.'

Maya dozed with Deborah sitting on the edge of her bed reading to her. Her favourite books were about princesses in castles waiting to be saved. Why is it, Deborah thought, that princesses never get up, walk out and save themselves? Maybe because these books are read to little girls who can't and they listen in solidarity. Deborah changed the ending of the book to entertain herself.

'The gallant Prince came but the Princess said, 'it's fine, I've got this,' and he went away again.'

'That's not the story,' murmured Maya.

'I thought you were asleep.'

'Nearly.'

'Don't you think it's a better ending?'

Maya didn't answer and Deborah waited with her until she was sure she was asleep then went back to her room. It was still torn apart from the altercation she'd had with Eva. Deborah had never seen anything like it. Eva had pulled her suitcase out from under the bed and between insults she was striding back and forth between it and the wardrobe stuffing Deborah's clothes in. Then she stopped next to the chest of drawers. Her body slumped forward and down. She slid down the side of the chest of drawers and froze on the floor. Then the moaning started and she pulled her knees into her chest with more agility than Deborah thought she had. The sound that exploded next sent a chill through Deborah. It was a primal, guttural scream. A sound from an insane asylum, or worse.

At just after two in the morning Deborah heard Connie arrive and Rabbi Rovner leave. She was glad there would be someone else there to deal with Eva. It was, she thought, a rehearsal for the end. Moments of action and high drama followed by worrying and waiting. Deborah went to check on Maya who was asleep and clutching a stuffed dog. She felt her face, it was damp. The room was too hot and Deborah went over to open a window. The sounds of the city forced themselves through the tiny crack in the triple glazed window; a siren, a voice calling out, the wind and tyres against the asphalt of Washington Square North. She turned back and Maya had opened her eyes lazily.

'It's alright, I just came to check on you. It's still night-time, go back to sleep.'

She left Maya's bedroom door open and met Connie on the landing outside. She was carrying spare bedding for the other guest bedroom where she was going to spend the night.

'Is Maya okay?' said Connie.

'I don't know,' said Deborah.

'Did she see it happen?'

'No, but she heard it. I think most of Greenwich Village heard it.'

'She'll be fine by morning.'

And she was. At seven thirty Maya was dressed and downstairs having breakfast with Eva. Eva looked Deborah up and down when she came to the table bleary eyed and in her nighty.

'Is Maya going to school?' said Deborah.

127

'Yes,' said Eva. And by her tone she might as well have added, 'why wouldn't she?'

Maya was eating a piece of toast and watching Connie scalp the top of her soft-boiled egg. Connie handed the egg cup to Maya and she dipped her crusts.

'Some coffee?' she said to Deborah.

'Yes, please Connie.'

Deborah sat and Connie poured her some. She brought the tray of milk and sugar around from the other side of the table. Nobody spoke. Eva leafed through a newspaper and Maya dug out the bottom of her egg with a tea spoon and ate it.

'May I be excused?'

'Yes,' chorused Eva and Deborah.

Maya ran off upstairs and Eva put her newspaper down. Deborah took a gulp of coffee. It was hotter than she expected and she struggled not to spit it out. Eva got up and walked towards the kitchen.

'Deborah, we don't come down in our night clothes in this house, it's undignified,' she said and then nothing more for days.

Chapter Nineteen

20th March 1999, Essex, UK

Eva hadn't phoned in person. Deborah wished she had because it was her boyfriend Pete who picked up the phone and she wasn't convinced he believed everything she'd told him about Eva. Not that she'd told him it all.

'It's an American woman,' he said, before he handed her the phone. 'Corrine or Connie, something like that. I didn't catch the rest; she sounds upset.'

Deborah snatched the phone.

'She's alright? Is she alright? Connie, tell me now,' she said down the receiver.

All Deborah could hear was Connie sniffling.

'Connie, tell me right now, is she alright?'

In movies people deliver bad news with such eloquence. This was nothing like that. All Deborah could hear was sniffing and sobbing. Pete put his hand on Deborah's back. She turned and shoved him away and walked as far as the spiralled telephone cord would let her.

'What?' said Pete, 'what's happened?'

'Just tell me, Connie, tell me, is she alright? Is Maya alright?'

Then Connie said one word, his name. After a long time of sitting in silence and listening to Connie pull herself together

Deborah heard that he'd been found dead. They suspected it was an overdose.

'In unfortunate circumstances,' had been Connie's description.

'What does that mean?' Deborah said.

Connie blew her nose and Deborah paced.

He'd been staying out for days on end. Connie knew this because Eva sent her over daily to clean his apartment. The place looked unlived in. Mostly she would empty the refrigerator of food that was out of date and replace it with fresh. Then she would change the sheets and bleach the bathrooms and all this could be done inside of half an hour. It was much quicker than the de-brief she would then give to Eva. Eva had him followed and found out he was passing out in apartments and hotel rooms all over town. There were drugs, she knew there were drugs. She confronted him, she pleaded with him and he denied it. But on 19th March 1999 an anonymous female caller rang for an ambulance to a room in a cheap midtown hotel. The call handler said the woman sounded out of it and when the paramedics arrived she'd left. He was pronounced dead at the scene.

'I called as soon as I could, please don't tell Mrs Goltz I told you. I knew I had to, I'm sorry Deborah. I'm sorry.'

Deborah could say nothing.

'The funeral's tomorrow. I'll be thinking of you,' said Connie.

She hung up.

'Who's Maya?' said Pete.

Deborah ignored him and ran upstairs. She locked herself in the small and windowless bathroom and turned on the sink and bath taps. The extractor fan let out a squeal as it kicked in and then whirred like a hairdryer in her ear. She pressed her face into a bath sheet and cried so hard that her body convulsed. After a while Pete knocked on the door and she told him to go away. He wouldn't. To begin with he tried to gently cajole her out. Half an hour later his tone had gone from concerned to accusatory.

'Why are you this upset about an ex?' was the question that made Deborah open the door. The usually steady and sane Pete was pacing the landing. Maybe he could feel the temperature changing in their relationship and the inevitable drop.

'Back off Pete,' she said.

He put his foot in the doorway so she couldn't close the bathroom door.

'Look, I'm sorry about your ex, but honestly Deb, don't you think you're over-reacting? What's this all about?'

'You have no ideas what I've lost,' said Deborah.

'I didn't realise,' said Pete. He rested his hands on the top of his head as if he was trying to keep it on. Suddenly he looked spiteful, not at all like himself, 'You really are slumming it with me, aren't you?'

He went to his parents' house for the night.

Deborah double locked the front door and put the chain across. The rising panic and anxiety that she felt made it impossible for her to keep still. She went from room to room as if looking for something and forgetting what it was until she was in the bathroom. She opened the bathroom cabinet and rifled through a case with old nail varnishes inside. At the bottom were the prescription painkillers she'd hidden. She got them out and shook the container. They were from the day Connie escorted her back to London and a doctor came and prescribed her a cocktail of drugs that would keep her numb and sedated for weeks. She remembered deciding to keep some back, wondering if there was even more pain to come. The pills were out of date but she felt the effects all the same. It had been such a long time since she last felt the delicious release of everything that ought to matter. She turned off her mobile phone and unplugged the house phone from the wall.

She watched television with the sound off and fell asleep on the sofa.

Deborah didn't go to work the next day— instead she spent it at home with the curtains closed and she covered over the mirrors with a tablecloth and bed sheets as she sat a solitary and make-shift shiva. It surprised her how different the house looked this way, lonelier without so much as her own reflection.

It was getting dark outside and Deborah switched on the lamp next to her. The funeral would be happening right now, she thought. There would be streams of sharply dressed New York society going into the synagogue. She'd upped her painkiller dosage. She could no longer feel sadness, or anything else. This allowed her to imagine a grieving girlfriend sitting straight backed, elegant and stony next to Eva. He was bound to have a society girlfriend, someone who looked like Ralph Lauren assembled her every morning. Would Maya be there? Do children go to funerals? Someone would have held her hand and tried to explain why Daddy was gone. Deborah took another pill and then another. She switched her phone on. She had a message from Kirsty asking if she was feeling better. She could honestly say she was, because it was better that she feel nothing instead of anything for him. She thought about how different it would all be if she was there. She should have returned before Maya remembered her leaving. She had believed Eva that nobody wanted her, that she was irredeemable and unloved. She should have paid back the money she was given and flown back in economy class and taken the bus to Washington Square. She should have walked if she had to, and knocked on the door, demanding her child back. Instead she took $12,000 a year which was deposited in her account every January and with it the knowledge that no judge would deem her fit to claim her little girl. Eva promised that any attempt to remove Maya would be a long, expensive and drawn-out battle.

Going back was like a holiday of a lifetime she never saved up for but thought might just happen.

The pills, just a couple too many, had made her face go numb and she squeezed her cheeks until there were nail marks. It felt like a strange thing to do but she checked the weather forecast and it was a bright day in New York City. Mourners would be able to stand by the grave a while after the casket was lowered. It mightn't be such a desperate affair. There could be crocuses scattered around the graves and birds singing in the trees. Deborah counted the pills left in the pot. There were seven and a litre of vodka in the kitchen. She could go too.

Her mobile phone rang, it was Pete again. She ignored it and seconds later a text message appeared.

'I'm worried, please call me.'

Deborah wrote back 'go away, Pete' then deleted it.

Pete was who she ought to want. But she was like a recovering alcoholic constantly reminiscing about the fun times with a beer in hand. She'd had counselling, talked it out, rationalised to everyone who would listen and even visited a hypnotherapist to try and rid herself of this attachment to a man she had left but loved.

'I'm alright,' she texted Pete. 'Let's speak tomorrow. I didn't mean what I said yesterday.'

It was the right thing to say. When all of this was dissected in a long and drawn out conversation she would need to sound kind and rational. It was the only way their relationship had a chance and she had to give this other life a chance.

Everyone except for Rabbi Rovner, Jona and Connie had gone home. Darkness had long hung over the den. Eva would not get up and turn on the light and she would have nobody else do it either. Connie came into the room and laid a glass of water next to both Eva and Joseph and tidied away uneaten plates of food.

Down the hall everyone could hear Jona, howling with grief in the kitchen. Connie stood in the doorway making fists with her hands and biting the insides of her cheeks.

'Mrs Goltz, should I ask Mrs Rovner to leave?'

'No, let her do it,' said Eva.

Connie left the room, her Cuban heels thumping the tiles in the corridor. Minutes later Rabbi Rovner came into the den and sat down between Eva and Joseph.

'Jona's grieving, forgive her, all she can think of is how she'd feel if it were her boy.'

'All my life I've had to share my grief with people who've had a much smaller helping of it than I have,' said Eva. 'Let her do it.'

Rabbi Rovner got up and went over to the mantlepiece where a photograph of Joseph's mother and father and Eva's Aunt Sal and Uncle Ira sat. Next to them were five fresh white roses that were replaced every five days and never allowed to sag. Not many people knew this but they were for Eva's mother, father and three sisters.

'Where's Maya?' said Eva.

'Connie put her to bed,' said the rabbi.

'What time is it?'

'A quarter to eleven.'

'Why did people stay so long?' said Eva.

'Because they care about you. Me and Jona will spend the night if you'll have us?'

'What about the boys?'

'Jona's sister is staying.'

'No, Samuel, let her go home to them.'

Rabbi Rovner shook his head.

'She'll refuse.'

'Not if I tell her to,' said Eva.

Eva got up and went down the corridor, closer to the sobs that had calmed down enough so that she didn't need to ask her not to wake Maya.

Joseph began to shake.

Rabbi Rovner sat down where Eva had been and laid his hand on Joseph's back.

'Let it out, Joseph,' he said.

But Joseph couldn't. It rampaged through him like a horde of pumped-up kids on a jungle gym. His heart felt like it was hitting his rib-cage and his stomach swelling in an attempt to push the organ that he just couldn't carry around anymore up and out of his mouth.

When Eva came into the kitchen Jona was wiping her face on a wad of paper napkins and taking deep breaths. Jona turned her back and Eva saw her crumple again.

'I'm sorry, I'm sorry,' she said between sobs.

Eva went over to Jona's hunched back and wrapped her arms around her and laid her head down on it. It felt like holding a baby with hiccups; her boy suffered terribly with hiccups as a child. Are these, she thought, the moments people talk about when they think they're being sent a sign from the other side. You know what I've done and you're still talking to me?

Eva took Jona's hand and led her back down the corridor to the den. Inside the men were sitting in silence. Eva sat Jona down on the opposite sofa.

'We used to do something, in the camp,' said Eva.

She saw everyone jump a little and look to her. She never spoke about those times and nobody ever asked. Jona stopped crying, Rabbi Rovner had moved to the edge of his chair. Joseph stopped shaking and squared his shoulders.

'We would say the names of the people we'd lost. We said them to the wind in the hope that it would carry them to somewhere better. It sounds silly now...'

Jona reached out and took Eva's hand. Jona took a deep breath and started by naming her grand-parents who had died in Hungary, her father and still-born brother. When she went quiet Rabbi Rovner began, his mother, his father, his sister Mag, his grandparents, his aunts and uncles, a dog from his childhood that he'd called his brother for thirteen years. Jona shot him a look that promised she'd be having words about this but he didn't care. How often in life does the sacred reveal another room in the house of the heart? He finished and there was silence. Joseph looked to Eva and she reached across the coffee table and squeezed his leg. He began, his mother, his father, his older sister, his best-friend, he didn't know the names of his grandparents. Words so painful were not permitted in his childhood, 'you're here, that's all you need to know,' was what he made do with. He said, 'Granny and Grandpa Goltz, Granny and Grandpa Abelman,' in a voice so sweet that Jona started to sniffle again. He finished with his son's name. The room went silent again and they sat with eyes fixed on the coffee table, like seekers at a séance, waiting for something to happen. Eva began. The list went on and on. Despite them being taken while she was so young she knew the name of each of her grandparents, her aunts and uncles, cousins and family friends. She knew the name of every one of her neighbours. She named the baker, his wife and their daughter Therese who was older than Eva but her closest friend. Everyone said Therese would have died early anyway because she had downs syndrome but she couldn't have been more than nine or ten. She listed her classmates and teachers and the man who delivered the school lunches. She listed the soldiers who had helped her, though she only remembered the nicknames she'd given them, 'big ears,' 'waddle walk,' and 'dirty boots,' they would definitely be gone by now. She ran out of names and eventually she said her son's.

There was a pause.

'Good company,' she said.

'Amen,' said Rabbi Rovner.

'Amen,' said Jona.

'Amen,' said Joseph.

Eva got up and switched the lights on.

'Go home,' she said to the rabbi and Jona. 'Shiva's been sat.'

Chapter Twenty

There was still picture but no sound between Eva and Deborah. Deborah had to get out. She jogged three blocks and back and stretched out against the slippery outer edge of the fountain in Washington Square Park. She was getting cold and would have to return to the house soon. The benches were icy, the light sparse for eight thirty in the morning and the gutters mealy with snow and grit. It was the kind of day when Christmas, New Year and the hope of newly implemented habits had been failed at and forgotten. A gathering of dog walkers chatted about the spring because January had gone on too long and there was nothing left to praise it for.

Deborah opened the front door to silence. She could smell pancakes being fried in the kitchen down the hall and bread in the oven. The warm hallway made her frozen sinuses run and she reached out to the hallway table to take a tissue. It was, she thought, an art to set up a house like this. It wasn't just money that made everything in the Goltz house run so smoothly, it was a system and a thought behind everything. It gave the house a feeling of permanence, like it was part of the bones of the family. She took her running shoes off and carried them upstairs. She was hungry but had to change for breakfast otherwise who knew what Eva would say. She blasted herself in a hot shower and quickly dressed in a pair of black trousers and a cream cashmere sweater and went downstairs to a bowl of berries, granola and yogurt while Maya ate pancakes and Eva buttered, but didn't eat, a slice of the freshly baked loaf.

Eva reminded Deborah that it was Saturday and Maya would need to be taken to synagogue. She mentioned it lightly, as if it were a continuation of a conversation they'd been having for days. Eva tried to hide her breathlessness and fatigue and said she'd go with them next week. Maya believed her, Deborah did not.

Deborah sat down in the chauffer driven car and lifted her legs in behind her. It was the way Eva got in and out of cars, as if she was the Queen Mother. They arrived at the synagogue a little late, and at the door to the synagogue they were ushered in by an elderly gentleman and shown to three seats reserved for them up the front next to Jona. Deborah and Maya sat down. Deborah couldn't concentrate on the service— this time if felt like an incomprehensible babble of English and Hebrew. Maya twirled her French plait around in her hands and whispered with the children in the seats behind. But Deborah wasn't bored; she scanned the people around her, this was the synagogue of New York royalty. And yet they sat there quiet and humble— willing to be carried along.

Once the service ended and everybody got up Deborah tried to rush Maya out but Rabbi Rovner caught them and made a long conversation about the weather and then suggestions of restaurants she had to try. This was followed by an interrogation as to her plans for super-bowl Sunday. Maya drifted off with a group of little girls and he asked after Eva. Deborah repeated what Eva had told her but the rabbi wasn't satisfied and promised to come over later. By that time, Maya was engrossed in a game with other children and she couldn't persuade her to leave without causing a scene. Deborah went to the bathroom, back to her stall, and stayed there for as long as she reasonably could before she emerged and tried to catch Maya's attention. There was a circle of the congregation's elders around the rabbi and they looked at Deborah. Deborah went over to Maya and took her by the hand, Maya shook her off.

'My daughter was like that about going home,' said one of the women to Deborah. 'She's doing it because she trusts you.'

'It doesn't look that way,' said Deborah.

'Kids play up the most for the people who are closest to them.'

The woman left the cluster of elders and offered her hand.

'I'm Irene,' she said.

Deborah shook her hand.

'Deborah.'

'Oh, we know who you are,' said Irene.

'Come on Maya, we have to go,' said Deborah. 'Nana will be expecting us.'

To her surprise Maya came over.

'Keep coming back,' said Irene. 'We'd like to know you better. You're going to be very important to this community soon.'

In the car Deborah thought about what Irene said. Surely Irene realised she wasn't really one of them— faithful and steady, committed and trustworthy. She had nothing to offer. The car took a different route home, the driver needed to pick up some medication for Eva, it idled outside the doctor's office while he went inside. Deborah rolled down her window and stuck her head out for some air. Maya complained she was getting cold. Deborah got out the car and slammed the door shut. Her legs wanted her to run again but she knew it was impossible in heels, on a busy street and with a child on her own.

From a juice bar across the road Jon noticed the car pull up and a man in a chauffer's uniform get out. He hadn't lost the habit of constantly scanning his surroundings but he had no idea why he was drawn to watching that car. The military will do that to you, he thought. He didn't miss a thing, even if he wanted to. Then he saw Deborah get out. He drank the end of his juice, thanked the girl behind the counter and walked out and across the street.

'Where's your scarf?' he called out.

Deborah turned.

He saw her taking him in and the pout on her face relaxed.

'Are you stalking me?' she said.

'Yeah, I follow your car around the city on foot all day long.'

She smiled.

'How was the party?'

He adopted a hillbilly accent. 'We got the banjos out and had ourselves a time.'

Deborah laughed.

'Is that your daughter in the car?' Jon said.

'Yes, that's Maya. We've just been to synagogue. Now I need a drink.'

'You're still doing that?' he said. The words came out before he could stop them. It never usually happened to him. All of his training; the control, discipline and vigilance just fell away. 'All these drinks aren't making you any braver. Whatever you think you're running from I'd say it's got you pinned down.'

Deborah looked downcast.

'Listen, I'm sorry, it's none of my business.'

Deborah didn't look up.

'No, it's not.'

'You were right about me when we first met, I am an arse.'

He said it with her accent.

Deborah's eyes met his and she smiled.

The chauffer came out of the doctor's office and got into the car.

'I better go,' said Deborah.

She opened the car door and got in. The car pulled away and she looked back. He'd turned and was walking in the other direction. It really was none of his business, she thought. It was none of anybody's business. Nobody else knew what it was like to watch the effort she made at life, first in New York then back in London, end up messy, fraught and too humiliating to talk about.

Chapter Twenty-One

They got home to a silent house. Eva was in her room asleep and Connie had left after breakfast. They cobbled together a lunch of left-over roast chicken, salad and bread.

'We're going shopping after this,' said Deborah.

'I'm not,' said Maya. She had stuffed her mouth so full of bread that the words came out as little more than a noise.

'Come on, Maya, it'll be fun, I'll buy you something.'

'Like what?'

'A new dress, a toy, some shoes...'

'I don't want any.'

Deborah felt the urge to reach across the table and whip away Maya's plate. Let the child know what it is to want. Deborah took a deep breath in and sighed it out. She immediately felt bad.

'Fine,' said Maya. 'I'll go.'

'You don't have to, sweetheart,' said Eva. She walked into the kitchen and towards Maya. 'Don't waste your afternoon.'

'Nana,' Maya cried and got up and ran to Eva.

'Rabbi Rovner says he'll call in later,' said Deborah. And she wanted to add, 'since you'll be housebound and then dead soon enough.'

Deborah temporarily felt less angry but then sad again. The winner loses and the loser loses. Deborah could go home. A few new suitcases and trunks could carry her new wardrobe. In just nine days she would have completed her month with Maya and Eva would owe her enough money to start again. But she had been recalled with the seriousness of a sentence not yet spent. There was no hiding Maya anymore and she never deserved to be hidden in the first place. That child knows what it is to want, thought Deborah and she took herself upstairs and sat down in her walk-in closet, the only place that she felt was truly her own.

When she came back downstairs she could hear Maya cackling with laughter behind one of the heavy velvet curtains in the hallway. Meanwhile Eva was somewhere down the hall calling out for her.

'Shh, don't tell her where I am,' said Maya.

'Are you supposed to be hiding?'

'Yes, shut up now, go away.'

'Jesus Christ my child has such beautiful manners,' said Deborah.

'Get lost,' whispered Maya.

'I'd have got a smacked bottom if I'd spoken to my mother like that,' said Deborah. She was teasing Maya who was now pushing her away from beneath the curtain.

'Oh, hello Eva,' said Deborah to the empty hallway. She pulled back the curtain to see Maya's furious face, 'kidding! See you later.' Deborah left and hailed a cab. In Bergdorf Goodman three sales assistants flitted around her as she changed her mind.

'Are you shopping for a special occasion?' one of them asked.

'Just meeting up with a guy I used to know. You might have heard of him actually— he used to date Donatella, Robin Ash?' said Deborah.

The women looked at each other and then both looked back

at Deborah and nodded.

'I need to look like I did eight years ago,' she said.

The women laughed but Deborah didn't see what was so funny. Nobody who wanted to look like themselves spent that much money on clothes.

'Lucky man to be taking out someone with such good taste,' said the assistant.

She would never tire of this, she thought. The attention, the compliments, the admiration. She looked in the mirror at herself, all in black, in fifteen hundred dollars' worth of clothes, shoes and accessories. She wished she could capture the moment and hold on to it forever because she had peaked. She was beguiled by her own image and even in that precious moment she feared she might never look quite as elegant, fashionable and rich again.

'Kate Hudson bought that dress,' said one of the women.

'She did?' said Deborah.

'Just the other day.'

'You've got the same body and style as she has,' said another of the sales assistants.

'What else did she buy?'

'Quite a few things,' said the first assistant.

'Will you show me?' said Deborah.

It was just after midnight when Deborah got home, Robin in tow.

'Quite an address,' he said.

She showed him through to the den and poured them both a glass of Eva's most expensive whiskey. Deborah wasn't that keen on the taste but it looked good in the crystal tumblers that sat on top of the bar.

'How come you didn't get married and move to the suburbs like everybody else?' said Deborah.

'I haven't died inside, that's why,' he said. He took a slug of the whiskey and set it down on the polished wood table in front of the leather sofa, ignoring the coasters.

'You?' he said.

'I tried it for a little while. It didn't suit me. I was living with this guy, Pete, he cared about things like having barbeques in the summer and buying the biggest TV we could fit through the door.'

'Knuckle dragger, eh?' said Robin.

Deborah held her breath and emptied her glass.

Deborah excused herself a moment and went to the downstairs bathroom to look at herself. Her make-up had pretty much stayed in place, her hairstyle too. The clothes were the same but they no longer held her together as they had earlier. When she got back to the den Robin was on his feet and looking around the room. He pointed at a painting.

'Great artist, I've got his work at my place in the Hamptons. You see I've got this house on the beach.'

Deborah went over to the bar and while his back was turned she threw down a shot of vodka and then poured herself another whiskey.

'Me too,' she said. 'Well actually it's my daughter's. All of this is my daughter's really.'

'You have a daughter?'

'She's seven, so it's in trust.'

'Of course, you were with the Goltz boy weren't you.'

Deborah looked over to the picture on the mantelpiece. Robin followed her gaze and she went over to stand between it and him. She drank down her whiskey.

'Shame about that, Mr Goltz too.'

Robin spent a long time telling Deborah about his houses and what a great investor he was. Like the others in that set he'd been given it all to play around with. She was bored but something about the way he was showcasing himself seemed desperate. She let him talk on, repeating and reiterating all the things he thought interesting. This passive listening is how women become wives to men like him, she thought. It's also how they become alcoholics. With nothing to do she poured them both another drink. Now she was hearing about his golfing. He had an aggressive swing, that's what everybody told him. When he hit the ball the sound was like a gun going off. He was drunk, but not a sloppy drunk. He just couldn't stop talking and everything he said seemed to remind him of something else he had to say. Since she wasn't required to do anything but keep her eyes open for this conversation she started to think about how she'd always been willing to be bored, made uncomfortable, even used, because she felt she owed the men in her life something in return for being with her in the first place. The thought annoyed her and she pushed it away. She tried hard to be interested in what Robin had to say.

'You see, this year I'm going to do some serious sailing, it's second nature to me,' said Robin.

It was hopeless. She pinched one hand with the other to keep herself alert. He talked on. It wasn't worth it, she thought, the boredom and fawning, the hoping and waiting. She wondered who she would be if she took off the glass slippers and instead took the crown?

'The Goltzes must have a yacht? There isn't much they don't have,' said Robin.

'What we have and don't have is nobody else's business,' said Deborah.

Robin stopped. He looked irritated.

'We?' he said and smiled without any warmth. 'You've wheedled your way back and suddenly you're a Goltz?'

He took a swig of his drink.

'I mean I get it, if you're going to have a kid with anyone…' He looked up to the picture on the mantlepiece. 'I guess you've got it made now.'

Deborah hadn't expected tonight to go this way. She'd

hoped for phone numbers of old contacts in the city, some invitations to tightly listed events, maybe a boost to her ego and a goodnight kiss.

Deborah got up and stood by the door.

'I'd like you to leave,' she said.

'Debs, let's not fall out. You used to be fun.' Robin raised his glass in the direction of the picture on the mantelpiece. 'So did he.'

He finished his drink, put his glass on the coaster and left, promising to call. She told him that when he did she'd be busy. He left and barely under his breath he whispered 'cunt'.

Despite the drinks she felt sober and clear. She thought back to the night she'd arrived back in the city. How she'd drank herself stupid and mouthed off to Jon and anyone else who would listen. She took the drink she hadn't finished to the bar and threw the rest of it away. She switched the lights off, double checked the locks on the front door and went upstairs and into her en suite. In the bathroom mirror she saw someone entirely different from the girl flitting around a changing room in a department store. She saw a woman bone tired of her own bullshit.

It was almost one o'clock in the morning, eight o'clock in the evening in London. If she sent the emails now nobody would see them until morning and she would be fast asleep and miles away from their reactions. She would send just two emails. One to her mother and another to Kirsty's work email address. Kirsty would keep a lid on it for as long as she could but soon word would go around among the girls in the office. She expected people who thought they were her friends to complain about being deceived and others would enjoy the scandal. It didn't matter, she had few true friends. What her mother would say would depend upon Patrick, so whatever happened she'd have no idea of what she really thought.

Deborah went to her room and cleared the bed of Kate

Hudson's clothes. She pulled out the phone from the wall and plugged in her laptop to dial up to the internet. With her laptop switched on she smiled at the screensaver of her and Maya sticking their tongues out. The email she sent to Kirsty to forward to their boss was brief and grateful for the time she'd spent there and she asked if he'd be willing to recommend her to their New York office. Her mother was harder to explain it all to. 'I'm really sorry not to have said anything...' she began. Then deleted that. 'Perhaps I ought to have told you...' she wrote. Delete. 'This is going to be a surprise, I think, but...' no, not that. 'You're a grandparent,' delete. 'I now wish I had told you before I came here why I was coming,' she wrote. 'I had a baby while I was here seven years ago, a daughter, Maya. She has lived with her grandmother (you might remember me talking about the formidable Eva Goltz). I wish I could have stayed and done it myself but I wasn't strong enough.' If the truth wasn't good enough she didn't think it was her who was lacking. 'Eva has taken good care of Maya for all these years.' That, she decided, was what she would say about Eva's involvement from now on, both to Maya and everyone else. Because she would not take Maya's adoration of Eva and stamp all over it for her own salvation.

Chapter Twenty-Two

When Deborah and Maya got back from ballet class the next morning the house was silent.

'Where's Nana?' said Maya. 'Why isn't she up?'

'I don't know,' said Deborah.

'I'm going to look in her room,' said Maya.

Maya ran before Deborah could stop her. Deborah kicked off her heels and chased her up the stairs.

'Don't go in,' said Deborah.

'Why not? Nana doesn't mind.'

'She must be sleeping.'

Maya stopped at the top of the stairs and studied her digital wristwatch.

'It's eleven seventeen, she isn't sleeping.'

Deborah took hold of Maya's arm and she shook her off.

'Fine, let me knock the door first,' said Deborah.

'Do you think she's dead?' said Maya.

Deborah laid her hand on the shiny brass door knob and put her ear against Eva's bedroom door.

'Go downstairs a minute.'

'No way.'

The door opened and Deborah and Eva almost knocked

into one another.

'You're wrong,' said Maya to Deborah, 'she isn't dead.'

Deborah stepped back while Maya pushed past her and held Eva around the waist.

'I was hoping for some breakfast,' said Eva.

'Why are you getting up so late?' said Maya.

'If you go to your room and change you can have a muffin with me,' said Eva to Maya.

Maya skipped off down the landing.

'I won't be going as quietly as that,' said Eva to Deborah. 'Walk with me, will you?'

Deborah offered her arm and Eva ignored it and they walked down the staircase side by side. At the bottom Eva turned to her. 'Don't bring your men into my house while I'm still in it.'

'I won't be seeing him again,' said Deborah.

'Oh?'

Deborah thought before she answered.

'He wasn't who I thought he was.'

'Give up now and you'll save yourself some misery,' said Eva and carried on down the hall.

'But you don't mean that,' said Deborah. Surprised by how bold she was being. She followed her down the hall and into the kitchen. 'You wouldn't have been without Joseph.'

'I'm not talking about me,' said Eva.

'It's alright for you to have a husband but not me?'

'Give up on men like that. I know that boy, his family used to come to our parties. They're the kind of people who'll tell you what everything cost, it's vulgar. You'll have put a jewel in his crown inviting him here.'

Deborah sighed and sat down at the kitchen island. She put her head in her hands. Eva poured herself a cup of coffee and put another next to Deborah.

'You must watch out for collectors; you'll be just their sort of treasure.'

Deborah looked up and smiled.

'I've never been someone anyone wanted to collect.'

'Welcome to what I can tell you is an unrewarding club with very high membership fees.'

Deborah laughed.

'Thanks.'

Eva reached out and held Deborah's arm.

'Don't be fooled,' said Eva. 'None of those pretenders will give a damn about Maya.'

Deborah's smile faded.

'I know.'

Eva searched Deborah's face as though looking for a tell. Satisfied there was none she nodded and let Deborah's arm go and went to the refrigerator for some milk.

'Let me see what I can do,' said Eva.

'What do you mean?'

'I'll send you someone.'

'How?'

'I don't know yet, but when my Uncle Ira died I think he found a way to send me Joe.'

Deborah laughed and Eva poured the milk into their cups.

'It's true. Sweet old Ira did it for me. He wasn't that old really, but seemed ancient to me at the time. He knew I didn't find courting easy. I wasn't light and wispy like the popular girls. 'Always so serious, Eva,' he said. 'You're a miniature schoolmarm. You're scaring them away.' Uncle Ira died on the Tuesday night and on Thursday afternoon I met Joe. He was dropping off his mother's casserole and he dropped it on the front step. I called him an ass and I suppose he liked it because he came back the next week with another and asked me to go and see a movie with him.'

'What did you see?'

'I can't remember.'

'I see,' said Deborah. She raised an eyebrow.

Eva playfully smacked her arm.

'I'll send you someone. You watch me,' said Eva.

Deborah didn't have the heart to dissuade her. Let her think she's going to perform acts of kindness from the grave, she thought.

Maya flung open the kitchen door and made a beeline for the muffins on the counter top. She climbed up on one of the high stools on the kitchen island and picked up every muffin until she found the chocolate chip one. Eva and Deborah drank their coffee and for a while they were like any other family, just sitting around on a Sunday morning.

Chapter Twenty-Three

21st December 1991

It was Deborah's first Christmas away from home and she was invited to attend a party at Lois and Dash's Manhattan apartment. It was the first invitation she'd received as part of the Goltz family. She spent the weeks running up to the event shopping for outfits, trying them on and then returning them. In the end she wore her back up dress and spent the cab journey scrutinising the skirt and berating herself for not having it dry-cleaned. As an afterthought she realised she ought to have worn a longer coat because when she stood up the skirt dropped below its hem and she felt like Orphan Annie. She took her coat off in the backseat of the cab and decided to suffer the cold for a few steps and leave it there.

They arrived at the apartment block where the doorman came out and opened the car door for her. She stepped out and offered her hand, immediately realising that nobody shakes the hands of doormen unless they're giving them a tip. He was gallant and shook it,

'Good evening, Miss.'

They were ushered inside. While they waited for the lift Deborah looked around, they could have been in any basic hotel lobby. And yet Eva and Joseph both said that if there was one other place they'd live in Manhattan it would be this building. The lift came and the doorman stepped in. There were no buttons to press but the doorman turned a key in one of the many locks on a brass panel and ushered them in and stepped back out again.

'Have a good evening,' he said.

'Thank you,' said Deborah.

The doors closed and the lift went up.

'You decided against a curtsey then?' he said.

'What?'

'The handshake.'

Deborah gave him a shove.

He pulled her in close and she could feel the metal buttons of his coat pushing against her.

'My ears just popped,' said Deborah.

'We're going all the way to the top. You know, they've got a private pool up there.'

'No way, nobody in Manhattan has a private pool.'

'They're rich.'

Deborah looked at him, expecting a laugh. It didn't come.

The lift stopped and the doors opened right into a marble hallway.

'Oh my god,' said Deborah.

He ran his hand down her back then took hold of her hand. There were already thirty or so guests there chatting in clusters in the living room which overlooked the city and the marble edged outdoor pool with steam coming off it.

'I'll give you twenty bucks if you dive bomb into the pool,' he said.

A waiter immediately came over with a tray of champagne and martinis. They both took a drink. He shrugged off his coat and gave it to a woman wearing an apron.

'Thanks Guadeloupe,' he said.

'No problem Mr Goltz,' she said, a glint of amusement in

155

her eyes. She winked at him and went on her way.

'Who's that?'

'Lois and Dash's maid. Where's your coat?'

'I must have left it in the taxi.'

'We'll give them a call in the morning. Lois'll lend you something to go home in.'

And, Deborah thought, it would be better than anything she could have picked for herself. She started the evening comparing what she was wearing to everyone else and wondering if they knew it was a backup dress and had been worn before. But despite how small she felt next to these big players, people came up to her and shook her hand and asked her questions about where she came from and what she was doing in the city. She noticed Eva was watching her and listening to what she said.

He kept bringing her drinks and she kept up the small-talk. More people arrived throughout the evening and there were more hands to shake, more toasts to lift a glass to and more questions to answer. It only let up after midnight when only the Goltzes and a few other stragglers were left sitting by the white stone fireplace that sat in the middle of the living space surrounded on all sides by deep, comfy sofas and plush rugs. Lois took Deborah to one side and invited her to choose a coat from an entire wardrobe full of them. She took what she thought was the least expensive one and slipped it on. Lois held her at arm's length and declared,

'I'll never be able to wear that coat again now you've shown me how great it could look— keep it.'

Deborah protested weakly and Lois chuckled and told her to scoot.

She found him outside by the pool talking to Guadeloupe, who was in jeans and stiletto boots now with a leather jacket hanging over her shoulders. She leant from foot to foot, her hips swayed and her long dark hair swished down her back.

Deborah went over, put out her hand to shake Guadeloupe's and stood a little closer than she normally would.

'I'm Deborah by the way,' she said and looked Guadeloupe squarely in the eyes.

'Hi, I'm Guadeloupe,' she said and stepped back a little. She smiled at Deborah hopefully.

Deborah could tell that was enough.

'I've got to go, see you later guys, have a good evening' said Guadeloupe and left.

He didn't say a word. He slipped his arm behind Deborah's back and together they looked out over the skyline beyond the steam lifting from the pool.

'You dated her?' Deborah said.

'No.'

'What then?'

'She's just friendly is all.'

A lie. An obvious lie. She'd seen him do it before. He used the same breezy tone with the girl he was with before her. But the moment was so unlike any others Deborah had had or was likely to. When else would she be invited to a place like this and with people like this and be treated like it was all meant for her.

The door opened and Eva poked her head out.

'It's freezing out here, come back inside,' she said.

'In a minute,' he said.

Eva tutted and closed the door.

Deborah had to shake the picture of him and Guadeloupe together.

'I bet you twenty bucks you won't dive bomb into the pool,' said Deborah.

'Get your money out,' he said and started to strip off on the spot. Through the glass doors Deborah could see Eva on her feet again and coming over. He took a run up and belly flopped into the clear turquoise water. Deborah laughed hard

157

and he tried to convince her to join him. Eva was at the door and shouting for him to get out.

'You should come in Mom.'

Moments later Lois and Dash came out and laughed heartily at him confidently swimming lengths.

'He's showing off for you,' Lois said to Deborah.

Lois took Deborah's hand and squeezed it. Eva gave up trying to convince him to get out and went inside, followed by the others. A couple of smokers cheered him on and blew plumes of cigarette smoke up into the air and Deborah felt that she too was drifting up, by no fault or force of her own she was drifting up.

Chapter Twenty-Four

Eva missed going to synagogue two weeks running, which she had only ever done when summering in The Hamptons or travelling. She watched Maya, Deborah and Connie coming and going in and out of the house and knew she would likely never do the same again. Rabbi Rovner came along to see her at least every other day along with her friends from the congregation. The doctor was right; she wouldn't be going to see him at his office in the hospital anymore. So he visited her and she quizzed him.

'How close to dead am I?' she said, a mischievous look on her face.

'Some way yet, Mrs Goltz,' he replied. He would never be more specific. If his first estimate of four months was correct she had twenty-four days left. She was granted the chance of an extra day because it was a leap year. Though in two weeks she'd gone from marching around the house to needing to sit most of the time, sleep often and up the painkillers.

'What comes after these pills stop working?' she asked the doctor.

'Diamorphine, Mrs Goltz.'

'I'm at the second to last stop.'

She glared at the wheelchair that people kept insisting she use. It sat, ungainly and awkward, a pile of metal in the corner of the den. She could still walk. She just got more tired than she used to. When she was in good humour, she saw the timing as win, win. If she went on time she would see her son before the first anniversary of his death came around. If not, she could be eating slices of Connie's simnel cake when April came. Along the way there were milestones still to be marked. Eva had resisted having a full-time nurse but soon someone would have to relieve poor Connie of the burden of helping her take care of herself. And she would take care of herself until the end. She would not be a pasty faced, sickly sight for everyone to pity. She would be well dressed, made up, her hair set, jewellery on and fragrant. It just all took so long these days. She noticed that Connie had been arriving early and staying late; she often worked fourteen hours straight. Connie complained about nothing except for how much Eva was over-paying her, but how else to show her gratitude?

Maya came thundering into the room, the sound in contrast to her agile pastel dressed form; a pink practice skirt, cream leotard and tights.

'Why weren't you at breakfast?' she said to Eva.

'I've only just got up, sweetie, Connie brought it up to me.'

'What did you have?'

'Just some coffee and a little toast.'

'Remember that I don't like lies,' said Maya.

Eva noticed that Maya had taken to saying her own words back, as though mothering her. Eva hadn't eaten any solid food for days; she had no appetite. All the foods she spent her adult life trying to resist; Godiva chocolates and marzipan fruits, warm madeleines and fruit tarts, Connie's cheese souffle and potatoes dauphinoise couldn't tempt her now. She ran her hand along the side of Maya's puffy practice skirt and Maya's arms folded around her neck. They stayed this way for a breath or two. Eva appreciated these moments and so they stretched out. A clock ticking and Maya's breathing and nothing else. Maya stepped back.

'Watch me,' she said.

She flitted around the room showing Eva a portion of her ballet exam dance, it was new to Eva and Maya danced it perfectly. She finished and Eva clapped and beckoned her close again.

'Sensational,' she said.

Maya was a gifted dancer, though she wasn't always given the lead in the dance school's productions because at that age everyone is told they're good but when Maya danced she wasn't herself anymore. She had what her teacher called 'presence'. She accented movements she was taught while the other girls merely followed. She'd been moved up to a class of older girls, though she was shorter by a head and shoulders. Eva had expected to see her rise up through The School of American Ballet. Ballet class was the only place Maya would go to for months after her father's death. She was comforted that it would be there for Maya this time around too. How wonderful, Eva thought, to truly belong, to know what it is you're good at so young. She wasn't sure she ever found her niche. She was a determined mother but that didn't make her good. She'd done better with Maya than she had her son. There's nobody in this world or beyond it she would say this to but she knew where she had gone wrong and to her intense irritation she saw that Joseph had been right. She taught him no restraint, he had no sense of measure or discernment. He had flabby morals; some would say she had them too. Perhaps he'd have behaved the same way no matter where he'd come from, if he'd been born into a family of mechanics instead of multi-millionaires. As Eva got closer to her god, she was atoning and she wondered why she hadn't done this sooner as well. Chasing off the stark and frightening feeling that came to her whenever her family were out of sight was always more pressing than self-reflection.

Maya had her grade two ballet exam the following weekend. Eva had never missed a single recital but Deborah would be going in her place. She agreed with Rabbi Rovner that this was the right order being resumed but she hadn't told Maya and now looked like the best time.

'Honey, Deborah's going to take you to your exam next week.'

'I want you to take me.'

'I'm sick honey, I can't go out.'

'You'll be better in a week.'

The words hurt Eva sharp as a bee sting.

'Maya, you know this, I won't be,' she said.

'Try, Nana.'

Eva thought a moment.

'I can't try, Maya, my body is failing.'

'You need a new one,' said Maya. She came over to Eva and lay her head on her shoulder.

'I do, sweetheart. But that's something you can't buy.'

'One day it'll be possible,' said Maya.

'You think?'

'Could you hold on a little while?'

Eva stroked the side of Maya's face.

'You have Deborah now.'

'I want you.'

Eva could say no more. They sat, Eva upright, Maya leaning in to her for a minute or more. What a portrait it would have made, Eva thought. As macabre as it was Eva wanted to have her last weeks available to Maya's memory forever. She couldn't stand to be erased or replaced by Deborah like her Uncle Ira and Aunt Sal unknowingly took away the faces of her parents.

Eventually Maya sidled off and started marking her dance again.

The trouble with sitting still, thought Eva, is that it invites other parts of your being to stir. To begin with thoughts of the past are like an orchestra warming up. The odd creak of a violin string and rumble of a drum, a memory here and there. You can push them away but before long all the instruments are chiming in and you know that in no time at all they'll come together. In all its complexity, beauty and horror the symphony of everything you have been busy dodging and ducking underneath will be played in full, if not today then soon and perhaps many times over.

Eva peeled the cashmere blanket from her lap and stood. Her legs shook from the effort. She walked towards the light shining in from the window and stopped to close her eyes a moment. The warmth of the sun through the glass, even in February, transported her. Perhaps, she thought, in the right conditions she could feel well again. A trip to Aruba or Tobago could warm her through and somehow the heat would refuse the chill that was accompanying her more and more often. But she couldn't travel, not now, not in this body. The right conditions for this body were a bed warmed by a heating pad. She couldn't stay with it for very much longer.

She walked over to the window and sat on the window seat, gripping the window frame to steady herself. Out front snow drops bloomed in the large planters and she could see the green shoots of daffodils growing. I'll see the daffodils, she thought, and then I'll go.

Chapter Twenty-Five

On the platform Eva, Ira and Sal waited to board the Long Island Railroad train out of Manhattan to the Hamptons. They were half an hour too early because Sal didn't like to run late, but didn't mind waiting around. Eva nudged a stone with the toe of her shoe. It made a mark and she bent down and drew a compass, writing N, E, S, W at the four points. Above her a conversation went on.

'We should have agreed to visit Aunt Violet in Buffalo,' said Sal. 'The Hamptons isn't a place for us.'

'Says who?' said Ira.

'It's expensive,' said Sal.

'I don't know when you went there to find that out.'

'It's what everyone says.'

'Who?' said Ira.

'Pamela Levy, you know, old Mrs Rose's eldest. She lives on the floor above, you know, used to have a family of Russians in it before they moved to Connecticut. Anyhow, her hairdresser went there on honeymoon and Mrs Rose said they came back with barely any change from $20.'

'Jonathan Klimkowski's grocer's second cousin's butcher's sister went there and said the opposite.'

Sal smacked Ira on the arm and laughed.

'I'm just saying I think it's going to be expensive,' she said.

Eva turned to face east and then slightly to the north and ducked her head around all the legs, suitcases and holdalls and looked as far off in to the distance as she could, shielding her eyes against the sun. She still didn't see anyone or anything familiar. Just people moving fast and purposefully, and she felt that she should follow them.

Ira ducked down and took Eva's hand.

'What you doing, Eva?'

Eva pointed to the horizon.

'Home?' she said.

Ira stood up and walked Eva to the back of the platform and turned them to face north.

'You see that building there?'

Eva nodded.

'That's how you know you're facing north when you're downtown. We live seventeen blocks from there.'

They walked back to Sal who was checking the letter from the boarding house they were going to stay in.

'Not America home,' said Eva. 'My home.'

'Your home is America, Eva. There's nobody left where you came from.'

'Ira! Do you have to keep telling her?' said Sal.

'I do when she keeps asking.'

Sal put her hand in her purse and pulled out a flat red lollipop the size of a milk bottle top, she unwrapped it and handed it to Eva. Eva put it in her mouth.

'Let's just try to keep it light, shall we?' Sal said to Ira. 'I intend to enjoy my vacation.'

After another twenty minutes of anxious shuffling around, Sal clapped her hands when the train arrived. Eva watched the faces of the other men, women and children closely. Nobody was crying or whispering quickly to each other and everyone had their things with them and were allowed to keep them. When the train was ready to board they all looked happy to be bundling on. Sal and Ira shuffled along behind other tourists, encouraging Eva when she hung back. When it came to their turn to climb in Eva's legs wouldn't move.

'Up you hop,' said Ira.

'Just one big step, honey,' said Sal.

Eva couldn't budge.

Sal climbed in and held her hand out to Eva.

Eva stretched up her hand, still sticky from the lollipop but she couldn't reach Sal's from where she was standing and her legs didn't move even though she wanted to stay with Ira and Sal.

'We're holding people up now,' said Ira. 'Shall I lift you?' he said to Eva.

Eva stood solid, like the statue she'd seen on the boat she arrived on ninety-three days earlier, but instead of a torch she held a lollipop stick. Ira and Sal had tried to take it off her to put in the trash but she balled her fist around it. Ira picked her up from behind and lifted her up to Sal. Eva's stiff and unyielding body, still so light and weak, felt as if it could break under the force of Sal's grip. Eva started to cry.

'What's the matter?' said Ira.

'Am I holding too tight?' said Sal to Eva.

Eva shook her head.

'I lost my stick,' she said.

She'd dropped it when Ira picked her up. Ira got down on his hands and knees and searched the ground. There were mutterings behind him and Sal smiled apologetically at the impatient faces that looked up at her. Eva anxiously watched Ira. Sal awkwardly reached into her purse and pulled out another lollipop.

'Here, Eva, have another. You'll have a new stick when you've finished.'

Eva took the lollipop and stopped crying.

'Ira, get on will you. These people have waited long enough.'

Ira climbed on and between them they carried Eva and two suitcases to some seats.

Eva curled up small in her seat and sucked on her lollipop. The train pulled away. The journey was much shorter than she expected and there was a window to look out of. A man came around and saw their tickets and another sold them a packet of potato chips and a soda. Ira opened the chips for her and she crunched her way through them happily. But she was afraid of the feeling of soda in her mouth and spat it out in the empty packet of potato chips. Then when nobody was watching she drank it again later when it wasn't so fizzy on her tongue.

While the train slowed down and people started to get up and collect their luggage Eva gripped Sal's arm until she complained that it hurt. They arrived at the station but there was no shouting or pushing. Uncle Ira carried the luggage and Aunt Sal carried Eva. They got down to the platform and were carried along in a group of other families. A man in a uniform blew a whistle and Eva jumped. Sal stroked her back.

'Remember we're on vacation,' she said. 'We're visiting a new place. It's going to be fun.'

'I want to go home,' said Eva.

'We'll go home next Saturday,' said Aunt Sal.

Eva scanned the platform over Sal's shoulder. The train was pulling away again. Suddenly her arms and legs were fighting Sal.

'Mama on the train,' screamed Eva. Sal had set her down and she was pulling at Sal's skirt so hard that she fought to keep it up.

'Judith. Mama on the train.'

Sal ducked down to Eva.

'I'm Sal, do you remember, your Auntie Sal and this is Uncle Ira.'

'Mama, Judith, Marion, Papa,' Eva named everyone she knew, every single

person she could remember from home. They had all got on the train, so why was she alone now? Why had she got off again?

Ira walked away. He pulled his handkerchief out of his pocket. Eva saw him put

his head against a wall. Sal put her arms around Eva.

'They're gone, baby, they're all gone.'

Sal started to cry and Eva broke free from her and ran towards the departing train.

She would catch the train and be gone too and they would be gone together. She pushed past the last people on the platform and there was just a little way to go before she got to the last carriage. But then hands grabbed at her and she was lifted off her feet.

They stayed at the East Hampton Hideaway Boarding House. Each morning a bell went at seven thirty and they were expected for breakfast by eight. They were to go out by nine o'clock and not return until after five. Eva had an egg and toast put in front of her every morning and how happy Ira and Sal would be that day depended on how much she ate. It didn't count when she balled up some of the toast in a paper napkin and stored it up her sleeve. That made them sad even though she intended to share it with them later.

A five-minute walk away was the ocean, where families lounged on the sand. Sal laid out a picnic blanket and asked Eva if she wanted to put on her bathing suit, but Eva shook her head. Ira couldn't sit still and went for a walk.

'Don't those children look like they're having fun over there?' said Sal. She pointed out a gang of three girls and two boys whom she guessed to be around Eva's age. They were running in and out of the sea laughing and splashing each other. 'Shall we go over and say hello?'

Eva didn't reply. She scanned the horizon in the direction that Ira had gone.

'He'll be back, sweetheart. He has ants in his pants is all.'

Eva scratched at the back of her neck, hard and determined.

'Not again,' said Sal. She took Eva's hands and placed them in her lap. 'Those scabs are just about healing.'

Sal lay down on the picnic rug and sighed. When she'd closed her eyes, Eva went back to scratching. The children on the shore line kept running past the blanket. Eva watched them. Eventually a girl about Eva's size but a little younger stopped and watched Eva back.

'There's a shark in the water,' she said.

Eva didn't reply.

'There's a shark in the water. We have to go and see him then run away.'

Eva looked the little girl up and down. She wore a red bathing suit and her hair was gathered up on top of her head. Eva looked to Sal. Her eyes were closed beneath her sun glasses.

'Wanna come?' said the girl.

Eva stood up. She'd never seen a shark before.

The girl took off, running to the water's edge. Eva looked back at Sal, who had propped her head up on a rolled-up towel.

'Go on then,' said Sal.

From that day on Eva, Lois, Nancy, Beth, Ronald and James met on the sand at nine and couldn't be dragged off the beach until dinner time. Ira went for his walks and came back with hot dogs and potato chips, soda and ice-creams throughout the day. Eva was so hungry from teasing the imaginary shark that she ate everything he put in front of her. Sal was content to sun bathe and read and every evening over dinner Eva regaled Ira and Sal with stories of how close she had come to being eaten by the shark. Or sometimes it was Lois, Beth or Nancy.

'But you weren't eaten,' said Ira. 'You got away. You were

169

fast and you were lucky.'

On the last day Sal and Lois's mother, Mrs Greening, got talking. Even though Eva looked busy with the sandcastle she was building with Lois and James she could pick out some of the words Sal was whispering to Mrs Greening.

'War...Austria...camp...mother...father...sisters...all gone.'

Eva looked up and saw Mrs Greening put her hand over her mouth. Both adults sat quietly for a while. Eva decided that she wouldn't talk about her life before this to anyone again. It made everyone put their hand over their mouth, which is what her mother did to her just before they were discovered and taken away by the soldiers. Perhaps she'd cried out and not realised it and that's why they were found. Maybe she made it happen— her mother said she was noisy and Judith said she tattled about everything. She scratched her neck again, the itching got so bad sometimes she wished she had something sharper than fingernails to relieve it. Eva felt Sal gently catch hold of her arm.

'Eva, you're bleeding.'

Eva looked down at her hand and there was blood on her fingers.

'It was the shark, he scratched me with his teeth.'

Sal spat on a handkerchief and wiped at Eva's neck.

'Certainly looks like he did,' said Sal.

'Sharks ate my mother, father and sisters,' Eva said to Mrs Greening.

Mrs Greening looked at Sal then back to Eva.

'Shame on them,' she said.

Chapter Twenty-Six

Deborah could hear Connie buzzing around outside her bedroom door. Deborah had tried to persuade Connie to stop tip-toeing around her and to let her make her own bed, but still Connie waited until her room was empty before she made it perfect again. Deborah went out, without plans or anywhere in particular in mind. There was nowhere to go in the cold except for a coffee shop and after an hour of reading a magazine she was restless. She knew she was avoiding the inevitable task that would be waiting for her when she'd stopped being a coward. After sending off her late-night messages more than a week ago she had waited to feel ready to see the responses. Eva was twitchy about anyone going on the internet at home and blocking the phone line and she'd felt busier lately— she was looking for a job and taking Maya to her after school classes. There hadn't been a right time to find out what everyone thought of her news. She walked to the internet café and pulled open the door to a room of people who didn't look up. Deborah used to like that about city life— there was no small talk expected and people acted like they couldn't see each other. It was unlike the nosey neighbourhood she'd grown up in. But now she missed someone striking up a conversation just for the hell of it. It had happened to her only once since she'd been in town. She was outside a convenience store and a woman asked her the time and then started to tell her she was running late to meet her daughter. She went on to say that her daughter was in school and had band practice; she was a great musician in the making. Deborah offered up some information about Maya and the woman nodded and smiled. Deborah enjoyed the chance to talk until she realised the woman was singing 'Under the Sea' to herself and then started to dance then asked Deborah for the time again. She was shaken by how normal the woman was for an instant before she joined the ranks of the lost, sick and sad of the city. Deborah wondered if this flavour or madness could have been hers had she not got away. Had she stayed Maya's father would never have been faithful to her and it would have driven her as crazy as this woman, perhaps worse. It was a moment of grace, a second where she could see her response had been pitiful, not dumb, or cruel instead it was plain old sad. Her poison was him, or more accurately her addiction to him, to someone, a fantasy.

Deborah typed in her email address and password and waited with a tightening in her stomach. There was a list of unread emails, mostly newsletters and adverts which she scrolled down and deleted. Then she saw that Kirsty had emailed her seven times in seven days. The last one read, 'If you don't reply to this one, I'm coming out there to get you.' Deborah quickly typed back. 'Stand down. I'm fine. I'll call soon, I promise.' Though she wouldn't call for a while, or else she would unravel and Maya needed her calm and focused. She searched through the remaining emails. Some were from other friends who wondered why she wasn't home yet. There was an invitation to a hen party and another for a gig. Jonty was organising the annual skiing trip and wanted to know why she wasn't coming. 'Still in NYC, not sure when I'll be back, sorry I'll miss it,' she wrote to every invitation. She busied herself with answering and deleting the other emails. Nothing from Mum. She double checked the 'sent' folder. The message had gone. She checked the deleted emails but there was nothing from her mother and Patrick's joint email address. She started another email. 'Did you get my last message?' she copied and pasted the last message underneath and pressed send. She gathered her bag and coat and left before her time was up.

She put her coat on and wrapped her scarf around her. She mumbled thanks to the cashier, swung the door open and hailed a cab.

Over the other side of the cemetery people were standing in a cluster of dark heavy coats. Deborah walked on with her head down. The wind blew in her face and made her eyes water. She found a stone on the path and carried it in her gloved hand until she reached his headstone. The stones that she'd laid with Maya were still there and she added to them. She ducked down and felt the inscription on the headstone, running her finger across the grooves of the dates and letters. 'Loving son, devoted father.'

'Maybe,' said Deborah aloud.

Because now she knew where he was on the morning Maya was born. At least she knew the story Maya had been told. The night before he'd been out in a club uptown with some buddies. Maya listed some names— they were the usual clutch of rich kids who were a bit too old to still be partying all night but too pampered to have real jobs. They decided to go back to someone's apartment and keep on drinking and play cards. He didn't have a cellphone, only city boys and pretenders had them back then and Maya wasn't due for another five days so it didn't occur to him to call anyone. They played all night and when morning came, they walked to the Barking Dog Diner and the winner drank his coffee from a dog's bowl. Maya had been keen to stress that it was a clean bowl but had paw prints around the outside and usually had water for dogs in it. The gang drank enough coffee to start another game of cards and by the time he was tracked down by his father's fury he had a two-day old daughter and no mother for her.

'You didn't call me, you didn't even try,' said Deborah.

Eva warned him off saying Deborah said she wanted time to herself to get her head straight and that she was coming back. Weeks passed; he searched his memory for everything Deborah had told him about her life in London but Eva counselled him to leave Deborah alone. A month passed, six weeks, two months— nothing from Deborah. But the calls were coming in from Deborah and Eva was intercepting them, she told her to wait until he calmed down. Unprepared for the rejection he began to listen to the whispers in his ear; deserter, liar, gold-digger. She had taken everything he'd given her and been looked after by his family and this is what she did.

She rested her hand against the cold headstone. He wasn't there. He was too fleeting and exciting— his eyes always on the horizon. Deborah knew that if she'd stayed they'd have made a go of it for Maya's sake, but they would have taken chunks out of each other until there was nothing left. Then she felt a sensation like someone standing behind her and turned quickly to see the rabbi's wife.

'Mrs Rovner,' she said. 'I was just, I'm just, I...'

Deborah could feel her face getting hot. Jona bent down and rested a hand on her shoulder.

'I'm surprised to see you here— glad actually. I always come by and visit when I'm here checking on my father's grave. You'll ruin that fancy coat of yours sitting on the ground.'

Jona offered her hand. Deborah took it, and got up off the cold damp earth and dusted off her coat. They stood looking at the headstones with their hands in their pockets. Jona's arm reached out to link with hers.

'Have you ever made a mistake so big that you feel like any

chance of a decent life was gone the moment you made it?' said Deborah.

Jona lifted her arm and put it around Deborah's shoulders and Deborah leant in and let herself be propped up.

'I made two mistakes like that but I couldn't help but love them. Now they're grown up I'm beginning to think it's possible to start again. I'm going back to school. I just had my interview and I got in,' she said. 'You're the first person I've told— well apart from my father, and that was out of spite. Come for coffee one day,' said Jona.

'Thanks, I will,' said Deborah. 'Though not yet, not until Eva…'

Jona nodded.

And they left the cemetery with their arms linked.

Deborah arrived at the school gates just in time to collect Maya and meet the car that had come for them. There was a jubilant Friday night feeling in the school yard. Maya bragged that she'd got five gold stars that week and on the way home they stopped off to pick up donuts and Hershey's syrup. When they got home Eva was asleep and Deborah entertained Maya by making hot chocolate and trying to eat a donut without licking her lips. They got out a huge encyclopedia from the den to do Maya's history homework together and then sat down for supper.

'Do you think Nana will come down since it's Friday night?' said Maya.

'Maybe,' said Deborah, not believing it. 'But I think we ought to start. Nana wouldn't want us to let the food go cold.'

'Who'll light the candles and say the blessing?'

Deborah paused.

'Do you know it?' said Deborah.

Maya rolled her eyes and grinned, 'What do you think?'

Deborah lit the candles and Maya said the blessing and

then hooted with laughter when Deborah blew the candles out afterwards as if they were on top of a birthday cake.

Chapter Twenty-Seven

On Saturday Rabbi Rovner came and said prayers with Eva while she sat propped up in a chair in the den. By Monday morning she was back in bed again. Deborah came in from her class at the gym. Connie was waiting for her in the hallway.

'Mrs Goltz wants to know if you'll be collecting Maya from school this week or if you would like me to go,' said Connie.

'I'll go,' said Deborah.

'Yes Miss.'

Connie walked back down the hallway, her plastic soled moccasins squeaking as she went. This was the routine now. Deborah followed Connie around.

'Connie?' she called out.

She heard Connie turn on her heel and walk back.

'Yes,'

'Please check on Mrs Goltz every hour or so, will you?'

'Of course,' said Connie, smiling.

Connie was happy when Deborah gave her jobs to do and even happier when they all acted like a family. Deborah went upstairs and changed out of her workout clothes. She picked up the phone and dialled Maya's school.

'Good morning, this is Maya Goltz's mother. I'm wondering

if you could tell me how to join your PTA?'

Deborah listened and made some notes in the back of her diary. She thanked the school office receptionist and hung up.

Perhaps it was because of Eva's retreat but Deborah no longer felt as though the house was merely tolerating her, like a fleeting discomfort to wait out. She walked along the hallway to outside Eva's room and stopped. The door was closed. She wanted to crack it open and see if Eva was alright but she didn't know what side of her she would get and so she waited, willing a sound or sign to beckon her in. A sound on the landing startled her and she walked on purposefully past Eva's room. She looked back to see Connie emerge from the back stairs. She was carrying a tray with soup on it with a napkin and a pile of pills. Deborah went down the main stairs to the den. She would only have a few minutes, ten at most, but there was something she had to do and nobody else must see it.

Maya sat next to Illana at school most days but today she was next to Sophie because Illana was at home with strep throat. She panicked a little when Miss King told her and spent all day wondering how long strep throat lasted and whether or not she could find out and be off school for as long as Illana was. Maya knew her own telephone number by heart. Nana said she could go to the office and tell them to send her home any time she wanted. For now, she was content to sit next to Sophie and fill in the missing numbers on a worksheet. At recess she sat in the library and looked at the book she always took out on days like these, 'Children's Encyclopedia of the World'. There was a picture on the Asia page— a woman and a man with two children walking through a Japanese garden. One of the children was on the man's shoulders and the other was walking holding the woman's hand. There were pink blossoms on the trees and everyone was smiling. In the picture nobody looked worried. Afterwards she ate lunch and joined in a game of 'it' but left the moment she was caught. She found her favourite lunch supervisor and walked around the playground with her. If she could get past lunch, she would normally be able to last all day. She got a gold star on a chart for every full day she completed. If she got five gold stars in a week, she would visit the principal's office and be offered a cookie on a Friday afternoon along with the other children who had been nominated by their teacher. If she could make it until 3.30pm she would have one gold star for this week. Maybe Illana would be back tomorrow and it was easier to stay when Illana was there.

Deborah did a quick check around the hallway and kitchen before she went to the den. She opened the door, stepped over the creaky floorboard and went to the mantlepiece where his picture was. She slipped off the engagement ring she'd been wearing on the third finger of her right hand and laid it in front of his picture— like an offering on an altar.

'No.' she said. 'I wouldn't have married you.'

She didn't know if that could have been true all those years ago. But now she was sure. Still, she felt no spite towards him. She imagined him being in a place where it's always summer and he could have the top down on his Ferrari and drive as fast as he pleased. She sighed and the petals of the white roses next to his picture quivered. Deborah did not. She had handed the ring back now along with what might have been. With her ritual complete she slid the ring off the mantlepiece and on to the palm of her left hand and listened out to hear Connie come down the stairs.

'Connie? I'm in the den, can you come in here please?'

'Yes?'

'How is Eva?'

Connie turned her face away. Deborah reached out her right hand and held Connie's arm.

179

'She won't eat a thing,' said Connie. 'Second day running.'

'What can I do?' said Deborah.

Connie shook her head. Deborah stepped back. They were both helplessly orbiting a dying star.

'I need you to put something in the safe for me. I don't know the code.'

Deborah opened her left hand to show Connie the ring.

'I need to make sure that it's left to Maya,' said Deborah. 'I don't know how all of this works but Eva must have insured it. We need to make sure it's in Maya's name.'

Connie nodded earnestly.

'Oh, yes Miss, it is. Mrs Goltz had me organise that a while ago. I think it was the first or second week of January.'

'About the time she gave it to me,' said Deborah.

Connie looked down.

'Sorry, Miss.'

'It's not your apology to make, Connie.'

'But I'm sorry— not about the ring but for what I did, and I owe you that. Deborah, I'm beyond sorry for what I helped to do.'

Deborah reached out to put the ring in Connie's hand and Connie took hold of both of Deborah's hands in hers.

Deborah searched her mind for what to say. Tears sprang from Connie's eyes and fell down her face. Deborah took her hands away, leaving the ring behind in Connie's hands.

Connie left the room clutching the ring and wiping her eyes with the cuff of her shirt. Moments later Deborah went after her— she was uncertain of what she'd say when she found her. What is there to say to an apology without excuses or blame- except for 'thank you'.

At 3.28pm Maya went to Miss King's desk and peeled the gold star off the plastic backing and transferred it to the chart in the back of her exercise book. She followed the other children on her table out to the hallway to get her coat and school bag and then lined up at the door.

'Good afternoon, class,'

'Good afternoon, Miss King,' said the line.

'Good job. Now let's show the rest of the school what a well-mannered class we are and walk silently to the front gates.'

Deborah was standing next to Sophie's Nanny, who was looking at her phone. Deborah tapped her watch and Maya ran over. They climbed in the back of the car.

'Why are we in a hurry?' said Maya.

'You'll see,' said Deborah.

'Good or bad?' said Maya.

'Good,' said Deborah. 'Maya, I wouldn't keep it from you if anything bad had happened.'

'Like Nana dying.'

'That's right, I promise to be the person to tell you.'

'I don't mind if it's Connie.'

'It'll be me.'

'Even if it's night-time?'

'Yes.'

'Even if I'm in school.'

'Yes.'

'Even if you're in the bathroom when it happens.'

'Maya!'

They drove through busy shopping streets, past shop fronts full of hearts.

'Did you give the card we made to your valentine?' said Deborah.

'No,' said Maya.

'Why not?'

'Didn't want to. Did you get any cards?'

'No,' said Deborah.

'You can have it,' said Maya.

'Thanks,' said Deborah.

'Unless you're taking me shopping. If you are, I'm keeping it.'

The car stopped outside the Lincoln Centre and they got out.

'Why are we here?' said Maya.

'You'll see.'

Deborah took Maya's hand and they walked in through the foyer. Deborah spoke to a lady on reception who Maya couldn't stop staring at. She had so much make-up on that Maya wanted to run her finger across the lady's face and then look at it. Sort of how Connie ran her finger across shelves at home and then studied it. The receptionist made a call then asked them to follow her. They went through a door that was marked, 'no entry' and along strip lit corridors. Maya kept looking behind her, expecting to be told they'd gone the wrong way. Every now and then Deborah turned her head and smiled at Maya. Maya smiled back thinking, 'you might be the goofiest person I know.' She could hear piano music and then voices too. The corridor became smaller and then opened out to the wings of a stage. On the stage a dancer in a practice skirt and leotard pounded ballet-shod feet against the boards, a sound Maya wished she could make, but she was too light and not in pointe shoes yet.

'Brava, brava,' said the voice, which came from the auditorium, 'great work, take a moment, you've got guests.'

The dancer shielded her eyes from the lights and turned to look in Maya, Deborah and the receptionist's direction. The receptionist began to speak but Maya couldn't hear a thing for the blood rushing through her ears. The dancer's hand reached down and Maya shook it, then Deborah too.

'This is Maya and she wants to be a ballerina when she grows up. She's the best in her class, honestly. Every mother says that, don't they, but my daughter is a talent.'

Maya couldn't move, but if she could she didn't know if

she'd kick Deborah or run away. Deborah wouldn't shut up. Every word she said was more excruciating than the last.

'We're rehearsing,' said the dancer. 'I'm dancing Sleeping Beauty.'

Maya nodded.

'Would you do some steps with me?'

'I don't have my—'

Deborah riffled in her handbag and pulled out Maya's ballet shoes.

'Take off your blazer,' said Deborah.

Maya did so and slipped on her pink satin ballet shoes over her school tights. Deborah and the dancer both ducked down at the same time and Maya stood still as they wound the pink ribbons around her ankles and tied them in a bow. Maya wished the dancer had done them both, her bow was a lot neater than Deborah's. The dancer took Maya's hand and they walked on to centre stage. Maya had been in a ballet show before but never on a stage this big. The dancer said something to the pianist and he began to play. Maya looked over to Deborah. She was holding both thumbs up and grinning. She was definitely the goofiest person Maya knew. Then the dancer started to call out instructions and nodded to Maya to join her as she moved first on the spot and then around the stage. To begin with Maya couldn't stand it. Her skin felt the way it did when Connie brushed her hair and accidentally ran the hairbrush down her neck. But she watched the dancer and every part of her wanted to move in the same way, like her body wasn't her own but a toy being played with by the music. She began to follow along with the dancer's steps. She strained to get up on the tip of her toes as they did the last pique turn and the dancer took her hand. They walked to the front of the stage and curtseyed. Maya could hear Deborah clapping loudly and whooping from the side of the stage. She didn't know that you don't scream like that at the ballet. Deborah walked on to the stage and shook the dancer's hand again. Maya felt her legs hot with effort and she was out of breath.

'Your mother's right,' said the dancer. 'You're exceptional for your age, Maya.'

Maya didn't speak for the entire journey home.

Deborah pestered her, 'Wasn't that amazing? What's the matter? Talk to me Maya.'

Maya just looked down at a t-shirt she'd been given which was signed by the dancer and then out of the window and then down at the t-shirt again and again. They pulled up outside the house and got out on to the curb.

'I don't want to go in,' said Maya.

'Why not? Connie's making heart shaped fishcakes.'

'I want to go back.'

'You'll go back again one day, that dancer will be you if you want it to be.'

Maya nodded.

'That was a weird Valentine's Day gift,' she said.

'I'm a weird mother,' said Deborah. 'Do you mind?'

Maya shrugged.

Deborah was embarrassing sometimes, thought Maya. But everyone says their mothers are embarrassing. Maybe that's what having a mother is supposed to feel like.

Chapter Twenty-Eight

18th February 1991

'We met at a party,' is the line they would tell people when asked how they met. And they did, on Presidents' Day. But what they didn't say is that they were at two different parties. The party Deborah attended took place in a basement apartment beneath the townhouse where he was. Despite the cold the basement party spilled outside on to the street and joints and cheap wine were passed around.

He was at his girlfriend's parents' party and eager to get away. When the smell of the smokers below wafted up through the open bathroom window, he slipped his hand around his girlfriend's waist, kissed her neck and said he needed to get out for some air. She said she'd come with him but he dissuaded her.

Deborah was outside smoking with a group of people who in that moment she would have called friends, even though their only time together was spent drinking. She saw him throwing on his coat as he walked down the steps to the pavement below. She remembered his first words so well because she couldn't imagine ever being confident enough to turn up among a bunch of strangers and say, 'Hey, I'm bored to shit up there. Pass me that joint will you?'

She handed him the joint. Without thanks he took a pull and handed it back. She took a drag and sized him up. He carried himself like someone for whom life just couldn't go wrong and yet he was escaping a party just like she was and sucking on a spliff to make it all more bearable.

A suited man walked past with a mobile phone pressed against his ear. It was the size of Deborah's clutch bag. She smirked.

'What an asshole, right?' said her acquaintance.

'Totally.'

He reached out his hand for another drag. She passed him the joint.

'I'll bet he's talking to his mom.'

Deborah smiled.

'What's your name?' he said.

'Deborah.'

He passed her the joint.

'Yours?' she said.

Just then the front door of the townhouse opened and a young woman stuck her head out. He stood up a little straighter.

'Are you coming back?' she said to him. She looked at Deborah and cocked her head. Deborah lifted her hand in a half-hearted wave.

'Sure,' he said.

'Ok,' said the girl, 'don't be long.' She hesitated a moment as though waiting for a reply but he'd turned his back and she closed the door.

Inside the basement party a ruckus had begun and someone was being bundled out the front door.

'Rowdy down here,' he said.

'Who was that?' said Deborah, pointing up to the front door of the townhouse.

'My sister,' he said.

'Hmm, weird vibe.'

'You've got a decent bullshit-ometer,' he said.

Deborah nodded.

'We're breaking up,' he said. 'It's just her grandfather died last month and I don't want to be a dick.'

Deborah shook her head. 'So you're being a dick.'

She handed him the joint.

'You're honest,' he said and pointed at her.

On the street next to them two guys were pushing each other. He steered her away to the other side of the townhouse steps.

'Listen, the kindest thing you could do is go up there and do it now.'

He took a puff and choked on it.

'No fucking way.'

'Then give me my joint back and go back to pretending.'

He handed her back the joint and pulled his coat tight across his chest. And that's the moment she really saw him. He was scared.

'What do I know? Do what you want,' she said.

He paused and looked away.

'I want to get the fuck out,' he said.

She passed him the joint and he took a drag and blew the smoke up into the cold air.

'Then why haven't you? Is she pregnant? Are you married? Are you afraid of being lonely?'

'I'm already lonely.'

'You know you're really on your own when you're at a party, and you disappear outside but nobody comes looking for you,' said Deborah.

He passed her the joint and looked towards the lit windows where his party was.

'Do you want to get out of here?' he said. 'Go have a drink, or coffee or something?'

'Not like this,' she said.

He paced the sidewalk. Deborah pulled out a cigarette paper and wrote on it with an eye pencil.

'Here's my number,' she said and passed him the paper. 'I'm going home, via somewhere I can get something to eat.'

He looked at his watch. She looked at his watch— he was wearing a Rolex. She couldn't imagine where a guy his age got a Rolex from.

'It's late, they might be closed. There's an Italian bakery around the corner. They know me in there and they'll make you whatever you like.'

'Flash guy, you've got connections,' she joked. She had no idea. 'I'm gonna go, I'm starving.' She passed him her joint. 'A parting gift.'

He reached out and took hold of her arm and squeezed it gently.

'Don't,' he said.

She lingered a moment and looked into his eyes.

'You're stoned,' she said.

'And you're not? I'm not the one about to take off into the night with the munchies.'

Deborah smiled and without thinking she cupped his cheek and at that moment the front door opened again and the girl came out.

Deborah stepped back.

'Shit,' he said.

'Call me,' said Deborah.

She walked away with the girl's voice carrying behind her. She heard him telling the girl that Deborah was someone who worked for his parents and they were old friends. The same girl followed him around for a long while after. She appeared at events they were at together and left awkward messages on his answerphone. Deborah went from wanting to set her hair on fire to pitying her. For in time she was to know what it was like to try and give him up.

Chapter Twenty-Nine

Presidents' Day wasn't the occasion Eva most favoured to hold a soiree. And on a Monday night no less. The fourth of July was more her style, but she wouldn't make it and needed a theme for her last party. It was too late for Valentine's Day and too soon for spring so Presidents' Day it was. Kitty Kelsey, the city's most sought-after event planner was organising. Kitty had put everything together in six days flat and arranged for Eva's friends on the West Coast to fly in. Eva had seen the invitations— they said nothing of her condition but word must have spread, or Kitty had shared it. Everybody of importance was coming— even the mayor.

Eva had to subdue Kitty's enthusiasm. Kitty wanted to deck the house out in red white and blue with star spangled banners on every surface. Subtler, insisted Eva. Kitty dialled it back to red, white and blue glassware and crockery, crisp white linen, canapes with little black silhouettes of the presidents poking out on cocktail sticks and a single flag stationed at the front door.

Eva's stylist at Saks Fifth Avenue came to the house with a selection of outfits for Eva, Deborah and Maya to choose from. Eva rolled her eyes at Deborah's obvious excitement, of course

Deborah didn't know that that's how Eva always shopped. She wasn't going to tell her it was unnecessary to schlep to the store every time she wanted something new to wear. With the kind of money the household spent Eva's stylist was always available. Maya was at school and Eva weeded out the dresses she wouldn't see her granddaughter wear; anything that was above the knee was out of the question, anything with sequins too trashy, and there were designers she wouldn't begin to consider putting Maya in because she thought their styles looked cheap. This left two dresses, one in navy blue satin with a plain white organza sash and the other a plain white dress with a red velvet sash. She would make it appear to Maya that she could choose between the two but it would be the white dress with the red sash that she'd wear. Eva could tell the stylist was enjoying dressing Deborah, a young, slim, attractive woman, someone she could take a picture of and boast about. Eva chose black, she almost always wore black. Black made her feel severe and put together and she needed that when she wobbled on her feet so often, caught tears coming at the most inopportune moments and could feel the thread between her body and her life being worn down. This would not only be Eva's last party but her last new outfit, she thought. She kept reprimanding herself for marking all the lasts. The last party, the last new dress, the last visit to synagogue, these were the lasts she could handle. It was the other lasts she couldn't face; the last Shabbos, the last moment with Maya. Would she know when it was, or would she be taken unawares?

Maya was in Gym class when Deborah arrived at school. It was an hour before the end of the day. Maya was on the parallel bars when she saw Deborah standing in the doorway of the gymnasium her hands on her hips and talking to the teacher in a way that looked as if she was putting her right. Maya gripped the bars hard, she was suspended, her elbows locked and arm muscles shaking. She looked down at her feet swinging in the air and waited. Nobody could tell her any kind of news, let alone bad news while she was here.

'Maya?' called Miss King.

Maya continued to look at her feet— she clenched her toes tight and released them again, over and over while her teacher continued to call her name. Out of the corner of her eye she could see movement next to her and Miss King was about to place her hand on her arm. Maya whipped her arms away and landed heavy on her feet on the crash mat below. She turned her head to look at the doorway— Deborah was still there, and she was checking her phone.

'Your mother's here to collect you.'

'Why?' said Maya. Though she was pretty sure she knew.

'She'll explain. Run along to her, she's in an awful hurry.'

Maya chewed the inside of her mouth on her way over to Deborah. The other girls were all looking at her and she could feel her face getting hot. Every movement felt like a deliberate step she'd learned in a dance she wasn't yet sure of.

'Will you stop dawdling, I've got dresses and shoes for you to try on at home and it's taken me a half an hour to get from the front office to here. They're that worried about security anyone would think the president attended this school.'

Presidents' children had attended that school, Maya could have told her. But she was waiting to find out more of why she'd been collected before the end of the day. Rabbi Rovner had told her that when the time came the funeral would be very soon. It was always like that; she didn't need telling.

'I'm thirsty,' said Maya. Wait a while Deborah, not here, she thought.

'You can have a drink in the car. Nana's waiting for us at home— she won't let the assistants from Saks go until you've tried on your outfit and they're getting in the way.'

Not here and not today. In elation Maya cartwheeled the

last few feet to stand in front of Deborah and hugged her around the middle. She felt Deborah's arms close in around her. When Maya stepped back her friend Celeste was standing next to her.

'Are you alright, Maya?' she said.

'This is my mother,' said Maya. 'Her name is Deborah and she's from England.'

Celeste extended her hand to Deborah. Deborah looked surprised but she shook it. Maya saw Deborah and Miss King give each other a look that Maya understood to mean they found what was happening funny and she wanted to get out of class and home as quickly as possible.

'Pleased to meet you, Mrs Goltz,' said Celeste.

'It's Deborah.'

'I told you I had a mother,' said Maya to Celeste. She took hold of Deborah's arm and led her out.

On the way home Maya felt relief give way to a swell of irritation and by the time their car pulled up outside the house she wasn't talking to Deborah. Nobody had told her about the party which was unfair, in fact it was bad manners and it was nasty to trick her into thinking Nana had gone. When it was just her and Nana she would know everything that was happening in the house but now she'd been demoted. Maya folded her arms and sighed heavily in Deborah's direction.

Nana always told her not to make a scene in public or in front of the staff, she waited until they were through the front door.

'Nobody told me,' she raged.

Deborah acted dumb and asked her, again, what the matter was.

'The party,' she shouted. She threw her school satchel down and kicked it across the polished black and white tiled floor.

'What's bad about a party?' said Deborah.

'Nobody told me.'

'You can't expect to be consulted on everything that happens, you're seven years old Maya, stop making a stink.'

Maya stopped a moment, she sniffed the air. Deborah laughed at her and she lashed out and pummelled Deborah with her fists.

'It's an expression,' said Deborah. 'Stop hitting me.'

Deborah kept on laughing. Her stupid laugh and ugly face, thought Maya. She wished she could reach her face and hit her in it. She opened her mouth wide— she would bite Deborah, and that would stop her laughing. Deborah saw her coming and held her away at arm's length.

'Maya, stop it, really, you're acting like an animal.'

'You're an animal.'

'Maya, I mean it— enough.'

'You don't tell me what to do, you're a money grabbing whore.'

'Maya, come on,' said Deborah.

'You're trash and a thief, a bitch and I wish it was you who was dying.'

Deborah looked wounded and let go of her arms and stepped away. Maya immediately felt better, but soon after afraid she would be in trouble. To her surprise Deborah turned her back and went up the stairs without saying a word.

Eva was in the den. Maya walked in still in her school uniform.

'Sweetheart, come here,' said Eva, her arms outstretched.

'But I haven't changed,' said Maya— usually Eva would have reprimanded her for this.

'I don't care, come here.'

'Deborah's upset,' said Maya.

'Oh, Deborah's always upset about something, come here.' Eva embraced Maya.

'I swore,' said Maya. 'I said bad words to her.'

Eva couldn't resist a moment of glee; Maya had turned on

Deborah. She wanted to say that it didn't matter, that it was them against the rest of the world.

'What did you say to her? Tell me the clean version.'

Maya told her, replacing the words 'female dog' for bitch and she didn't know what the word whore meant, she spelled it out badly.

'Oh dear,' said Eva. 'The trouble here honey is that it's my fault. You've heard me say these things.'

And she had. She had said it so often and in every way she knew how and to everybody who would listen.

'And Daddy,' said Maya.

Eva had made her son hateful— she'd had to in order to keep him away from Deborah. Eva didn't realise just how much of their shared vitriol against Deborah Maya had contracted.

'None of these things are true,' said Eva. 'You know I don't like lies but I was very upset at the time I said them, Daddy too— we were wrong.'

Hear that, thought Eva as though God was listening in, hear that. I'm sorry. I was wrong, enough of this now. Eva could feel an ache in her heart, deep and frightening. How different things might have been if she'd done this sooner. Eva held her chest.

'Sorry, Nana, sorry, I was bad.'

Eva fought to take deep breaths. It was made worse by the look of terror on Maya's face.

'I'll apologise,' said Maya. 'I'm sorry, I'm sorry.'

At that moment Connie walked in and gasped. Before Eva could stop her Connie said she was calling the doctor and ran out of the room. But it's not the physical pain, thought Eva, it's worse than that. The rabbi was right, we can't choose who we hurt when we go out into the world with bad intentions. Connie came back with Eva's pill box and a glass of water. Eva pushed both away and Connie escorted Maya out of the room and temporarily distracted her with a cookie. When the doctor came Eva told him she was just tired, nothing more. He gave her something to help keep her energy up for the night.

'These are good ones,' he said.

'I never took drugs, ever,' said Eva.

'You'll feel great on these.'

'I'll want them every time,' said Eva.

'Well the good news is if you get hooked now it doesn't matter,' the doctor said.

They laughed. Eva liked him more now he'd relaxed and was being her friend as well as her doctor.

Deborah came out of the en suite bathroom and found her long red gown hanging up on the outside of the wardrobe. Her navy-blue Manolo Blahnik heels stood on top of their box, her accessories were laid out on the dressing table and a clutch to match the shoes nearby. Connie had also brought up a plate of canapes and a bottle of mineral water and a glass.

Maya was hiding in her room. Deborah had tried to forget what she said but she suspected she was the voice of every person coming to the party. She got dressed and then looked out of her bedroom window at the dark and freezing evening. On the street a man was opening car doors and welcoming guests. Deborah had never seen anything like this. There were security guards dressed as waiting staff and a doorman. A fleet of real waiting staff and caterers had taken over the kitchen and a florist delivered enormous floral arrangements for every downstairs room. Kitty Kelsey had been shouting orders into a mouthpiece all afternoon.

There was a gentle tap on her door,

'Maya?'

'No Ms Goltz, it's Kitty.'

Kitty had called her Ms Goltz— what should she say to that?

'Come in.'

Kitty's head appeared around the door.

'You look amazing,' she said. 'I wanted to let you know people are arriving and there's a man called Jon downstairs who wants you to know he's here.'

'Thank you.'

'That dress,' said Kitty. 'Wow.'

The door closed and Deborah checked her make up in the mirror once again. She wondered if she'd see anyone who knew her before. If she did she expected them to blank her or treat her with half-hearted kindness only to save face in a room full of well-behaved people. But this is what she must expect. It might take more years to prove her worthiness than it did to tear it away. She got to wear fifteen thousand-dollar dresses but there would always be somebody to look her up and down.

She was intrigued that Jon didn't notice her outfit, or if he did, he didn't say a thing about it. He'd left the airport and was working security now.

'Now I'm convinced you're stalking me,' Deborah said.

'I'll admit I found out where this party was and said I could work it. Now I know you're as rich as a Rothschild I don't feel so bad about you buying me lunch and not letting me return the favour.'

Deborah smiled.

'It's not my money,' she said.

'About what I said to you last time...I'm sorry, it wasn't my place.'

Deborah could see Eva watching them talk. She couldn't read Eva's expression but she thought about how Eva had called Joseph an ass and he'd still come back. There are people, none of whom she'd ever given more than a moment of her time, who just see past it all. All her bluster, preening and posing had nothing to do with his interest in her. She had no idea what his attention had taken hold of, she was yet to see it herself. Deborah batted away the apology.

'For what it's worth I'm not drinking tonight,' she said.

Jon looked bashful.

'Besides, I've absolutely no idea why Presidents' Day is an event,' she said.

'It's in the name,' said Jon.

'But what's to celebrate?'

Jon laughed.

'Is it just more flag waving?' she said.

'I suppose it is,' said Jon.

'The land of the free and the home of the brave,' said Deborah.

'On our best days,' said Jon.

'Do you think that the 2000s are going to be good days for this country?'

Somewhere in the distance what sounded like a tray of glasses was dropped and a voice called out for help.

'I need to go,' said Jon. 'Enjoy your party.'

The party went on almost all night. Well-dressed guests piled in, and the house was full by ten thirty. The mayor gave a toast to Eva and the Goltz family and Deborah noticed glasses held in her direction. There was a cake decorated with stars and stripes and it was cut into thin slivers and circulated. Deborah watched Maya going back for seconds, thirds and fourths—Maya looked happy and so she let her. The next time this many people would be gathering at the house it would be a wholly different atmosphere. The heart of the house was Eva and she beat loudly that night. Maya fell asleep on a chair in the den and every time somebody tried to carry her to bed she argued to be allowed to stay up. She could have asked for anything at all that evening and she knew it.

At 3am there were still people sitting around Eva while she talked animatedly and drank cups of coffee. Lois and Dash, who had flown in from California, were the very last to leave.

Dash had spoken to almost nobody but Eva all evening, despite getting a lot of attention. Others had tried to talk to the well-known Hollywood producer but he only had time for Eva. Deborah wondered if they'd ever had a fling. Time had stood still for Lois, even though she was about Eva's age her face had been pinned, tucked and plumped. She could pass for a Hollywood fifty-year-old. She told Deborah that if Eva needed anything in the coming weeks to be sure to call her or Dash. There was nothing Eva would need now except for care but that had been bought. Soon there would be somebody to wash her, sit with her and keep her comfortable. Nobody else needed to do a thing except to wait.

Connie managed to persuade Maya, drunk in her tiredness, to walk up to bed. Kitty Kelsey and the skeleton staff of waiters and security who had been paid overtime to stay until the party finished began the clean-up. Eva and Deborah were left alone.

'What a party,' said Deborah.

'It's important to throw a good party, make sure you do it often when I'm gone.'

Connie gently knocked on the door to the den and Eva told her to come in.

'Miss, Maya says she wants you to tuck her in.'

Deborah looked over to Eva guiltily. Eva was getting tired now, she wasn't sure she'd make it up to bed.

'Go on, Deborah. She's your daughter.'

Deborah looked to Connie and Connie understood that she was to stay with Eva.

Deborah swished down the hallway, her gown now dirty at the bottom, and some of the underskirt brushing the floor where her stiletto heel had caught it. She skirted around piled up boxes of dirty cutlery and crockery and stacks of silver gilt chairs. The floor was sticky and a glass of red wine had gone down one of the walls and was being soaked up by some tissue paper. She could hear voices in the kitchen laughing and complaining that rich folks make as much mess as a frat party. She took off her heels and went up the stairs and to Maya's room.

'Connie says you want me,' said Deborah.

From beneath the covers Maya nodded.

Deborah sat down on the edge of Maya's bed.

'Did you have a nice time this evening?' said Deborah.

Maya nodded again.

'Let me see your jammies,' said Deborah.

She pulled back the covers a little and smiled at Maya in powder pink pyjamas covered in ballerinas. Maya had drawer upon drawer of nightclothes. Deborah had never seen her in the same set twice and it had become a nightly ritual to make a fuss of what she was wearing.

'Shall we say goodnight?' said Deborah.

Maya nodded.

Deborah tucked the covers in around Maya's small and delicate form, just like Deborah's own mother had done for her for all the years before Patrick came along. Deborah leant down and kissed Maya on the forehead.

'I love you,' said Deborah.

Maya reached out to Deborah and when Deborah ducked down Maya wrapped her arms around her tightly.

'Goodnight.'

Maya turned on to her side and Deborah tucked her in again. She switched on the ballerina shaped nightlight that Maya depended on and turned off the main light. Connie had placed Maya's dress on a hanger which hung off a hook on the back of Maya's bedroom door. The skirt had hand wiped smears of cake frosting down the sides and the bow of the sash was sticky with chocolatey fingerprints. Deborah lifted the dress from the hanger and took it into the bathroom. She sponged the frosting and chocolate out as best she could and left it to soak. It would take some work but she would make it new again.

Chapter Thirty

14*th* June 1980

In the corridor outside the restrooms at the Waldorf Astoria hotel, where so many well-heeled feet had trod Connie was using napkins to surreptitiously mop portions of the floor. Whenever anybody came by she stood up and tucked the napkins behind her back and smiled. She went into the women's bathroom to get some hand towels to assist with the job.

Eva walked out of the men's bathroom and met Joseph who was on his way in. She pushed him back into the hall.

'He's eaten too much,' said Eva.

'Don't cover for him. Connie told me she found him and the Gutterman boy both holding an empty bottle of wine. Which you'll know cost us $150 apiece.'

'Joe, don't be crass.'

An elderly couple walked down the corridor excruciatingly slowly and Eva and Joseph stopped talking and smiled at them with their teeth. When they'd shuffled on a bit Joseph mumbled,

'Your newly Bar Mitzvahed son is puking his guts up in there and I'm crass.'

'There was a lot of pressure on him,' said Eva.

'And yet most thirteen-year-olds don't turn to drink.'

The couple were out of earshot now so Eva could raise her voice.

'Why can't you be proud of him for once?'

'I am proud of him, Eva. But really all he had to do was say a few words, receive a tonne of presents and party with his friends here, in a place that neither you or me could have afforded to walk through the door of until a few years ago.'

A teenage boy was headed towards the men's bathroom. Eva reached out her arm to block the entrance.

'There's a leak in there, I'd use the other one if I were you— it's that way,' she pointed.

The boy shrugged and walked away; Eva turned back to Joseph.

'Everyone said he recited the Torah beautifully.'

'And you mouthed every word for him.'

'No, I didn't.'

'I was sitting right next to you. And you were miming.'

'I was supporting our son, is there anything wrong with wanting him to do well?'

'I just want him to deserve something.'

'You're nasty when you've had a drink, Joe. I don't think you ought to have any more.'

'I've had a single beer.'

'Who drinks a beer in a place like this?'

'I do.'

Eva tutted.

'I'm going back in to see if he's alright. When he comes out you won't say a word will you?'

'I'm going to say plenty.'

'Not in front of anyone else and not here.'

'It might do him good to get bawled out in front of his friends. My father did it to me and I learned the value of shame.'

'You'll spoil today for everyone if you do that and it's all anyone will remember.'

'Fine, but I'll leave it to you to explain that.' Joseph pointed towards the Gutterman boy who had appeared from around the corner and was dancing a sloppy version of the can can outside the ladies' room.

Eva shook her head.

'Such a proud day,' said Joseph.

Chapter Thirty-One

Eva woke and could hear Connie showing the nurse around the house. Connie sounded bright and perky, not at all like somebody who had hardly slept. She glanced at the clock— it was almost eleven— she couldn't remember the last time she'd slept so late. The doctor would soon be over to check on her. It seemed that every day brought a new ailment or limitation. She rolled on to one side carefully and pushed down on her elbow to try and lift herself out of bed. She felt pain in her back and had to lie down again. She didn't want to call out to Connie and for the nurse to come in and see her without her make-up on or her hair done. The nurse would see a lot worse before their time together came to an end, she knew that, but she had to try for a good first impression. Aunt Sal used to say that a good first impression was like a decent handshake, you had to get in there first before the other person had time to square you up. And this stayed with Eva as proof of her love since when she arrived in Aunt Sal's care she spoke almost no English and never smiled, she ate her hair and dragged her teeth beneath her fingernails, chewing on what she found underneath.

Eva kept her make-up bag on her nightstand and she did the best she could in applying some concealer, mascara and lipstick with only a handheld mirror and an intermittent pain that made her hand shake. She ran her fingers through the top of her hair and smoothed it down, she hoped the style her hairdresser had set the night before had held. She tried to get up again. The pain warned her against it.

'Connie?' she called.

Moments later the door opened.

'Mrs Goltz?'

'I'm having some trouble; will you help me.'

Connie came in. She closed the door behind her.

'Mrs Goltz, the nurse is here.'

'Where is she now?'

'Downstairs with a cup of coffee. I thought you'd like to be up and ready when you met her.'

'Yes, Connie, thank you.'

'The doctor is here as well.'

'Lucky me,' said Eva.

The drugs that had kept her going into the night had faded now and it felt like

somebody else had attended that party but she had their hangover. Perhaps, she thought, he'd give her some more. But for now, she had to sleep a while longer. Suddenly it didn't matter that people were waiting and the world was trying to push her into another day. She set down her make-up and hand mirror and lay back.

It was almost midday by the time Connie helped her up and she was ready to go downstairs. Eva took Connie's arm and they toddled down having to stop after every two or three steps for Eva to rest.

'I'm lazy these days,' said Eva.

'Mrs Goltz,' said Connie, in a warning tone. A tone that said, I'm going to give you a talking to if you persist with this nonsense.

'Let me believe I'm lazy, Connie.'

Connie tut tutted.

'Mrs Goltz, fancy sleeping until past eleven o'clock, you must have had a whole seven hours last night.'

Eva gripped Connie's arm, afraid she was going to fall. Connie stopped.

'I'm not sure I can take much more of this laziness, Mrs Goltz— look sharp!'

Eva felt pain like fingernails digging into her insides but still she laughed, a laugh from deep down in her belly, the kind that makes you weak. Connie caught her laugh and by the time they reached the bottom they had to sit down on the chairs in the hallway and compose themselves.

In the kitchen, Connie made Eva a plate of breakfast that she pushed around her plate— she didn't have an appetite anymore. Maya came down dressed in a strange ensemble of a fairy dress-up outfit on top of a pair of jeans and an Arun jumper tied around her waist. Eva thought to tell her to go upstairs and change but Maya was buoyant, talkative and too full of the excitement of the party to be corrected. Eva watched her climb up to sit on a high stool around the kitchen island. Connie fixed her scrambled eggs, toast and a glass of orange juice. Maya wolfed it down and asked for seconds. Eva kissed Maya on the head and went to the den to meet her nurse and see the doctor.

Eva could hear them talking but they went quiet when she opened the door.

'Eva Goltz,' said Eva, offering her hand to a small and serious-looking woman dressed all in white, she introduced herself as Viola Peters. 'Whatever the doctor tells you about me understand that I knew his father and I've known him since he was in kindergarten. I have stories I could tell you about him that would embarrass a Bush.'

The nurse gave a polite smile. Perhaps, Eva thought, she was a Republican. Eva tried to appear engaged while the doctor talked to her and the nurse looked on, apparently rapt by everything he said. But on the mantelpiece next to the pictures and flowers there was a champagne flute from the night before. Somebody had put down a champagne flute between the picture of Joseph and her son. Who would do such a thing? Who would be so thoughtless as to put their drink down there? And it was half full. Why hadn't Kitty's team cleared it away? Hadn't Connie noticed it? Eva felt the doctor gently touch her arm and she moved her attention back to him for a moment. He wanted re-assurance that she'd rest. She told him that she would and she meant it with the same sincerity as she did when Maya expected to be checked on five minutes after being put to bed. He either believed her or let her win this battle and agreed to leave and come back that evening. He asked to see the nurse in the hallway and they left Eva alone in the den.

She went over to the champagne glass and picked it up. She inspected the rim for lip marks, as though that would expose the culprit. It was a clean glass— it hadn't been drunk from as far as she could tell. She took it over to the bar in the corner and set it down. Suddenly, too tired to stand a moment longer, Eva went back and lay on the leather sofa glaring at the wheelchair in the corner. The items of equipment that were appearing piece by piece in the house hadn't escaped her. Connie had been canny in hiding them but she knew what they were. She'd come across a stand for a drip in a closet just that morning. She heard the door and tried to quickly move her feet from the sofa to the floor. The pain came again and she changed position fast enough. Connie came in, followed by Maya.

'Mrs Goltz, can I bring you something up?' said Connie.

'Up where?' said Eva.

'You told the doctor you were going back to bed.'

'You know me, Connie, I can't stay in bed all day.'

Maya came over and sidled up to Eva.

'You know I don't like lies,' said Maya.

'Oh hush,' said Eva. She stroked Maya's face. 'Go upstairs and take the dress off, you look like a hobo.'

'Where's Deborah?'

'She went out,' said Connie.

'We've something else to talk about too,' said Eva to Maya. 'You were rude to Deborah yesterday, what'll you say to her when she gets home?'

'Sorry?' said Maya.

'I think you can do a little better than that.'

Maya searched her mind a moment and then nodded excitedly when she came up with an answer.

'I'm sorry for what I said to you, it was cruel and untrue.' Maya said.

'Very good, anything else?'

'And I'm glad you're here really.'

'Lose the 'really'.'

'Then can I have the candy Lois and Dash brought me?'

'Once you've said it to her— nicely. Don't tell her about the candy, understand?'

Maya nodded and pulled a skipping rope out from her back pocket and began to skip around the room. Eva winced as she watched a near miss between the rope and a vase of flowers. There were mounds of wrapped gifts from the night before stacked up in front of the fireplace which for the first time that year hadn't been lit. Outside had thawed and February was about to slip into March, though nothing else in nature seemed to know it yet. Eva felt herself retreating from time to time. Maya would call her name and she would awake and be back in the room. The nurse came in so Maya stopped skipping and sat down, she eyed Eva suspiciously. The pain was back and she was shaking. Eva heard the nurse say to Maya to call Connie in.

'I'm just tired,' said Eva.

'Mrs Goltz, we'll call Connie so that you can go to bed and she can watch Maya until Deborah gets home,' said the nurse, as though her white lace ups had been under the Goltz family table for months. She tucked blankets around Eva and knelt down so she could look Eva in the eye.

'No,' said Eva.

Eva didn't want to be taken upstairs and put to bed like a sickly child. Every morning she could get up like a normal person and have Maya around her was a blessing that, it seemed, was about to be revoked. The nurse retreated to a chair in the corner and was asked by Eva to leave the room. She did so.

'Come over here,' said Eva to Maya.

Maya walked over and leant against the side of the sofa. Eva managed to untangle her arm from beneath the blankets she'd been tightly tucked into and wrapped it around Maya.

'I want to tell you what's happening.'

'I know what's happening, you're going to die.'

'Yes, my organs are very tired and they're going to stop working.'

'Today?'

'No, I don't think so. Soon.'

'Tomorrow?'

'Probably not that soon.'

'When?'

'It's hard to say, a week, maybe two.'

Eva closed her eyes for just a moment and when she woke Maya was still sitting on the floor next to her, this time eating a cookie. Maya was no longer wearing her dress from the night before and Eva wondered how long she'd been out.

'What time is it?' she said.

'Connie said I could have this cookie.'

'What time is it?'

'It's not after dinner yet but I didn't eat all that much last night. I don't know what time of day it is but lunch was a little while ago and I'm particularly hungry today.'

Eva smiled.

'You're a special girl Maya— not everyone appreciates girls like us.'

Maya offered Eva a bite of her cookie, Eva shook her head. She heard sounds in the hallway and Deborah's voice calling out to Connie to help her with her bags.

'Deborah's back, do you remember what to say?'

Maya nodded. Deborah came into the room with several shopping bags in her hands.

'I'm sorry for what I said. It was cruel and untrue and I'm glad you're here,' said Maya.

Deborah put the shopping bags down and sat.

'Can I have my candy now?' said Maya to Eva.

'Go, have it,' said Eva.

Maya ran out of the room leaving the floorboards trembling behind her.

'She meant it,' said Eva.

Deborah laughed.

'She'd say anything to make you happy,' said Deborah.

'Wrong, she'd say anything to have the candy Dash and Lois brought her.'

'Where does a little girl learn those words?'

Eva looked into her lap.

'I think you know. She was just repeating words she'd heard,' said Eva. 'It was a long time ago. I didn't think she was listening— but she was— they always are.'

Eva was so close that she could almost hear Rabbi Rovner's voice in her ear, willing her on. An apology was as close as a bite of a donut the moment the sugar touches your lips. I'm sorry, I apologise, I deeply regret it.

'What did you buy at the store?' said Eva.

Not now.

Deborah delved into a bag pulling out a lime green and fluorescent orange sequined dress. It reminded Eva of the pictures of provincial child beauty pageants.

'Look what I bought for Maya.'

Eva grimaced.

'You couldn't just pretend to like it?'

'I'm a woman who can tell a lie, you know that, but that is the ugliest dress I've ever set eyes on.'

'I know it is. It's for Purim.'

'For Purim?' said Eva.

Deborah stood up and shook the dress out.

'I thought it was a sort of Jewish Halloween? I went looking for the silliest dress I could find. You'd be surprised how difficult it is to find ugly dresses.'

Deborah fluffed the skirts up on the dress and held it at arm's length, smiling in pleasure at her find.

'It's in a few weeks, right? I'm going to take Maya to synagogue. Irene what's-her-name told me about it, she said it was a big deal.'

Deborah turned the dress around and unfurled a garish train with fluorescent pom poms adorning the hem.

Eva couldn't hold her shoulders back and slumped, giving in to convulsions that shook her chest and choked her.

'Oh no,' Deborah dropped the dress and ran over to Eva. 'Connie? Connie? Help, Nurse, Oh my God, Eva? Eva?'

The nurse ran in and moved Deborah aside— she was followed by Maya who tried to push the nurse out of the way. The nurse and Maya were both upon Eva. The nurse checked her vital signs and Maya lifted her head up so she had to look straight at her.

'She's just crying,' said Maya.

'Is it the pain?' said the nurse.

Connie ran in, her heel hit the squeaky floorboard.

'Mrs Goltz, I'm calling an ambulance.'

Eva found her breath.

'I'm perfectly comfortable, will you just let an old woman weep.'

'I can call the rabbi?' said Connie.

'No, really Connie, do you get counselled every time you shed a tear?'

'It's my fault, I upset her,' said Deborah.

'The opposite,' said Eva.

The nurse left and Connie lured Maya to the kitchen with the promise of another cookie. Eva heard Maya discussing the merits of the various cookies on offer as she walked away up the hall. She was still a little girl, easily distracted, it made Eva hopeful that when she was gone Deborah would be enough of a distraction. Deborah put the ugly dress down and went over to the bar.

'I'm having the tiniest drink, don't judge me,' she said.

'It's too late for that,' said Eva, with a smile on her face. 'But I'll leave you alone on this occasion if you pour me one.'

'Scotch?'

'No, something sweet.'

Deborah poured out two amarettos and found cherries to plop in each glass.

She handed Eva hers and sat down.

'I don't know if cherries belong in amaretto but I like it that way,' said Deborah.

Eva sipped her drink.

'I never normally drink before seven,' said Eva.

Deborah lifted her glass. Eva joined her and they both drank.

'I heard Kitty call you Ms Goltz and you answered to it,' said Eva.

'I was in a rush, I couldn't be bothered to correct her.'

'I'm not scolding you,' said Eva. 'You'll have a better time of it here as a Goltz. It would help Maya— there's nobody she shares a name with.'

'Nobody?'

'Just me.'

Deborah finished her drink and thought a moment.

'You expect me to convert as well?'

'That's not mine to offer.'

Deborah put her glass down.

'Listen Deborah, it's vulgar to talk about money like this but—'

'The agency I worked for in London has a branch over here. I've already enquired about a job. Now I have some savings behind me I can get an apartment for me and Maya and support us.'

'If a job is what you want?'

'It is.'

Eva waited— there had to be a caveat.

Deborah went to stand up and Eva could wait no longer.

'Maya's school fees will be covered and she'll have an allowance. But please, Deborah it would be better for Maya if you both lived here, at least for a while. The house will belong to her, it can't be sold until she's twenty-one. Get a job if you want one but I'm leaving you enough money to keep up with the people who'll be around you now.'

'No, thank you.'

'Don't be stubborn— do it for Maya.'

'But I want to be my own person,' said Deborah. 'I need to prove I can be.'

'You already are,' said Eva, 'I stole from you. The deficiency is mine. There will be no conditions on this money, except that you take care of Maya and now I see that you'd do it anyway. Just do me a favour and see my financial adviser— don't spend it all in Barneys.'

This was the closest to an apology Deborah was ever going to get.

Chapter Thirty-Two

Rabbi Rovner had another conversation with Connie which involved her repeating word for word what Eva had told her to say and at the very end of their conversation giving him the truth. Eva wouldn't be in synagogue on Saturday morning. She wouldn't share a Friday night with him, Jona and the boys or fry up the best latkes he'd tasted since his mother was alive—pray nobody tell Jona.

Rabbi Rovner put his elbows on the desk and his head in his hands.

'I can't stand it,' he said to the mustard-speckled mouse mat beneath. He thought of the words he often recited at funerals, 'God takes nothing from the world until he puts something else in its place.' It gave him no solace, though as he often told grieving relatives what comes in its place is usually only apparent after some time. And who would read the mourner's kaddish for her without a parent, child or sibling left? He got up from his desk and went over to the third drawer of the filing cabinet. It was locked and he had to fish around in his desk drawer for a key. After five attempts the drawer slid open. He quickly looked over his shoulder through the glass panel on the office door. He took out two candy bars and slid it shut, then changed his mind and pulled out one more before closing the drawer and locking it.

'You're a terrible pig, Samuel,' he said to himself and opened the first candy bar. He crammed it in his mouth in one go and chewed quickly so as to get it down as fast as he could. Immediately he felt better. If his brain were wired up the reward centre would be flashing like a slot machine. Then he ate the other and with a mouth still full he pressed the third bar in.

It annoyed him that people would say he was a humble servant of God and that they didn't know how he could walk through the valley of the shadow of death with so many. This is how he did it, with God and with food and if anyone said that his love for God should make the other unnecessary they had no idea. His own father died of a heart attack at 52. Rabbi Rovner didn't tell people this but he saw the sins of the father inherited every single time. If a parent didn't find their way through their addiction or trauma, the sad and damaging defects didn't slink away when their host was gone, no, like an ugly heirloom someone would have to house it. He'd heard it called 'second generation trauma'— his father had called it making a fuss.

He wanted to go back to the third drawer and have just one more but he knew he had to wait. He watched the clock as a reminder that the craving would pass. He felt ashamed to be worrying about candy bars when Eva was still suffering. After what happened, can she be absolved? He asked God again and again. Will she be forgiven when she hasn't yet fully atoned? God's love was unconditional but he didn't believe there were no consequences for the missteps we take in this life. They were forgiven if we atoned, but it wasn't enough to starve ourselves for a day, and tell a rabbi and whisper a few secret prayers. We had to change.

He got up from his desk, went out of his office and into

the main sanctuary. He stood still a moment and then closed his eyes. His body knew shuckling as well as it did the right maneuver to get the synagogue refrigerator open without it making a sound. He began swaying back and forth like a flame in the wind. When the movement began he felt he had about as much control over it as he did his cravings. He swayed to loosen the grip of stillness and inertia, to pull out the tendrils of material concerns and worldly priorities. His addictions and habits anchored his soul in this most inhospitable place when all he wanted was to be free. The rapture that others spoke of was never there, but he was gone. Samuel Ernest Rovner took leave and a light, a feeling pure and crystalline took up residence. Who would come back? Which is why the body must be as it is, and ache, need, want and feel until it is heard. By the time he returned his back was sore and his ankles hurt so much he could hardly move and the swaying stopped. He took his hands to his heart, feeling the residue of its visitor.

'For Eva,' he said aloud and sent his hands out.

He sat down in the front row and bent down to rub his ankles. He could hardly reach them these days. He said it was because his back was stiff, but even with the spine of a yogi it would be difficult to get around his stomach. He groaned and panted from the effort.

A shadow appeared over him and for a moment he was afraid to look up. Who would intrude on such a personal moment except for the uninvited?

'Samuel?' said Jona. 'What have you done?'

He looked up and smiled.

'Just my ankles again.'

Jona sat down. She tapped her thighs as though inviting a lap dog to pounce on them.

With the help of both hands Rabbi Rovner swung his right leg up and she took hold of his ankle and gave it a pull.

'Ah, that's it,' he said.

She placed a hand either side of his ankle and began vigorously rubbing it.

'That's the stuff,' he said.

Finally she pressed her thumbs around the ankle bone. He put his right leg down and swung the left one up. She began the process again. This time the pull on his ankle made him moan. She moved on to some determined rubbing of the ankle and the moaning continued.

Adam came into the sanctuary through the back doors and gasped,

'Rabbi, I'm so terribly sorry... Mrs Rovner please accept my apologies, I, I, I'll wait outside your office.' He backed up as if trying to avoid attack and then suddenly turned and strode away.

Rabbi Rover swung his leg down and grimaced as his foot hit the floor.

'Adam, stop!' he called out. 'Jona was just rubbing my ankles for me.'

Rabbi Rover was on his feet and in pursuit. He tried to pick up his pace but anything more than a slow walk was beyond him now. What stopped him half way up the aisle was the roaring laughter he hadn't heard in such a long time. A sound of mirth that could make anyone believe that everything was going to be alright, that no matter how frightening, dark and hopeless it all seemed, there was joy in this life and it was God given. He turned to see Jona doubled over on her seat.

Rabbi Rovner turned back and went to sit next to her. He giggled as she tried to compose herself. She wiped tears from her eyes and then collapsed in snorts of laughter again.

Chapter Thirty-Three

13ᵗʰ May 1987

Eva was in the den trying to watch an episode of Moonlighting to take her mind off of things. She kept looking up at the mantlepiece clock and was surprised that only minutes had passed between glances. She heard Joseph's voice and switched off the TV and got up and closed the wooden doors of the TV cabinet. Joseph said goodnight to Connie in the hallway and then the front door closed. Their supper was keeping warm in the oven. Eva decided it would be better to speak to him before they ate, and besides she didn't think she'd get anything down before she'd told him the cost of smoothing things over for their son. Joseph opened the door to the den with a scotch in his hand.

'$250,000,' said Eva.

'How much?' said Joseph.

'$250,000,' said Eva.

Joseph shook his head.

'There's a clause that means the girl won't be able to go to the press— it's not as much as it could have been.'

'Oh sure, a quarter of a million is nothing.'

Joseph put his drink down and sat.

'And what does the college dean say?' he said

'Their lawyer is now saying it's a private matter— it happened off campus.'

'He won't be thrown out?'

'No.'

A pause. Eva went over to the far side of the den and looked out on the bright spring evening. Just then a dog stopped and cocked its leg on the pot of irises Connie had planted earlier.

'I offered a donation to the new sports complex. We were going to give them some money anyway.'

Joseph shook his head.

'Not like this.'

Eva twirled her wedding ring around on her finger and sat down on the window seat looking out.

'He says it was a misunderstanding,' she said.

'Do you believe him?'

'Of course I do. Don't you?'

'What's her name? What was she studying? Will she be able to go back?' he said.

Her voice shook a little.

'She'll transfer,' Eva said. 'That's part of the deal.'

'Does he know what he's done to her life?' said Joseph.

'He says it was a misunderstanding— she was drunk— he thought it was ok— she didn't fight him. She would have known who he was,' said Eva.

'Don't Eva, don't you dare.'

Eva dropped her head.

'I'm sorry,' she said.

'And how is he punished for this if we make it all go away?'

'You'd like to send him to jail?'

'I'd like to do a lot of things.'

'He feels terrible. I haven't seen him cry like this since he was a little boy.'

'Has he tried to apologise to the girl?'

'Things went wrong, and he said some things he didn't

mean after she made the accusation. We think it's better if he doesn't say any more, for legal reasons as much as anything else.'

Eva walked back from the window seat to sit opposite Joseph. She looked up at the picture of Uncle Ira and the five white roses sitting so pristinely in the vase. There could have been more roses— one for Daniel, Abigail, Gabriella and Ben. People don't like it when you name a fetus and nobody ever told Eva whether they were boys or girls but she knew each time and named them in secret. Eva looked back to Joseph.

'I don't know why I'm having to run between the both of you like this,' she said.

'Because you always do.'

'Can't you talk to him about this properly, Joe? He needs to know you support him. Have a talk, man to man.'

'I'm the only man in this house,' said Joseph.

He swallowed his drink in one gulp and left the room.

Chapter Thirty-Four

Inside The School of American Ballet Deborah stood in a corridor and through a crack in the door she watched Maya in the exam studio. Behind her the other mothers were grilling their daughters about their exams in loud whispers or giving last minute pep talks.

Maya curtseyed to the examining panel. Deborah could make out a slender old woman with silver grey bobbed hair and a pair of Chanel sunglasses on her head. Next to her was a younger woman dressed in tweed with a mousy brown bun. Both women had their long slim legs cast to the left, their tiny ankles crossed. Coming up from her curtsey Maya's gaze fixed higher than her natural eye line, and her chin poked out a little. It made her stand taller and gave her lift. There was nothing haughty about it; somehow it made her look sweeter, more innocent and hopeful. A tiny burst, a bleeding out of feeling came from inside Deborah. She wanted to push the door open wide and go in and pick up Maya. Behind her she felt a nudge and the door was pulled closed.

'The door is to be kept closed,' said a dumpy looking teenage girl who had been calling out the names of the examinees all morning.

'Says who?' said Deborah.

'It's the rules.'

'Let them arrest me,' said Deborah and she pushed the door open a crack. Another mother muttered under her breath and the teenage girl protested. Deborah put her foot in the door. She watched Maya dance her routine— it was faultless and serene. At the end of her number Maya curtseyed again, this time allowing a glint of a smile to show. Maya received a nod from both of the examiners and jogged towards the door— Deborah opened her arms wide and Maya jumped in, and wrapped her body around Deborah. The woman with the oversized sunglasses on her head turned.

'Mrs Goltz, please close the door.'

'The door is to be kept closed,' said the nurse to Connie. 'Mrs Goltz is sleeping.'

Connie was balancing a tray of lunch for Eva between her hip and her right arm whilst carrying a vase of flowers in her left. She walked backwards to push it with her behind, and it made a click and Eva woke up but paid Connie no attention. Connie could feel Eva withdrawing, even from her. She was quiet, slow, disengaged, and nothing like the woman who Connie knew. She no longer sat with Deborah and Maya for breakfast or lunch. If she came down at suppertime she would push food around her plate and sip iced water. She'd missed Friday night dinner the evening before and didn't seem to notice. It was Deborah who asked Maya about her day and if she had any homework. Eva could manage a few words at a time and then she'd be asleep for another hour. She spent many days in bed but it was a good day and she'd been downstairs all morning.

'Mrs Goltz, I've brought you some lunch.'

'No, thank you,' said Eva.

Connie had expected as much.

'Someone has sent you flowers— shall I read the card?' said

Connie. Eva didn't reply.

'A secret admirer perhaps?' said Connie.

Eva didn't react, not even a smile.

Connie put them down on the table to the side of the sofa and turned to leave.

'Stay a moment,' said Eva.

'Yes, Mrs Goltz,' said Connie. 'Though I expect Deborah and Maya will be home soon and I haven't finished with their lunch.'

'No matter, they'll manage,' said Eva.

The nurse got up from her chair and tapped at her watch to indicate she was leaving for her lunch break. Eva waited until the door was closed.

'You know how tired I am, Connie, and I don't want to repeat myself because you're interrupting me. You promise to let me finish?'

'Yes, Mrs Goltz.'

'Go to the drawer over there.' Eva pointed to the desk.

Connie did so and opened it to find an envelope with her name on.

'This one?' she said, holding it up for Eva to see.

'Bring it over here.'

Connie handed it to Eva.

'I've thought hard about this. I've been very selfish over the years. I've taken up all your time and what you've been paid for it isn't enough.'

Connie pushed her lips together hard and shook her head. She had always been paid fairly.

'This money is for you and your family. Go on that trip to Ireland with your sister, buy your boys a place of their own.'

'Mrs Goltz, are you letting me go?'

'I'm making sure you can if you want to.'

'Why would I want to?'

'Deborah will be your employer—surely that's reason enough.'

'Mrs Goltz,' said Connie in a warning tone.

'Give me one last swipe,' said Eva. She laughed a little and then she was gone again, her eyes glazed over and eventually closed.

Connie thought this was the last time Eva seemed like herself. Connie had heard it called the last good day. It ought to have been a good one— it was the first time in her life she had more money than she needed. When Connie had first taken the job she was only going to stick it out for six months. Her husband at the time had been laid off and they needed the money, he said that in six months' time they'd be back on their feet. She did part-time hours in those days and was home in time for the school bus and to cook the evening meal. Connie didn't understand why but despite working she came home with more energy than she left with. There was something about the newness of it all and spending time around people with so much vigour that was infectious. Mrs Goltz hadn't had help before and liked to work alongside Connie. They went through the chores together when Mrs Goltz was at home, and except for preparations for Friday night dinner parties the work was so light that Connie felt guilty some days. Mr and Mrs Goltz even asked Connie to look at the town house in Washington Square before they bought it. They wanted to know if she'd be happy working there and how much more help they would need. By this time she was living on her own with her boys. They were in high school and didn't need her around so much so she asked the Goltzes if they would take her on full-time. Mrs Goltz doubled her pay, which Connie felt bad about because she only worked three more hours a day. The new house was harder work but some afternoons her only chores were to bake a loaf of bread and receive the floral deliveries and distribute the new bouquets around the house— clearing away the only very slightly wilting flowers. Sometimes she took them home and they sat on her kitchen counter for another few days.

There were many perks to the job; the bonus Mr Goltz gave her each Christmas as well as hampers of food that came from stores Connie had never been to. She had four weeks paid leave, use of the coach house at the Hamptons whenever she wanted a vacation as well as first refusal of any clothes, shoes or handbags Eva no longer wanted. There was only one time when she wanted to leave. She took a week-long vacation to think it over and went to confession for the first time in thirty-two years. She told the priest of her trip to London and back. He was silent a while and then asked what she thought her penance should be. Connie replied that she deserved to have to leave her post and take work that was harder in a place with fewer rewards. But what with a new baby in the house she couldn't do it. She promised herself she'd go as soon as she could, waiting for the right time. But the baby became a chubby-faced toddler and then a smart-mouthed little girl and Connie could no sooner leave her than she could leave her own children. Connie sat looking at the cheque. She would hand it back in exchange for staying in Maya's life. But when Eva was gone Deborah would move on and take Maya with her. She would have to say goodbye not only to Eva but to Maya too. Perhaps that was the penance that had accrued interest over the years and would not be deferred any longer.

Connie heard the front door open and stood up. She folded the cheque and slid it into her apron pocket. Before she could get to the door Maya burst into the room. Her ballet bag was flung aside and its content spilled out and rolled along the wood floor, like glass marbles from a jar. Deborah followed behind. She picked up ballet shoes, a water bottle, a sweater, leg warmers, headbands and bobby pins.

'I got a distinction,' said Maya and she slid over to Eva and landed on her knees by her side.

Eva had woken and was stretching out.

'I knew you would. You're the best dancer there,' Eva said.

'It's The School of American Ballet, Eva,' said Deborah.

'One day I'll be the best,' said Maya.

'I know it,' said Eva.

Deborah put the bag down and went out to the kitchen. Maya had Eva and Connie watch her do her dance over and over again. She drew out her curtsey like she'd seen the principal dancers of the school do. Maya bounded over towards Eva and Connie had to hold her back before she leapt on top of her.

'Give Nana some room to breathe,' said Connie.

'I'm fine,' said Eva. 'Stop fussing.'

Maya pirouetted away, spinning along the wooden floor on the toe of her pink ballet tights. Her head whipped round on each turn, she was travelling in a perfect straight line, headed for the door to the hallway.

'Careful, Maya,' said Connie.

'Look at me,' she said.

'Slow down, Maya or you'll crash,' said Eva.

'I won't.'

'Now who does that sound like?' said Connie, looking at Eva.

Eva laughed.

Maya's right foot landed down on the squeaky floorboard. It moaned and she slipped and fell heavy on her side, her right arm whacked the bureau by the door as she went down. Connie felt Eva jolt, she was pushing herself up, turning to stand. Eva could no longer walk unassisted, if she tried to get up she would fall. Maya held her breath, she looked up at them both her eyes wide with horror. She clutched her arm and her breath came out in a huge wail. Connie's instinct sent her straight to Maya who was crying breathlessly and rocking.

'Nana,' Maya screamed, 'Deborah.'

When Connie looked back to Eva, she was down on the floor dragging herself in their direction.

Maya cried the whole way to hospital, though Deborah wasn't convinced it was the pain in her arm that was upsetting her. She hadn't wanted to leave Eva behind, none of them had. Eva had hit her head when she tried to get up and when Deborah came into the den there was blood on the silk rug and Eva had passed out. Eva came around quickly enough and her doctor was attending after she refused to leave the house in the ambulance the nurse had called. Connie and the nurse were at home with her and twice Deborah called them on the cellphone to reassure Maya that it wasn't her time just yet.

'You'll get a cast,' said Deborah to Maya. 'We can all write our names on it.'

Maya couldn't be distracted and sobbed quietly as they went into the hospital. Connie had called ahead and a nurse was waiting for them in the pristine foyer. She immediately took them to see the doctor who took one look at Maya's arm and sent her for an x-ray. They managed to make Maya laugh and she left with her right arm in plaster, a pink sling and a lollipop.

'Can I keep this plaster even when it's comes off?' said Maya to the nurse.

'Sure, get your friends to sign it.'

'Will you and Doctor Welsh be the first?' said Maya.

'She's got another patient but let me see if she can escape for a minute,' said the nurse and she winked at Maya. She went up the corridor and knocked on the doctor's office door.

'Do you want me to call home again?' said Deborah.

Maya shrugged.

'I'm so hungry— we missed lunch,' said Maya.

'I'm just going to call home,' said Deborah. She got out her cellphone and pressed speed dial.

'Why?'

Deborah put her finger to her lips. Maya got up and went over to the vending machine. By the time she'd decided what she wanted from it and gone back to sitting down Deborah was cheerily saying goodbye to Connie. She knew it was Connie on the other end because Connie always said, 'God bless' at the end of a conversation and nobody knows what to say back. There was a funny pause before Deborah hung up.

'I'm so hungry, I think I'm going to faint,' said Maya. 'I need a dollar for the vending machine.'

'I didn't bring any cash out.'

Maya huffed.

'We'll order in when we get home,' said Deborah.

'Pizza?'

'I think you could ask for just about anything today and get it,' said Deborah.

Maya thought for a moment.

'When Nana is gone can I have a puppy? Please Mom?'

Chapter Thirty-Five

That night Deborah went to bed just after Maya and dreamt her mother and Patrick turned up at her bedroom door and said they didn't want to see her again unless she came with them and never returned to Eva's house. She begged her mother to reconsider. Her mother held out her hand and Deborah wanted to take it. But she couldn't step over the threshold. If she went, she was lost to Maya forever. She half woke, taunted by the dream and afraid of the darkness that was standing over her. She lay perfectly still, playing dead to the looming darkness, so it would float off and oppress someone else. She told herself off for being so shaken by a dream and closed her eyes and fell back to sleep. Hours later she woke with a start when she heard a click. She opened her eyes and watched the bedroom door glide open, just a little at first, and then stop. She gripped the silk duvet and waited. The door opened a little more, then completely. She stayed perfectly still, watching and barely breathing. There was nobody in the doorway. She knew that if she could reach out and quickly turn on the bedside lamp the spell would be broken. It would be a breeze that opened the door and not some other-worldly force. It would be a broken catch on the door and not someone coming to lure her out of the room. I wouldn't go, she thought to herself, no, the answer is no, I won't go with you. I'm staying with my daughter. Then she heard a sound of footsteps on the landing. She didn't have time to feel ridiculous—there was somebody in the house. How had the burglar alarm not gone off? How had someone got in? She knew houses like these were targeted and the inhabitants tied up, beaten or sometimes worse. She knew where the phone was on the bedside table. She had to call 911, it would be too late for her but they might arrive in time to help Maya and Eva. In a quick movement that she expected to be cut off at any moment she grabbed the phone and started dialling.

'Mommy?' said a voice.

Maya was in the doorway. Deborah dropped the phone and switched on the light.

'It's you!'

'I had a bad dream.'

Deborah lifted up the covers for Maya to get in.

'Me too. What happened?'

'Everyone was taken away.'

'Everyone?'

'Nana, you, Rabbi Rovner, Mrs Rovner, Connie, Illana, Sophie, Miss King— everybody.'

'Taken where?'

'I don't know.'

'Dreams aren't real, sweetheart.'

'This was real.'

'It feels that way, but I promise they're not. You'll see Nana and Connie in the morning. You'll see the Rovners at synagogue and Illana, Sophie and Miss King at school.'

Maya lay down and watched Deborah. Her eyes closed dopily and then opened again. She did this until her eyes couldn't stay open any longer and she fell asleep. Deborah watched Maya sleep a while and the more she looked at her the more she saw the face that she thought was a young version of her own become more like Eva's. She stroked little Eva's face and smelled the top of her head. She cupped her perfect round forehead in her hand and covered over the small, angular shoulder that the covers had fallen away from. Deborah got up, closed the bedroom door and switched the lamp off. When she got back into bed Maya looked like herself again.

At half past five Deborah got up and left Maya sleeping. She crept downstairs and got her coat, made coffee and went out to the garden. She turned on the garden lights and saw the flowerbeds had been planted up and were full of colour instead of snow. The bird table was unoccupied and beyond the walls of the garden the city was still hushed. People say that early morning is the best time of the day but what hell it would be if everyone believed it. It was winning her over— she never slept late here. The ground beneath her wouldn't tolerate stillness. This was a place where everything changed all of the time and nobody wondered if they would know how to slow down now they were moving so fast. The boredom and inertia of the first few weeks here had gone. She was embedded now and people came to her in the way they used to come to Eva.

The lights came on in the utility room which meant Connie had arrived, early again. Connie said it was a coincidence but she just happened to be there whenever the nurses changed shifts and gave each other an update on Eva. Connie questioned, checked and double checked everything the nurses did. She insisted all of Eva's bedding be changed daily and ironed every kink and fold mark out of the sheets herself. She created an altar of sorts at the end of Eva's bed which had pictures of everyone she loved upon it and cards from her friends. Deborah admired her dedication but it was all-encompassing. She wasn't ready to face her. She wanted another moment to herself so she ducked into the summer house and out of sight.

It had been used as a potting shed over the winter and smelled of woodchips and soil. She found two planters inside with showy yellow and orange daffodils standing tall inside them. The gardener must have forgotten to put them back outside the French doors leading into the kitchen, so she dragged them in sight of the house where they could be appreciated. Connie was looking out and she saw her from the kitchen window and waved, she opened the kitchen door and spoke in a whisper,

'Any news overnight?'

'None.'

Connie held her chest and breathed out.

'Can I get you anything?'

'No, thank you, Connie. I'll be in in a moment.'

Connie gestured to the planters of daffodils.

'Shall we put these under the television room window so that Mrs Goltz can see them from the bedroom?' she said.

It wasn't worth arguing with her so Deborah agreed. They each took an end and carried the planters over and set the daffodils down again. They dusted off their hands and went inside. Connie had laid out boxes of cereal and poured jugs full of juice. The oven was on and frozen pastries were laid out on trays ready to be baked. She was feeding everyone who came over the threshold of the house now and there was a constant stream of visitors. Connie and Deborah stood together a moment and admired their handiwork out of the window. Connie shook her head.

'The planters aren't straight,' she said.

'They're fine,' said Deborah.

'It's not good enough.'

Deborah put her coat back on and followed Connie out to the garden once again. They moved the planters an inch this way and that until she was satisfied. It was getting light now and the next time Eva looked out she would see the daffodils in their perfectly symmetrical planters shining up proudly.

Chapter Thirty-Six

31ˢᵗ *January 1992*

Deborah rang her mother. She could hear Patrick's voice in the background.

'Nu Yawk, Nu Yawk,' he bellowed in the worst attempt at a New Jersey accent she'd ever heard. Her mother chuckled. He did it again. Deborah waited. It didn't stop.

'Mum, this is important,' she said.

'I'll have a cup of cawfee,' Patrick called out and her mother shrieked with laughter.

She would have to tell someone the news soon otherwise it would look like she'd been hiding it. Which she had. It wasn't so hard. She'd conceived on the morning of the day she threw him out after their last fight. They fought about a credit card bill with quite a sum on it from one of the city's fanciest hotels, an outing Deborah hadn't been invited to. She threw the keys to his Ferrari off the balcony and told him to leave.

'This is my fucking house,' he said.

'No, it's your parents' house.'

'You're going to tell them what you found?'

It depends, thought Deborah. Whether you grovel or just go. He went.

Deborah promptly rang Eva. This was the first time Deborah

saw Eva's ever so friendly mask slip. She'd been welcoming and generous all this time, if a little reserved when they talked of marriage. Deborah put it down to that generation taking everything so seriously. Eva defended his freedom, 'boys will be boys', she said. Deborah assumed Joseph had said something else because five days later he was back but beaten.

Patrick must have been tickling her mother or something even worse because she was squealing with laughter now. Deborah had to hold the phone a little way from her ear.

'The big apple,' he was saying.

'This is serious,' said Deborah. 'Mum, will you just listen?'

'Oh, serious is it?' Deborah's mother lowered her voice, and she must have scuttled away from Patrick because his voice was now just background noise, 'you're not phoning for money are you? Because I can't ask Patrick to pay your bills as well.'

'No.'

'Don't tell me you're phoning to say you're up the duff, Deb. You know what me and Patrick think about single mothers—nobody likes a scrounger.'

Silence.

Then her mum startled giggling again and Patrick was back on the line.

'Are you talkin' to me?' he said, still in the unbearable attempt at an accent.

'No Patrick I'm not talking to you. I'd like it if you could fuck off so I can have a conversation with my own mum.'

Silence.

Deborah waited. She would not be the one to break it.

'Deborah,' said her mother, in that voice that was so calm it was unnerving. So practiced and sure of itself that Deborah wanted to tell her to fuck off now. 'I don't appreciate that. I know that Patrick won't either. I'm going to put the phone down now and the next time you call it'll be with an apology to him.'

The line went dead.

Deborah burst into tears.

He got home from what he called work. These days Deborah called it lounging around talking cars. She met him in the hallway. He gave her a half smile and hung up his coat.

'I'm pregnant,' she said.

And he betrayed himself for just a second. It was as though he was looking into the abyss and the outer edges were smeared with dog shit.

But then his expression changed.

'That's amazing,' he said. 'That's fucking amazing,' he opened his arms and she leant into them, 'it's really fucking amazing.'

He was right, it was quite amazing since they fucked less often than they fought.

As hard as he tried she could still see terror in his eyes. She didn't want him like this. But she still wanted him. One in three pregnancies ends in a miscarriage, one in three, she thought and then hated herself for it— I'm sorry baby, I'm sorry. I'm an idiot, don't listen to me.

They had an awkward dinner together full of false excitement.

'She's due in October,' said Deborah.

'She?'

'I think it's a girl.'

'How do you know?'

Deborah shrugged and offered him the rest of her lasagna, nothing tasted like it should. He took it and cleaned her plate.

He got up from his chair and down on one knee.

No, no, not like this, not this way, thought Deborah. But then again what choice did he have now?

He reached out and put one hand on her stomach, and the other in the small of her back.

'I'm going to be the best father,' he said and stood up again.

Chapter Thirty-Seven

Another week went on, Eva was put to bed like a child too tired to complain and now she didn't expect to get out of it. She didn't want to, there was nothing beyond her bed that she had any desire to get involved in. Her world was all there and it was changing every day, becoming more interesting in some ways and more hopeless in others. The pain, when it came, made her wince and gasp. A nurse would come and fiddle with something attached to the drip in the back of her hand and all sensation would go again— usually she would drift off, further each time. Rabbi Rovner hardly left her side. She could smell the washing powder on his starched clothes and the pastries he'd finished just before coming into the room. Maya came by and talked about her days and what she and Deborah were doing. Connie was often alongside the nurses helping. But there were others.

'Ahh-merri-ca,' said Eva aloud.

'Eva, I didn't catch that,' said Rabbi Rovner.

She was too tired to explain.

She remembered practicing the word day after day on the boat over. She held a tatty old rag that she wiped her weeping nose with and a woman told her to hide it when she got to

America otherwise, they'd say she was sick and send her to quarantine. America, a word she was taught to pronounce by an English soldier who would occasionally walk through the hospital ward she was staying in once her camp was liberated. He brought light to the long days and pranced around trying to make the children laugh; some did, most did not. It could have meant anything but he pronounced it with such zeal that she came to feel the same about its sound as she did the word schokolade— he brought that too. Everyone said she was very lucky to be going to America, so terribly, terribly lucky. She had only vague memories of arriving at Ellis Island— others told stories of tears rolling down their cheeks at the sight of the Statue of Liberty and New York's shores. She didn't remember feeling anything. But it had all meant something because she refused to go back there, even when invited by the city. She must have got through immigration without incident and into the hands of Ira and Sal. She remembered meeting them. They smiled and acted cheerful but Eva saw Sal wiping her eyes all the way home. Ira goofed around just like the soldier and laughed every few words.

'Is it safe here?' said Eva, in German.

'You speak English now,' said Ira.

'Ahh-merri-ca,' Eva said again.

Her eyes closed and she went back to sleep for a few unconscious moments or hours, she couldn't tell. In the space between waking and sleep was where she spent most of her time— there she saw her mother and sisters. They were rounder than the tiny frightened skeletons in her memory. Her mother wore a powder blue tea dress, the front of the skirt covered with an apron dotted with embroidered red cherries and green leaves. Each time she saw her mother she noticed greater detail. The beauty mark on her face, the shoulder length dark hair with a kink at the bottom and that she tapped her wedding ring against her thumb when she felt impatient.

Judith presented herself as an elegant thirteen-year-old, her shoes shining and her long white socks pristine. Her hair was plaited so it hung over one shoulder and she stood tall with a defiance that reminded Eva of Maya. Judith had been the last to disappear— her long hair was gone and her tall slender figure stooped. She'd always been self-conscious of her height. Without an ounce of confidence left Eva imagined Judith would have one day snapped in the middle. Anna and Marion always appeared together. They were just a year apart in age and of similar height and build. They were round and with chubby cheeks that they ought to have grown out of at nine and ten. Sometimes they swapped clothes— a pink gingham summer dress and a white cotton applique two piece.

Eva's eyes opened— the room was empty apart from the rabbi.

'Remind me what I believe about the afterlife, ' she said. Her voice came from the cracks between slow and laboured breaths.

Rabbi Rovner shrugged.

'Why don't you tell me what you believe?'

She told him what she saw.

'And what about your father?'

Eva took a couple of stiff breaths and shifted around in the bed, trying to dislodge the weight that she felt pressing down on her chest and hugging her rib-cage.

'Nothing,' she said.

Eva opened her mouth to say more then closed it again. She hadn't spoken her thoughts on this aloud and wasn't sure how they would sound. She opened her mouth to try again.

'I don't know if…'

The rabbi watched her intently.

'No records,' she managed to say but could say no more.

'You wonder if he survived?' he said.

The weight on her chest increased and Eva made little more

than a grunt to say she did. For days she'd been watching her mother and sisters flit around but he had never appeared with them. She'd been told to assume he was dead. But unlike the lists that her mother and sisters had been on there was no trace of her father. While she was busy with life it was reasonable to assume he was dead and too painful to believe otherwise. Surely Ira and Sal had looked for him even if they never told her so. But during this long week in bed and with no future she had nowhere but the past to dwell and nothing but her own wrongdoings to confront. Like preparations for Yom Kippur she was being forced to pull out every splinter still under her skin.

'It's extremely unlikely he survived,' said Rabbi Rovner.

Eva nodded.

'Do you find seeing your mother and sisters comforting?' said the rabbi.

'Are they coming to get me?'

'That's what some people say,'

'So?'

'I just don't know, Eva.'

With a sudden strength, she reached out and gripped Rabbi Rovner's hand tight. It felt firm and muscular, like a steak before it's been pounded.

'Yes, but what do you think? ' she said.

'I think it's a memory from the past,' said Rabbi Rovner.

'I think you're wrong,' said Eva.

She let go of his hand and lay with her eyes closed as another wave of tiredness overtook her.

'From your lips to God's ears,' he said.

This time Joseph came and then her son. They too looked better than they had before they left her. Joseph was at least ten years younger and for once he'd remembered to untuck his tie from inside his shirt and button up his suit jacket.

He looked smart and handsome— she wanted to tell him so. He didn't need his glasses and his hair was darker. Her son looked as he had around the time he passed except he could hold her gaze again. It didn't feel as though he was waiting for something more interesting than his mother and father's company to come along. It took a while for her to see them but there were children playing in the background, two boys and two girls. Eva was aware of Rabbi Rovner sitting next to her rocking back and forth in prayer and she could see a nurse sitting in the corner. Looking at them was like looking at a photographic negative but her visitors came in full colour, as if one world were fading and another ripening.

'Go home,' she said, to Rabbi Rovner.

'Eva, I want to be here.'

'Samuel, go home, it's Friday night. I insist.'

The children came closer and she recognised them, though she didn't know how, when she'd never seen their faces. Gabriella did a cartwheel, Ben followed her, Abigail twirled on the spot and Daniel looked on. He was always a timid one, she could feel it from the start. The pain came again and she whispered, 'wait for me.'

Rabbi Rovner went home to have dinner with his family. Eva hadn't said he couldn't come back after and he quickly ate roast chicken, diced carrots, broccoli and as many roast potatoes as he could get on his plate before Jona whipped them away. His sons donated him their leftovers and when Jona cleared the plates he ate the rest of the challah bread. Afterwards he went upstairs to wash his face and came down to Jona waiting at the bottom of the stairs. She handed him a box with a slice of apple pie inside and a tiny Tupperware pot of Chantilly cream.

'Nothing else, Samuel, I beg you.' She cupped his cheek, 'I'll know it if you stop for a hamburger on the way home.'

She was warmer these days. School didn't start until

September but she'd had him dig out all of his old training materials and she spent her days reading and asking him better questions than he'd ever thought to ask his teacher at rabbinical college. This proved his theory that we use our gifts or they become our pain, and our pain will become our gift if we let it. Rabbi Rovner poked his head in to the dining room. His sons, both students at NYU, one a freshman the other in his final year were good-naturedly debating the pros and cons of euthanasia.

'Dad, what do you think?'

Jona came in with the rest of the apple pie and cream and placed it down on the table.

'Life is sacred,' said Rabbi Rovner.

'Cop out,' said one of his sons.

'That's just what you were taught to say at college,' said the other.

'We don't know what happens in the final days and hours of our lives,'

'Pain and suffering mostly,' said his younger son.

'We don't know what else though,' said Rabbi Rovner.

'Send Eva my love,' said Jona and she sat down at the table.

'Ours too,' chorused his sons.

He felt the richness of his family— his boys raised by a mother so firm and fierce that they were the kind of men he trusted in the world. A wife who had grown so bright and bold that she was absolutely loyal to herself and so to him.

Samuel kissed the top of Jona's head, wrapped his coat tightly around him and left the sweet smell of home baked apple pie and their comfortable apartment for the cold night.

He walked the four blocks between his home and Eva's. Walking was the only time he had to himself and he enjoyed the anonymity of the city streets. Nobody would stop and ask him for advice or tell him their problems. To serve is to

240

live but he wouldn't give up the luxury of walking between appointments. Though the day had been bright and clear, smog obscured the stars and all he saw above him was a dark sky and the flashing of plane lights heading in and out of the city. He thought about all the people arriving for a reason and all with hope. He thought about all the arms that would open to receive their loved ones and faces kissed in recognition. What greater purpose in the world is there than that?

He recalled stories of people re-united years after being separated. His father, who spared him what he could of the horror of his young adult life, had told him about the chaos at the end of the war. People got lost, lost their minds, lost every shred of their identity. If Eva's father was alive he'd be in his nineties, as implausible as it was it was not impossible. Rabbi Rovner took out his cell phone and fumbled with it beneath the light of a street lamp. His sons teased him that he shouldn't use it in public— they said he was the least streetwise man in New York City and made bets with each other about how soon he'd be robbed. He found Adam's name in the caller list. He was just out of rabbinical college and could find everything Rabbi Rovner ever wanted to know just by tapping away at the keyboard of his laptop. Adam picked up the phone after the first ring and Rabbi Rovner apologised profusely for asking him to work on a Friday night then explained that he'd like him to look back over Eva's family history. Adam sounded excited by the project and he promised to keep going for as long as it took to get an answer.

'You'll need Eva's maiden name. Look up Messer, Evangeline Sarah Messer,' said Rabbi Rovner.

He repeated the name several times, uncertain of the reliability of the signal.

'She was born on September 18th 1937, Vienna. All we know is her father's name was Jacob Messer, her mother Lise and she had sisters— Judith, Anna and Marion.'

Adam repeated the information back and asked after Eva.

'She still has a lot of questions,' said Rabbi Rovner.

'Then she's like the rest of us,' said a voice coming from what looked like a dark pile of trash and discarded clothes but at a second glance was a man sitting on black sacks containing his belongings and wearing a large bottle green wax jacket, unshaven and unkempt. Rabbi Rovner realised he'd been shouting. He said goodbye to Adam and turned to the man sitting on the sacks beneath the canopy of a closed stationary store.

'Sorry Sir, my sons tell me I shout down the phone. It's all new to us isn't it,' said Rabbi Rovner.

He noticed the tired look of the man he was addressing. The tilt of his head, and the slump of his shoulders.

'Your sons speak to you, you're a lucky man,' he said.

Rabbi Rovner went over. He smelled the man before he got to him and he offered twenty dollars and his box of apple pie and Chantilly cream. The man took it. He opened the container and gulped down every delicious bit of the apple pie and drank the Chantilly cream straight from the tub.

'Is there somewhere for you to go tonight?' said the rabbi.

'Here,' said the man.

Rabbi Rovner waited a moment, unsure of what to say or do.

'There's a hostel six blocks away, twenty dollars will get you a bed for the night.'

The man laughed and shook his head.

'What's so funny?'

'It's not a bed I'm after.'

'I see.'

Rabbi Rovner knew what his sons would say about this—he'd once again been duped into giving a man the money to ruin his life some more. He stepped back a little and eyed the containers he'd handed over, knowing full well that if he came home without them he'd have Jona to answer to.

'What's your poison?' he said.

'Anything I can get,' said the man. 'Yours?'

'I like a decent Sancerre and my wife says I eat too much.'

The man looked him up and down then examined him closely.

'You're alright,' he said finally. He said it as if he'd adjourned with the highest company and they'd deliberated long and hard and come back with this verdict.

The rabbi felt oddly touched by this.

'Thank you, sir. So are you.'

The man handed him the empty containers.

'I'm a rabbi, can I say prayers for you?'

The man sighed.

'Well, the thing is I've got a twenty burning a hole in my pocket.'

'Not now, oh no, I mean another time.'

'If you like,' said the man.

'And your sons too?'

The man thought a moment.

'Do them first,' he said.

The rabbi nodded and held out his hand to shake the man's.

'Pleased to meet you, I'm Samuel.'

The man took his hand. His was smoother than he'd expected— he was younger than he looked. The man didn't offer his name.

'Like I say, I've got this twenty burning a hole in my pocket,' he said.

'Goodnight then,' said the rabbi and wandered on.

Just a block away the front door of the Goltz house was open and inside the hallway two nurses were talking as their shifts changed over. He heard one of them say Mrs Goltz was nearing the end. It was then that Rabbi Rovner wondered if this would be the last trip he would make to the Goltz family home. Deborah might not let him over the threshold. He could

243

lose Maya in the way he'd lost so many of the young people, more often to apathy than pure disbelief. Connie came to meet him in the hall.

'Mrs Goltz woke up while you were gone. She said 'tell the rabbi I saw my father.' I don't know what she meant but—'

'Thank you, Connie.'

'I'll bring you up something to eat.'

'Please don't, I won't be able to face my wife,'

Connie smiled and walked up the hall towards the den.

Rabbi Rovner got his phone out and dialled Adam to call off the search. He felt stupid for putting Adam on a trail that must have been followed before and found to have nothing at the end. Hardly anyone in Eva's position came across their missing relatives after the war. We remember the exceptional when we want to, he thought.

The lights were so low in Eva's bedroom that it took his eyes a while to adjust. The air smelled floral and there were several vases of flowers dotted around between pieces of equipment that beeped and paused with calm regularity.

Eva opened her eyes and spoke so softly that he had to lean in close.

'After what happened during the war I should have lost my mind,' she said. 'Why didn't I?'

Rabbi Rovner sat back in his chair. There was a pain in his chest and for a moment he wondered if the heart attack that Jona promised he'd have one day was coming at this most inopportune moment.

'You lost enough,' he said.

'But who can see what I saw and ever be ordinary? I should have spent my life rocking in an asylum, not living like this.'

'You lived as you did by God's will,' said Rabbi Rovner.

'What I did to my son, Deborah and Maya wasn't God's will,' she said.

The rabbi shook his head. Eva had closed her eyes. He

didn't know if she could hear him. He hoped not because he couldn't stop himself from talking to the only other presence he felt in the room.

'God, you ask us to be devoted to you and yet you won't explain yourself.'

Eva's eyes opened.

'I don't want pity or anger. I want people to change.'

'Amen,' said Rabbi Rovner.

The pain in his chest got worse and he brought his hand to it. Maybe God would take him instead. He'd be willing. He was ready, she was not. She closed her eyes.

The pain faded away into a dull and constant ache, like a tooth pushing up through the gum. He pulled his kippah out of his jacket pocket and placed it on his head and began to pray for Eva— he said the confessional prayer aloud and hoped Eva was saying it in her heart. When he was finished there was a tap at the door.

'Rabbi?' said Deborah.

He stood up.

'Maya's woken up and wants to come in and see Eva. Will you sit with her? I can't.'

'Certainly.'

'Thank you.'

A few moments later Maya appeared from behind Deborah and went over to sit next to him. Eva stirred and Maya stood up and leant over her. The nurse was on her feet and came over to guide Maya away.

'Miss,' he said and held his hand out to the nurse.

The nurse stepped back a pace but kept a watchful eye on Maya.

Eva's eyes opened for a moment and she looked in Maya's direction. The rabbi couldn't resist— he knew he wasn't supposed to intervene now— he was meant to hand her over, but he would hold on a little longer.

'Eva, this is why you survived,' he said. 'Maya is why.'

She looked at him then Maya and away again, her eyes closed once more.

Maya was asleep on the chair with her arm in a cast resting on a pillow and the rabbi was taking a break from his prayers and stretching his back— it wasn't long before dawn and he decided that in good conscience he could eat something now and call it breakfast. He dunked one of Connie's homemade cookies into his third mug of hot coffee that night and chewed its sweet stickiness down. The doctor was in the room and two of the nurses, another shift change. The bleeping of the machines slowed down and just as it stopped completely the rabbi felt something behind him, as if someone were standing too close. He turned and saw nothing. He knew he was too weighed down by his dense, lumbering, human body and narrowly trained mind to recognise it.

Chapter Thirty-Eight

Deborah was downstairs in the den. Even there she could hear Connie crashing around in the kitchen, preparing breakfast far too early. The hours between two and six were the most helpless. She knew Eva had gone when she heard Maya shouting. She dropped the magazine she was pretending to read and paced out to the hallway, avoiding the squeaky floorboard. Rabbi Rovner was at the top of the stairs, with his arms outstretched and Maya threw herself into him. Over Maya's shoulder she could see he was crying. His face made the ugly shape that is so wild and terrifying in a man. The doctor was heading down the stairs towards Deborah with a serious look on his face. He arrived at the bottom.

'Don't say it,' said Deborah. She looked up to Rabbi Rovner and Maya again.

The doctor persisted with what he had to say like an arresting officer delivering a caution.

'I'm very sorry Deborah— at 5.59am Mrs Goltz passed away.'

Before that Maya had awoken in Nana's room to the sound of muffled voices and people moving around. Rabbi Rovner started stroking her back and she curled up tighter in the chair. There was a chocolate stain on the arm which proved to her that Nana ate chocolates in her room even though she told her not to.

'Maya,' said Rabbi Rovner, in a soft voice.

There were crumbs down the sides of the chair too, she could feel them with her toes.

Then he put his hands over her ears and she couldn't keep still any longer. She pulled away.

'Time of death 5.59am,' said the doctor.

That's how Maya found out. Deborah promised she'd be the one, or Rabbi Rovner. Instead the doctor who smelled like mouthwash and was serious all the time just blurted it out.

'Maya, Nana has gone now,' said Rabbi Rovner.

'Dead?' she clarified.

'Yes,' said Rabbi Rovner. He turned to the doctor and asked him to go and tell Deborah.

Then Maya started smiling and couldn't stop. She had a feeling that if she went over and shook Nana she'd open her eyes again. She knew she'd have to be fast because everyone would try to stop her, so she ran and jumped on the bed. The nurse, the doctor and Rabbi Rovner were saying 'no', 'stop her' but she was quick. But as far as she could tell it wasn't Nana in the bed. She thought they'd put someone else in there in Nana's nightdress and with her wedding ring on. This was not Nana. She smelled like Nana's perfume and had the same kind of mole on her cheek that Maya always wanted to pick off but it wasn't her. Nana had gone. Someone took hold of Maya around the middle and lifted her off the bed and out to the landing.

'Where is she?' she shouted.

'She's with God,' said Rabbi Rovner.

'That isn't her,' Maya said, even louder.

'It's her body, her remains.'

'But it doesn't look like her,' she said.

'People's faces change when they leave us.'

Maya didn't know that when a person dies they take most of their beauty with them.

Connie was in the kitchen. The pastries were just coming out of the oven and another batch needed to go in.

'This is where people go wrong with croissants, they don't rise properly if the oven isn't hot enough,' she muttered.

She heard voices along the hall but if she abandoned the cooking every time somebody called her name then breakfast would be at lunchtime, lunch would be eaten for supper and supper for breakfast. That's why she didn't come running the instant Deborah called out for her. Connie held a baking sheet with six perfectly golden croissants in one hand which she slid onto a cooling rack next to the basket lined with a red gingham napkin. She put another batch of unbaked croissants on the tray. Deborah was still calling but the oven was open and Connie was damned if she was going to let it go cold. Besides a hot baking sheet makes the bottom of the pastries crisp and stops them from sticking. Then she noticed the freshly squeezed orange juice in the refrigerator had run low and she had to go to the pantry to fetch more oranges and get the juicer out of the cupboard. The only fruit anyone could get into Maya was orange juice so she wasn't going to leave her without. The calling stopped so Connie assumed everything was alright. The misplaced sunglasses case will have been found, or the tiny little spider in the downstairs bathroom would have scuttled off without a helping hand. These were the usual disturbances. But of course it was nothing like that. Connie kept on going, cooking and fetching and putting on noisy pieces of kitchen equipment; three loaves of bread, two pints of fruit smoothie, whipped cream for the pancakes she was going to make and granola that demanded smashed up walnuts, pecans and brazils. These were stolen moments, the last gasps of air. She might not stand in this kitchen again. She was going to leave it brimming.

Then the phone in the hallway started to ring and she wondered how long they'd all known and how long she'd been hiding. It was just past six and it would be Lois or Dash. They were on vacation and no matter what time zone they were in they would call at this time every day. She left it to ring a while and then went out into the hallway. Upstairs on the landing Rabbi Rovner was holding Maya and Deborah was holding him. You would have thought he'd lost everything he'd ever known.

She left the phone ringing and walked up the stairs. She helped Deborah to hold the rabbi up. She whispered to her.

'I'm glad for Eva. I hope she left it all behind.'

In the gaps between Maya's tiny form, the rabbi and Deborah's, Connie could see inside the room. The nurse was switching off the machines and pushing pieces of equipment aside. She pulled the table at the bottom of the bed away and with it all the flowers, cards and pictures. She was tidying up after a job done and clearing the way for the undertaker. Connie helped Deborah peel Maya off Rabbi Rovner and left them sitting squashed together on one of the two seaters that sat along the landing and nobody ever used. Maya was now draped around Deborah and the rabbi had composed himself. Connie went into the room. Of all the nurses that came this was the one she'd warmed to the least— she was dignified in a 'been there and seen it all' sort of way. But Connie wasn't sure that she really cared because she searched her face for emotion and saw none, but she did her job proudly and that would have satisfied Mrs Goltz. She helped her move one of the heavier vases of flowers off the table and was glad the nurse didn't try and make small talk or comfort her. Some people are like that, they just know how to be with you when your heart's hanging out and it's grim to watch.

They shifted the chairs from the bedside and moved the nightstand to the corner of the room. Then the nurse went over to the window and opened it wide— she placed her palms together. She mouthed some words that Connie couldn't decipher and whispered 'amen'. She closed the window and packed her bag. She zipped it shut and offered Connie her hand, and she shook it.

'Thank you,' said Connie.

'God bless you,' she said and left the room.

Connie stood there awhile wondering whether or not to peel back the sheet that they'd put over Mrs Goltz and see her face one last time. She went over to the bed and fingered the edge of the Egyptian cotton. Mrs Goltz would have been horrified to be viewed like a curiosity and in life Connie would never have dared to loom over her while she slept. So instead she went over to her walk-in closet and pulled out the outfit she told her to find and hung it up on the back of the bedroom door. She picked out a brand-new pair of Christian Dior silk stockings, still in their wrapping from her lingerie drawer. She chose the bra that Mrs Goltz joked made her feel fifty-nine again and a pair of lace briefs that she would laugh herself pink about if she knew. She got out the pair of shoes that had been worn for the Presidents Day party and put all the make-up she would normally use in a black satin bag. She arranged it all into a large tote bag then hung it with the dress.

'Safe journey, Mrs Goltz,' she said and double checked she had everything she needed before she went down to get the batch of croissants out of the oven.

Chapter Thirty-Nine

The next morning had none of the peace of a usual Sunday. There were people in every downstairs room and a constant queue for the bathroom. Connie ducked in there every half an hour or so and spruced it up with a new hand towel, a spritz of air freshener and a fresh point folded on the end of the toilet paper. Security and catering staff trod the halls with mobile phones in hand and Irene and some of Eva's other friends from synagogue were covering mirrors with cloths and clearing away vases of flowers. Rabbi Rovner and Adam were sat up at the kitchen island each eating a plate of pancakes. Platters of food and cases of wine were brought in and Connie directed extra cleaning staff to get to the tasks she didn't have time for. She had to repeatedly go back and forth to the front door that kept banging shut in the wind. Eventually she pushed a door stop against it and looked out at the bright March morning, a day almost warm enough to go without an overcoat. Connie had been raised a Catholic so this wasn't how things were done in her family but it made sense to her that the funeral should happen soon after death. There seemed no point in leaving a body decaying in a morgue until a convenient date some weeks in the future. There had been two funerals in the last twelve months, both unexpected, both a shock. This time it would be easier, Eva had it all planned out. The caterers had been put on standby and Saks Fifth Avenue had been waiting for the call. They arrived in the early evening of the Saturday night and within an hour everybody had perfect black attire. Personally, Connie found Deborah's hat with a veil a little much and she knew Eva would have done so too. She would glance up to Eva in the synagogue and they would share one last eye roll. From upstairs she heard banging and Maya's raised voice. It sounded like a wild boar had been let loose and Connie strode up the stairs two at a time, a cloth in one hand and a bottle of disinfectant spray in the other.

'Maya?' she called. 'Maya? Are you alright?'

She could hear a shrieking sound but the banging had stopped. Connie ran the last few stairs. When she reached the top Maya was flat on her back on the landing still dressed in her nightie and on her chest was a Yorkshire Terrier puppy licking her face. It was laughter— thank god, thought Connie, it's laughter.

Connie was sure there would be many times when she'd think Deborah was making mistakes, but not this time. On the previous morning Eva's body was taken at 7am and Deborah was back home with a puppy by midday. The dog had slept in Maya's bedroom all night and relieved itself on the landing at its leisure. There was hardly time to get the house in shape let alone clean up after a dog but Deborah said it kept Maya busy and she couldn't argue with that. By the time Connie got to Maya she was on her feet and running up the corridor with the puppy nipping at the hem of her nightdress as he followed her. Downstairs she heard a thud as the front door banged closed again and she turned on her heel and went to open it.

Deborah closed her bedroom door against the noise of the game Maya and Lucky were playing and opened her laptop. The day before she had sent another message telling her mother that Eva had gone. She didn't know why this would matter to her when none of the other news had, but at the time she needed to tell someone— she needed to tell her mother. She might as well have told Lucky. There was still no reply.

She closed her laptop and went over to a rectangular box on top of the chest of drawers. She opened it up and took out a framed photograph of Eva. It would sit above the fireplace in the den. Eva, Joseph and Zach— his name no longer too sacred to be spoken. Unsure if she was breaking some kind of Jewish law, she quietly gave the five white roses that had been on the mantlepiece the night Eva died to the undertaker. She checked them all for any signs of spoiling but they were as perfect as the day they were placed in the vase. She asked the undertaker to put them into Eva's hands. She buffed the glass of the framed photograph with the sleeve of her dressing gown and tucked it under her arm.

Deborah stepped out of her bedroom and into a warm puddle.

'Connie?...Connie?'

She waited but nobody came. She hopped back to her bedroom and through to the bathroom. She placed Eva's photograph on top of the cistern. With her foot in the sink she ran the taps and gasped at the chill of the water. She dried it off and picked up one of the towels and threw it over the wet patch.

'Maya?'

The dog came first followed by Maya, out of breath and red in the face. 'Lucky's had an accident,' she said.

'I know, I stepped in it. Take him outside for a pee and then shut him in the laundry room. Rabbi Rovner's here. He wants to talk to you quickly and we've got to get dressed, we're leaving in half an hour.'

'That's ages,' said Maya. She skipped down the hall and ran

down the stairs with Lucky in tow.

'Come right back up,' Deborah said.

Her mobile phone rang and it was her realtor. Deborah told her she was sorry for taking up her time but she no longer needed her services to find an apartment— they were staying put. She called her mother and Patrick's house. It went to answerphone— the bleep came and she took a breath in and then realised she had nothing at all to say. It would be repetition, another attempt to reclaim her mother. She hung up and called out to Connie again.

Connie arrived at the top of the stairs, a bucket of water and cloth in one hand and carpet cleaner in the other.

'Thank you, Connie. The dog's had another accident,' said Deborah.

'Leave it to me,' said Connie. She dabbed at the wet patch with the cloth and sprayed carpet cleaner on it. 'At least he does it upstairs where none of the guests will see.'

'That's it, isn't it, we can live with making a mess so long as nobody else knows about it,' said Deborah.

Connie looked up at Deborah.

'For some people that's true,' said Connie.

'For Eva,' said Deborah.

Connie stood up and with her foot she dabbed at the wet patch with the dry corners of the towel.

'That's the best I can do.'

Deborah didn't know if she meant with the carpet or the loyalty she still felt to Eva that prevented her from saying more.

'Thanks Connie. The cars are going to be here soon, we'll leave everything else and get ready.'

Deborah watched Connie carry the bucket back along the landing and turn down the stairs. She hoped Connie wouldn't leave them.

Deborah looked at her watch for the fiftieth time that

morning and remembered that she needed to find nail scissors. She set off back up the landing to the big bathroom but was distracted by Connie's voice down in the hallway.

'Good to see you again,' said Connie.

Deborah craned her neck to look down at whoever had arrived but could only see the top of a man's head.

'Good morning, Ma'am,' said a voice.

'Call me Connie.'

'I'm Jon,' said the man and offered his hand.

'I recall,' said Connie.

Deborah was sure that there was girlish delight in Connie's voice. Was she flirting?

Deborah didn't know why but she kicked off her slippers and ran down the stairs. She almost fell down the bottom few steps and arrived in front of Jon barefoot and slightly out of breath.

'Deborah,' he said.

'You came,' she said.

'I'm sorry for your loss. I heard about the job here today and I'm friendly with the guy who does the rosters so he let me work.'

Deborah didn't know what to say next and stood dumbly looking at him.

'How are you doing?' he said. 'I mean, obviously not so great, but I just want to say...I wanted to say...I wanted...I'm here is all. Let me do what I can.'

Connie excused herself and chased Lucky, who was dancing around the ankles of a caterer carrying a cheeseboard down the hallway.

'The rest of the guys, I mean my colleagues are just setting up. We have instructions to have two on the front door and five plain clothed inside.'

Deborah continued to stare at him, unable to find a coherent thing to say.

Jon glanced down at his paperwork.

'I have your name down as Deborah Goltz now?' he said.

Deborah didn't respond.

'Just so you know we'll all be wearing ear pieces and we'll be in constant communication throughout. We're all ex-forces—there's nothing we haven't seen. These events are like a tea dance to us. You can relax, nobody comes in who isn't invited and we'll have eyes on everyone who is here. I have a note here that some of the mourners will have security teams of their own coming in. I have to tell you that in accordance with your mother-in-law's wishes we won't be allowing anyone carrying firearms inside and we'll be setting up metal detectors here at the door.'

'She wasn't my mother-in-law,' said Deborah. So she could speak. 'I changed my name so it's the same as my daughter's—we're the only surviving Goltzes.'

Deborah held on to the bannister and felt her face getting hotter and her throat tightening. Jon reached out and touched her arm. She sat down on the bottom step before her legs gave way. Maybe she was crying for Eva or perhaps for Maya. Or for the years they'd lost with each other.

'I'm going to change plans and swap with another of the team. I'll come to the synagogue,' said Jon. 'If that's alright with you?'

Deborah nodded. She wiped her eyes on her sleeve and Jon produced a Kleenex for her from his pocket.

He lowered himself down next to her and they sat together, shoulder to shoulder.

'Do you think we can try again?' she said.

Deborah was chivvied upstairs by Connie and after a protracted search she found a pair of nail scissors in the toiletries bag she'd brought with her. It had somehow avoided being thrown away like everything else from her other life. She peeled away the garment bag with her black Dior jacket and dress inside. She pushed the scissors into the fabric below the left lapel of the jacket and snipped just enough to get her finger inside, she made a tear downwards until a piece of fabric hung loose. She took Maya's dress out of its box and spread it out on the bed. She dug the scissors into the outer layer and ripped a hole. Maya came into the room, still dressed in her nightie.

'Did you see the rabbi like that?'

'Yes.'

'What did he say?'

'Nothing much— we rehearsed the mourner's prayer. We're going to say it together.'

Maya sat down on the edge of the bed. She lifted her knees up to her chest and hugged them tight. Deborah saw tears gathering in her eyes.

'Sweetheart,' said Deborah and she held Maya.

Maya let her.

'It's too much of a rush,' said Maya. 'I want some more time.'

'I'm sorry,' said Deborah.

'Sometimes you're the pilgrim and sometimes you're the turkey,' said Maya.

'What?' said Deborah.

'It's not 'what' it's 'pardon',' said Maya.

'Oh, excuse me,' said Deborah.

Maya wiped her face on Deborah's sleeve and got up from the bed.

'It means sometimes it's your day and sometimes it's not.'

'It's Nana's day today,' said Deborah.

'Do you think she's watching us?'

'I don't know, Maya.'

Deborah prepared to concoct a fantasy that might soothe Maya about Eva watching over them, though she didn't believe it. Eva felt further and further away with every hour that passed.

A sudden smile streaked across Maya's face.

'By the way, I heard Connie say a swear.'

'You did?'

'S-H-I-T. She trod in Lucky's.'

'Don't let me hear you say that again.'

And this, thought Deborah, is what motherhood is. The winnowing of your own childhood until you find the sort of parent you want to be. She hoped to be kind, safe and sensible and she trusted that with that would come some joy.

'You cut your suit?' said Maya. 'You're not supposed to do that. It's just me. Are you even a relative?'

'I think I am, Maya.'

And knowing that sometimes your efforts will be mocked and getting used to being told that you're doing it all wrong—hoping that when you do you'll be forgiven.

Acknowledgements

I'm indebted to my teacher and mentor Claudia Gould who read through many rewrites of this book without complaint. Claudia's skill and generosity is such that she made me believe that I was doing her a favour by churning out yet another version. Claudia, this really is the last. Thanks to Emma van Klaveren, your eagle eye and kind encouragement kept me going. Thank you, Marianna Kilburn, for our weekly catch-ups and your sanity and perspective when mine fails. Mum, thank you for your unwavering support and years of reading we did together. Bryan Webster, you read an earlier version of this book and gave me excellent notes, thank you. Thanks to everyone in my writing group. I'm grateful to Gill de Warren for the cover design and to my brother, Andrew, for the layout. Throughout this process I've had the company of two generations of four legged companions to sit by my side as I write and walk with me while I clear my head- Vivi, Maude, Dolly and Delilah, thank you for being the most compelling distraction.

Book Club Questions

Do you see Eva as having triumphed over her past, simply survived it, or become a victim of it?

Can you imagine being seduced by the luxurious lifestyle Deborah encountered when she first met Eva's son?

After Deborah arrived back in New York city in the year 2000 did you think she would leave Maya again? Was she fooling herself that she could?

If you were Maya, who could you forgive and why?

How do you think the relationship between Deborah and her mother affected Deborah's own ability to mother?

Why was Rabbi Rovner such a support to Eva even after he knew what she'd done?

Which character in Forgiven were you most intrigued by and why?

Contact

www.alisonstoker.co.uk/author-page